ABDUCTIONS
AND LIES

THE JESSE DAMON SERIES

ABDUCTIONS AND LIES

KM ROCKWOOD

A Jesse Damon Crime Novel

WILDSIDE PRESS

Published by Wildside Press LLC
www.wildsidepress.com

CHAPTER 1

The glare of headlights split the night, shimmering off the wet asphalt. A sharp metallic glint by the base of a discouraged tree caught my eye.

I glanced over my shoulder. A patrol car. It slowed as it went by.

I stopped and pulled my hands from my pockets, letting my arms hang by my sides. I didn't have a weapon, and didn't want anyone to think I did.

My gut tightened and I felt sweat crawl down the back of my neck.

Well, at least the car hadn't stopped. That didn't mean it wouldn't swing by again, but it did continue on down the deserted street instead of turning at the corner or pulling a U-ie.

The wall of Quality Steel Fabrications, where I worked, loomed next to me. Up ahead, the barred windows of the darkened offices were the only breaks in the solid brick wall.

Across the way was a big employee parking lot. During the day, it would be crammed with vehicles, but at this hour of the night, it was empty except for two pickup trucks. Neither one was mine. I walked.

There was nowhere for me to slip out of sight.

Going over to where I'd seen the glint of light, I scraped around the base of the tree with the toe of my boot, dislodging something. In the darkness, it was hard to tell what it was.

I picked it up and carried it to one of the windows, where a dull glow from the interior emergency lights let me see a little better.

It was a metal money clip. Silver, with a dollar sign welded onto the front. And it held a fair number of bills. I couldn't see well enough to tell what denomination they were. But I had a pretty good idea whose money clip it was.

Stebril Jenkins, the night watchman, was more than a bit eccentric. A couple of times, I'd seen him with a money clip like this in his hand, fingering the bills. When he saw me looking, he'd stuff the whole thing in his back pocket. Once he'd dropped it in front of me, and I'd pointed it out to him. He'd gotten mad, as if it was my fault he almost lost it. Even if I could manage to find him now—not likely since he could be anywhere in the darkened factory on his rounds—he'd probably get mad at me if I tried to give it back.

I could turn it into the office. They'd make sure he got it back. He'd never have to know I'd had it. None of us in the shop made that much money, but as watchman, Steb made even less than the rest of us.

The offices wouldn't be open until tomorrow morning, so I'd have to wait to turn it in. Steb would probably be worried about it, but he'd just have to wait.

Headlights appeared from behind again, this time followed by a spotlight. I glanced over my shoulder, but the bright light made me blink and I couldn't see anything beyond it.

Not good. I should have just picked up the money clip and kept going.

I shoved it into my pocket and turned to walk away.

The car pulled over to the curb in front of me.

"Stop right there, mister. We want to talk to you."

I stopped dead in my tracks. The cold sweat trickled down my neck and made me shiver. I didn't want to do anything that could be interpreted as threatening, so I stood still, my hands at my sides.

Two cops got out. A broad muscular man and a skinny woman with a hatchet face. I was familiar with a lot of the cops in the city, but I didn't recognize these two. It was too dark to read their name tags.

The street lights weren't working. The sharp spotlight mounted on the car cast long shadows across the sidewalk and onto the factory wall.

One stood on either side of me. No one said anything. The man stood back a bit, his hand resting on the flap of his holster.

They were waiting for me to talk. A standard interrogation tactic.

They'd have a long wait. I knew better than to volunteer any information, especially when I had no idea why they wanted to talk to me.

"So." The woman got tired of the game first. "What's your name?

"Jesse."

"You got a last name?"

"Damon."

"Jesse Damon?"

"Yes, ma'am."

"You wanna tell us what you're doing out here at this hour of the morning?"

"Going home from work."

"At..." she checked a watch on her wrist. Who still wore a wristwatch? Besides me. "three ten in the morning? Who gets off of work at three ten in the morning?"

"I work at Quality Steel Fabrications." I nodded toward the factory wall next to us. "Overnight shift."

She frowned. "It's pretty dark in there. Doesn't look to me like anybody's working now."

What she could see were the office windows, not the shop floor. No one would have been working there this time of night under any circumstances. "Well, no," I said. "It wasn't a full shift anyhow. Just getting ready for a retooling shutdown. The power went out. So the foreman sent everybody home."

She looked around at the otherwise empty sidewalk. "If he sent everybody home, where is everybody else? How come you're out here by yourself?"

"I drive a forklift. I had to run the after-shift checklist before I left."

"You know, I can check all this with the company when they're open in the morning."

"Yeah." That sounded like a good idea to me.

"Unless they're closed. You say they're doing a retooling shutdown?"

"Yeah. But the offices will be open. And a skeleton staff will be on in the shop. At least during the day shift."

"You got your driver's license on you?"

"I don't got a driver's license. But I have a work ID in my wallet." I also had my old prison ID in there.

"And you say you drive a forklift?"

"Yes, ma'am."

She pushed her hat back. "But you don't have a driver's license? That's odd."

It might be, but I didn't have any good explanation for her. Just that I'd never gotten it together to get a driver's license. And I certainly couldn't afford a car, so I didn't see much urgency.

"You got any weapons on you?" she asked.

"No, ma'am."

"Mind if we check?"

I did, really, but they were going to search me anyhow. No point in antagonizing them. "No, ma'am." I put my hands on top of my head.

The male cop moved forward and started running his hands over the outside of my pants.

"You on probation or parole?" the woman asked.

Their already skeptical attitude was about to get a lot worse.

"Yes."

"Which one?"

"Probation or parole?"

She snorted impatiently. "Yes."

"Parole," I said.

"Parole? For what?"

They'd find out soon enough anyhow. "Murder."

The male cop grabbed my left arm and pulled my hand behind my back, turning the palm out. I felt the cold steel bite of handcuffs on my wrist. He repeated the motion with my right hand. Then he finished frisking me, rougher this time. He removed my wallet, keychain and Steb's money clip from my pocket. He tossed them to his partner. "Run him."

The woman grabbed for them. She missed. They fell into a puddle on the wet, uneven sidewalk.

Steb would be getting his money back damp. Assuming I had a chance to get it back to him any time soon.

She fished them out and held them with her fingertips. She riffed the bills in the money clip and then looked into the wallet. That had the two IDs and six dollars.

"Where'd this money come from?" she asked, holding up the money clip.

Given the number of bills, it must come to a decent amount, even if all the bills were small ones.

I wasn't about to tell her I'd found it. She'd figure it was drug money. Or stolen. I shrugged.

"How come you got some money in your wallet and the rest in this money clip?"

I tried to come up with a reasonable explanation. "Savings," I said.

"Savings?"

"Yeah. The money in my wallet is spending money. The other is what I'm trying to save."

"For what?"

That I could be truthful about. "I wanna buy a pickup truck." I didn't know if I'd ever get that much money together, but I could hope.

"You know, we can call a drug dog to give everything a go-over. And if he alerts on the money, we can run tests for drug residue."

Would Steb have money with drug residue? It was possible—money circulated around, and no one could ever be sure that the bills they got hadn't passed through a drug dealer's hand at some point. But I was pretty sure Steb himself wasn't involved in drugs.

I knew I wasn't, so I said. "Go for it."

She glared at me, then slipped into the driver's seat of the patrol car.

As I stood there, the other cop gripping my arm, the rain started up again. He was wearing a weather-resistant jacket. And a hat. With my hands cuffed behind me, I couldn't flip up my hood, and anyhow I could feel dampness beginning to soak through the shoulders of the hoodie.

I was going to be cold and wet if they held me for any length of time. Which they could do if they wanted to.

The woman sat in the driver's seat, door open. After a few minutes, she called out, "Murder conviction for starters. Possession of a handgun. A few others. Paroled about three months ago. Armed and dangerous."

That designation was going to follow me for the rest of my life. When I'd first been arrested, twenty years ago, I was clutching a bag that contained a knife and a gun. The gun had just been used to kill someone. Dumb kid that I was, I had no idea what was in the bag.

I wasn't at all sure I was much smarter now.

The male cop reached over and opened the back door to the patrol car. "Get in." He held his hand over the doorframe to shield me from hitting my head.

I slid in. At least the car was one of the newer models. The seat was molded plastic with a cutout in the seat back for my cuffed hands. More than once I'd ended up with arms so numb from sitting back on too-tight handcuffs that it was hard to eat for a few days.

He leaned in to fasten the seat belt over me. Then he shut the door and got in the front passenger seat.

We drove around a few corners and stopped. From the back seat of the car, I found it hard to see what was going on. But I did see emergency lights flashing and people bustling around. I could also see a fire engine and an ambulance, with a truck and a few cars behind them.

The male cop got out and opened the door for me. "Get out. Stand still and face forward."

Climbing out of the back seat of a car with hands cuffed behind is awkward.

He reached in and grabbed my arm, pulling me out. I managed to get one of my feet out the door and under me before I fell. He held onto my arm again. Tightly.

I caught a quick glimpse of a car with its front crumbled against a utility pole. The pole was broken off near the base and lay across the car's roof. Wires draped onto the wet pavement.

Probably why we'd lost power at work. They'd have to shut off the whole neighborhood to get that fixed.

One of the vehicles sitting crosswise in the intersection was a utility truck. Still, it was going to be a while before they could get the power back on.

Rain dripped from my wet hair into my eyes. I shook my head.

The cop's grip on my arm tightened more. "Stand still."

A bright flashlight shone straight into my face. Blinking, I started to turn away from the glare.

Another squeeze on my arm. I'd have bruises there. "Look straight ahead."

I had to close my eyes.

A murmur of voices came from near the crashed car, nearly drowned out by the increasing drumming of the rain.

To the side, someone said, "He can't see you with the light in his eyes. Don't worry."

I was pretty sure they weren't talking to me.

My stomach churned. What was going on here?

"Is this the man?"

A strangled female voice said, "Yes! That's him!" and ended in a sob.

CHAPTER 2

That's him? Him who? Were they talking about me?

I had no idea what they thought I'd done, but this couldn't be good.

The cop turned me around and pulled me off to the side.

Could they possibly think I'd been driving the car when it crashed? And left the scene of the accident?

I wondered if anyone was hurt. Or killed.

Another car pulled up. A puke green hybrid.

I knew who that belonged to. Carissa Daniles, a reporter for the Rothsburg Register, the local newspaper. She might be the *only* reporter. Her uncle owned the paper.

Like most print news outlets, the paper was struggling to stay afloat. Carissa wrote most of the local news stories and features. She thought her true calling was investigative reporting, but she didn't seem to take the part about actually "investigating" seriously.

Rothsburg itself was once a small thriving industrial city, but now the major employer was the large state prison just outside town. A few factories like Quality Steel Fabrications were left among desolate railroad sidings and abandoned warehouses. The once-busy riverfront dock area was being transformed into a park with flood-control levees.

In a city like Rothsburg, there wasn't a whole lot for Carissa to write about. Unless she delved into the contentious political scene, which she didn't seem inclined to do, possibly because her uncle was active in local politics. A feature article, incongruously on the front page of the paper, appeared under her byline as often as she had material for it. She liked to write crime stories.

I had shown up in a couple of her features. And not in a flattering light.

Carissa didn't mind playing fast and loose with the facts if they interfered with her story. She might have a promising future writing for supermarket tabloids, but I didn't understand how she got away with her articles in a supposedly serious local paper.

That's probably where being the owner's niece came in.

I wondered how she'd found out about this accident so fast. Didn't she ever sleep?

Camera in hand, she hurried over to where I stood. I turned my head, trying to keep her from getting a good picture.

No one stopped her, so she just stepped around the patrol car and snapped a few pictures from that angle.

Then she went over to the officer in charge of the scene, notebook in hand. I knew she was also recording this. She thought the notebook made her look more professional. Or so she'd once told me.

She kept her coat belted tightly against the chill from the wind and the intermittent rain. Carissa's wardrobe ran to revealing clothes, although she was so skinny I didn't quite understand what some men found so distracting. They eagerly answered her questions, appropriate or not. But it did seem to work for her. She flipped her layered blond hair and turned her dazzling smile on the cop she'd targeted.

In a few minutes, she probably found out more about what was going on than I ever would, even if I ended up going to jail. I'd get charging papers, but they could be surprisingly uninformative. She glanced in my direction and smirked.

The cop who was holding my arm shoved me toward the patrol car. He opened the back door.

Carissa abandoned her target and hurried over. "Jesse!" she shouted. I could hardly hear her above the noise. "Do you have anything to say?"

I ignored her. The cops wouldn't let her get too close to me, for fear I'd lunge at her, but they sure weren't holding her back at a reasonable distance.

"How about the recent string of abductions and rapes? All those poor women? What can you tell me about that?"

I couldn't get in the back seat of the parole car fast enough, even if I wasn't sure where they were going to take me.

"Did you know they found a body yesterday afternoon, Jesse? Does that make you nervous?"

I slid into the seat. The cop slammed the door after me.

Carissa would report that when she tried to ask me questions, I'd refused to answer.

That part at least would be true.

What kind of convoluted thought process led her from a traffic accident that cut off power to half the city to the recent string of young women who had been abducted? Did she get the connection from talking to the officer in charge?

I hoped not. *Something* was going on, but I had no idea what. I did seem to be caught up in the middle of it, though.

As the patrol car pulled out, she took another picture of me. I hoped the glare of the uncertain lighting off the windows would ruin it.

I had no doubt my picture would be on the front page soon, although I could hope it was too late to make this morning's paper.

Carissa had started writing a series of feature articles about the women who had disappeared. That was certainly newsworthy, but I couldn't tell how much of what she wrote was true and how much was speculation. She said it looked like a serial rapist—five women had been targeted in the last three weeks. That part sounded true.

One of them had been found dead, one had managed to escape her captor, and the other three were still missing. Since all seemed to have been seized from around the new park and surrounding areas, Carissa had labeled the unknown perpetrator the "Riverfront Rapist."

The woman who survived was a well-known prostitute. It was unclear whether the other victims were also in the business.

If the article couldn't make today's paper, maybe Carissa would have enough time to check out some actual facts, instead of making most of it up. And maybe by then I'd have some inkling of what was going on.

The patrol car arrived in the center of town, where the city and county government buildings occupied a few square blocks. The cluster of stately brick buildings with white columns in front of them was the most prosperous-looking part of the city. Right now they were dark, except for the police station and the jail. Those operated twenty-four/seven.

The patrol car pulled up to the overhead door that led to the sally port for transferring prisoners. It paused while the door opened, then drove in.

Was I officially under arrest? No one had read me my Miranda rights, but then, discounting Carissa, nobody had really talked to me since the initial confrontation.

Not that it mattered. Since I was on parole, I could be searched and detained for any reason. Or for no reason at all. I'd had to sign away most of my rights when I was released from prison.

This had to have something to do with that woman who'd identified me. What did she tell them I'd done? Until just before the cops stopped me, I'd been inside the factory of Quality Steel Fabrications. John, the foreman, could vouch for that.

Was that girl who ID'd me trying to claim I'd been driving the car when it crashed so she wouldn't be blamed? That didn't make sense.

Could she have said I was trying to kidnap her and her friend?

That made even less sense.

If I'd hoped to find out anything when we got to the jail, or be officially charged, I was out of luck. I wasn't about to say anything I didn't have to, so I didn't ask. I was escorted into a cell in the booking area, but instead of starting the usual paperwork, I was searched again, more thoroughly this time. I had to hand over my steel-toed boots, hoodie and belt. They still had the wallet, keys and Steb's money clip.

They gave me back the rest of my clothes to put on instead of issuing me an orange jumpsuit. The concrete floor was cold through my socks.

My things were bundled up in a paper bag and the bag stapled shut. A bored officer shoved a paper across the counter to me. "Check this list over and sign it if it's right."

Boots. Belt. Hoodie. Keychain with one key. Wallet with two IDs, work and prison. Forty two cents in coins. Three thousand six dollars in cash.

I blinked. Three thousand six dollars?

Steb's money clip had three thousand dollars in it? Even if they were all hundreds, that was thirty bills.

Where would Steb get that kind of money? And why would he be carrying it around with him?

He had to be worried sick. I wondered if there was any way I could get in touch with him to let him know where it was. Not likely. He was secretive and suspicious, and I doubt anybody outside personnel knew where he lived.

"You wanna make a phone call?" the officer asked me.

I looked around for a clock, but didn't see one. Who could I call? Kelly, my some-times girlfriend, would be my best bet, but she wouldn't appreciate being roused from her bed. It's not like she could do anything anyhow. And she was mad at me right now, for reasons that weren't entirely clear to me. I could try Jumbo George, who was my landlord. I was renting a couple of rooms above his store. Theoretically, he lived up there, too, but he'd gained so much weight over the years that he couldn't make it up the stairs any more, and slept on a recliner in the back room of the store. It'd be cruel to call him now—he had enough trouble getting out of the recliner as it was, without having the phone ring in the early morning hours. I didn't see that he could do much of anything, either. Or why he'd want to.

"Could I wait until a more reasonable hour?" I asked the officer. "I hate to wake anybody up now."

He shrugged. "Suit yourself. I'll leave a note for the next shift that you didn't get your phone call. But I can't guarantee they'll let you have it."

"No big deal." Jumbo George read the newspaper every day. Even if I didn't manage to call him, he's see Carissa's article and figure out what happened. I wasn't sure what he'd do, if anything.

Kelly couldn't read, although she didn't like to admit that to people. If she saw the paper with my picture on it, she'd buy a copy and get someone to read it to her. Probably her young son, Chris. I wasn't thrilled with the idea of the kid reading what Carissa would write about me, but there wasn't a whole lot I could do about it.

And even if she didn't see the paper, eventually she'd try to call me at Jumbo George's place.

Work was shut down for the coming week, so there was no need to call my foreman, who was probably still at Quality Steel. With any luck, I'd be back out on the street before I was supposed to report for a shift. And if I wasn't, chances were good I'd be on my way back to prison, and it wouldn't matter if I lost the job.

I was escorted to a small holding cell inside the entrance to the jail. It looked like we were skipping the visit to medical which was a standard part of intake.

The CO, the correctional officer, stopped and gestured for me to enter. I stepped inside and, with the metallic clang of a cell door closing, I was locked in. The panic that had been rising in my throat threatened to overwhelm me. I'd spent most of the last twenty years of my life in prison. Ever since I was convicted of murder at age sixteen. And here I was again, locked in a cell.

I leaned my forehead against the coolness of the solid steel door and closed my eyes. My hands were clenched and I felt like I was going to throw up. I looked over to make sure I could make it to the stainless steel all-purpose plumbing unit if I needed to. Taking a deep breath, I forced my muscles to relax. I knew I couldn't make my situation any better, but I sure as hell could make it worse if I didn't suppress the urge to scream curses and pound on the walls. They'd just put me in a restraint chair and note that I'd been uncooperative.

A holding cell might not be my favorite place, but it beat a restraint chair any day.

I tried to make sense of this. I hadn't been booked. Or told why I was being detained. The processing had been minimal.

Decidedly not usual procedure. Possibly not entirely legal. But I was on parole, so that nobody was going to worry about how long I was held. They could be pretty sure I wasn't going to complain. If I did, no one would pay any attention anyhow, except maybe to call Mr. Ramirez, my parole officer, and ask him to start proceedings for a parole violation hearing. That would most likely be a ticket back to prison. I could do without the clock beginning to tick on that.

I should try to get some sleep. I'd reported to work at midnight last night, and now it must be near dawn. The cell didn't have a window. I would have to tell time as best I could by the meals I was served and the shift changes of the staff. I hoped I wouldn't be here for many of them.

Someone must have asked the jail officials to hold me for what they would call an "interview," but was more like an interrogation. When that happened, I'd want to be as alert as possible. I knew from experience how my words could be twisted around to make it seem as if I'd said things I'd never intended. Being tired would make it all the more difficult for me to keep my wits about me.

I leaned my head back against the concrete block wall. A cold lump had formed in my stomach, but I tried to ignore it.

My thoughts raced. What did Carissa know? Or think she knew? I tried to convince myself no one could make a connection between me and those women who disappeared.

I reminded myself to take deep, measured breaths and relax. My mind was a pond with a calm surface, I told myself. No thoughts at all. Any thoughts were ripples that spread out from the center and disappeared.

Breakfast showed up. The slot in the cell door swung open and a tray was shoved through. I grabbed it. The slot slammed shut again. It was delivered by a correctional officer, not an inmate kitchen worker. He didn't say anything.

Oatmeal, milk, a banana, coffee. The oatmeal and the coffee were even hot. The meal was very welcome.

Before I had a chance to finish, I heard someone outside the cell. "Pop the door on Holding # 2." That was followed by the sound of the remotely controlled door lock clicking open.

I shoveled the rest of the oatmeal into my mouth and downed the coffee, scorching my throat. Meals might show up on a regular basis, or they might not. I knew I'd better eat when I could.

Two COs stood there. They peered at me. One held a waist chain with attached cuffs in his hands. "You gonna cooperate?" he asked.

"Yes, sir," I said, straightening up and lifting my arms so he could slap the chain around my waist.

I'd worn lots of shackles and restraints over the years, especially in the first year I'd been incarcerated and was less inclined to be compliant, but I'd never been in this type of restraint before. The cuffs were separate from each other and attached to the waist chain at the sides. It was supposed to be more comfortable and more secure than regular handcuffs and a waist chain. For a minute, I was afraid the CO was going to cross my arms in front of me, which I'd seen happen to some prisoners, but he just locked each cuff around the wrist on that side.

Where were they taking me that I needed to be shackled up like that? Surely not straight back to prison.

No, I told myself. Usually those transports got done one night a week, when the prison bus made its rounds. And I hadn't had a parole violation hearing.

So far, I hadn't asked any questions, but these COs were acting professional and disinterested, so maybe I could find something out. If they knew.

I licked my dry lips. "Where're you taking me?"

The CO shrugged. "Somebody wants to see you, I guess. In the police station, though, not one of the conference rooms in the jail."

Sure enough, they escorted me to an elevator that lurched up to a secure area of the police station, and turned me over to an officer there. He deposited me in an all-too-familiar interrogation room with a battered wooden table between two equally battered chairs.

I sat down and stared at a mirror high on the wall of the room. It was almost definitely a one-way mirror for observation, although I had no doubt that there was a camera rolling and a recorder picking up every sound.

Part of the technique, of course, would be to leave me for an extended period of time in the hopes I would become increasingly anxious and ready to talk as soon as someone showed up. But I'd been through this kind of thing enough to know what they were trying to do, and while it gets to me, I would never let that show. I slumped in the chair and tried again to clear my mind of any thoughts. Especially thoughts of abducted women.

I shifted in the chair. This waist chain with separated cuffs *was* a lot more comfortable. My hands were at my sides, rather than in front of me, so my shoulders weren't so strained. I might even be able to manage a cup of coffee if they offered one. I leaned over to one side and tried bringing my hand to my mouth. No. It'd still take major contortions to drink anything. Which would mean I'd have to ask to have one hand released. Any time I asked for anything, it would improve their perceived psychological advantage over me. Which was already considerable.

The door opened, but I didn't turn to look. I caught a whiff of cheap cigars and stale whiskey.

Detective Belkins? I'd had a few run-ins with him before. He didn't like me much. That was okay—I didn't like him much, either. But he was an old-school cop, not fussy about how he got his information and evidence.

I'd heard a rumor that he'd been ordered into alcohol counseling. And was getting ready to retire. Or forced into it, as soon as he was eligible for his pension.

His retirement couldn't come too soon, as far as I was concerned. And where was Detective Montgomery, who often partnered with him? Montgomery wasn't exactly a sympathetic soul, but he was a cop's cop, professional and careful to follow procedure. If he was involved in a case, it would be as airtight as possible before the state's attorney presented it to the court. And he didn't want any convictions overturned on appeals that could be traced to investigative errors.

For a while, I thought he was looking for promotion in the police department. Now I knew he was planning to run for mayor. When he actually announced his candidacy, he would have to stop working for the city. So he'd have to resign or take a leave of absence or something.

Had he already done so? I had to admit I hadn't been following local election news in the paper. I couldn't vote anyhow.

I resisted the urge to sit up straighter, and continued to look at the surface of the battered table.

Belkins stepped into my line of sight and stood looming over me. This close, I could tell he needed a shower.

I guess I did, too.

But he could take one whenever he wanted to.

He had an unlit cigar clamped between his teeth. His shirt was wrinkled and his shoes scuffed. He stood there staring at me.

Finally he ripped the cigar out of his mouth. "I suppose you know what you're in here for?"

Although I was tempted to ignore anything he said, I thought that wouldn't be a good idea. I was on parole. He'd call Mr. Ramirez, my parole officer, and tell him I was being uncooperative. So far as I knew, Mr. Ramirez hadn't instituted official parole violation proceedings against me, but I knew he was getting pretty fed up with all the trouble I seemed to be getting into. I had another twenty years backup time if I got sent back to prison. And if I picked up a new conviction, I'd probably never see the outside of a prison again. Especially if it was a conviction on a violent charge.

So I answered. "No, sir. I don't."

He snorted. "Hard for me to believe that. You were identified. Eye witness."

I was still in the dark about what was happening. "For what? I just got out of work."

He took a couple steps to one side. "Quality Steel's shut down for retooling. I called and asked. And even I know you don't get out of work at three in the morning."

"The power went out. We got sent home early. You can check with my foreman."

"I don't know what you've got going with him. He's covered for you before. I wouldn't trust what he says."

"You can check my timecard…" My voice trailed off. No electric power, no timeclock. No timeclock, no punched timecard. That bit of evidence would be absent.

But he didn't pick up on that. "Someone else could always punch your timecard. One of your buddies."

"The power went out. The emergency lights came on, and John sent us home. It's too dark to work safely, even if there was anything we could do with no electricity."

"If that was true, how come you didn't go home with your girl-friend?"

Kelly, my some-times girlfriend, worked the same shift as I did, but she hadn't worked last night. "It wasn't a full shift working. Just a few of us. Tearing down the platers, moving equipment, stuff like that. They had me come in 'cause I drive a forklift and they needed a lot of stuff moved."

"Your girlfriend drives a forklift, too. And she's got seniority over you."

That was true. When she worked, though, she had to pay a babysit-ter for her two kids. It made more sense for her to get a full week's unemployment compensation. So when they posted a list for people who wanted to work a partial week, she hadn't signed up.

"No answer to that, eh?" Belkins said. "She finally come to her senses and kick you out?"

Kelly and I had never lived together, so she couldn't really kick me out, but ending the relationship might not be far from the truth. We hadn't had a fight or anything I could point to, but she didn't seem to have much time for me lately. Something wasn't right.

He was trying to rile me. I didn't rise to the bait.

It was all I could do to keep facing straight ahead. He walked around behind me, where I couldn't see him. He'd been known to smack me on the back of the head when he got frustrated. I fervently hoped the camera was rolling. Even Belkins wouldn't want to be taped smacking a handcuffed prisoner.

"Those girls…" he said, and paused.

Panic rose in my throat. "What girls?"

"The girls in the car that crashed."

I could hear him pacing behind me. "The one that hit the light pole?"

"Maybe. Tell me about the girls."

There he was, twisting what I said around. "I don't know anything about them."

"About who?"

"The girls in the car that crashed."

"You know the one girl identified you positively?"

Eyewitness identification is pretty unreliable. But it's hard to refute. "Identified me for doing what?"

"You know."

"No, I don't."

"Come on. Three o'clock in the morning. How many people are out? And they gave a good description of what you looked like. Before they saw you."

"I told you, I'd just gotten out of work. I was on my way home."

"Yep, that's what you said, all right. How about the other girls?"

"I don't know anything about any other girls."

"But you do know these ones?"

"No." I closed my eyes. No matter what I said, he'd make it sound like I'd done something wrong. Or was trying to hide something.

"I've got a call in to Mr. Ramirez."

Of course he would have called Mr. Ramirez.

"You know you have twenty years backup time?"

Of course I knew that.

"I'm going to have you held while I do some investigating."

I strongly suspected he wasn't supposed to do that. I should be charged or have a parole violation scheduled or something.

But he had his connections. I wouldn't want to take bets that he couldn't arrange for someone to keep me in jail and "forget" to process me on time.

And I wasn't exactly in a position to object.

CHAPTER 3

"Could I get a phone call?" I asked the CO who returned me to the holding cell.

"Didn't you get one when they first brought you in?"

"It was the middle of the night. I didn't know anybody I could wake up. They said maybe I could get one later."

He shook his head. "Not something I'm supposed to take care of. Looks like you missed your chance." He radioed for the cell door to be opened. It slid open and I stepped back inside.

This holding cell was getting old fast. Lunch showed up, once again served by a uniformed CO instead of an inmate kitchen worker.

I tried to sleep, but the cell was cramped. The only place I could lie down was on the floor, with my feet up against the plumbing unit and my head jammed up against the door. It was cold, and every time I dozed off, I woke up shivering.

When supper came around, I decided to see if the CO had any information he would share. Or if he was willing to find out anything.

The slot opened and a tray slid in. I grabbed it.

"Officer?" I asked.

He didn't say anything, but he paused.

"Do you have any idea how long I'm gonna be held?"

"No."

"Do I have any charges or parole violations pending?"

"No idea."

"Any way you could find out why I'm being held?"

"You don't know?"

"No, sir."

"What do your charging papers say?"

"They didn't give me any."

"No charging papers? Were you booked?"

"No, sir."

"That's weird. But not something I can do anything about."

"It's chilly in here. Could I get a blanket?"

"You weren't issued bedding?"

"No." He hadn't actually refused to bring me the blanket. I decided to push it a little more. "Any possibility of toilet paper?"

"You didn't get that, either?"

"No."

"How about a jumpsuit? And shower shoes?"

"I'm still in my street clothes."

"Really." He sounded mildly curious.

"Yes, sir. And I could use a shower."

"You didn't get a shower when you went through medical?"

"I didn't go through medical."

"Were you uncooperative?"

"No, sir."

"Were you processed at all?" he asked.

"Not that I know of. Just locked up."

"I'll see if I can find out anything. But that's not likely."

"Thank you."

Supper wasn't bad. Some kind of stew with lots of carrots and potatoes, but not much meat. Two slices of bread. A cup of coffee and a piece of something that may have been apple cake. I ate it and put the cup and spoon on the tray, waiting for the CO to return for it. Would he bother to try to help me? No real reason why he should. I was completely dependent on his good will.

A little while later the slot slid open.

"Here's a blanket." He partially unfolded it so it would fit through the slot.

I grabbed an end and pulled. "Thank you."

He shoved in half a roll of toilet paper. "Don't be clogging up that drain, now."

"I won't."

"I didn't find out much," he said. "But you can write a request for an update in your status and I'll put it in the lieutenant's mailbox. He probably won't get to it until day shift tomorrow, though."

"That's a whole lot better than nothing. I don't have a piece of paper, though. Or anything to write with."

With a sigh, the CO slipped a smudged request form through the slot, followed by a pencil.

I tried to come up with a reasonable way to ask my questions without sounding like a smart ass. I didn't know the lieutenant's name, but that shouldn't matter. I hesitated, the form resting on the edge of the slot and the pencil poised over it.

The CO shifted from one foot to the other. His keys jangled. "Just put 'Request status update' on it and sign it. Then put your commitment number on it."

I wrote down what he told me, but said, "I don't have a number."

"It's on your ID. Look at it."

"I don't have an ID."

"The wristband."

"They didn't give me a wristband."

"How could you be locked up like this and not have a wristband? Or a commitment number?" He made it sound like it was my fault.

"That's what I'm trying to find out."

I put the pencil and the request slip on the tray, and passed it through the slot.

"I'll put the request slip in the lieutenant's mailbox," he said. "But I don't understand how you could have managed to miss the processing."

I didn't understand it, either.

The blanket helped. I wrapped it around myself, so it not only covered me, it was between me and the floor. It wasn't exactly comfortable, but at least I didn't keep waking up freezing. I used the roll of toilet paper for a pillow.

Breakfast came just before the shift changed. I ate and handed back my tray. Then I settled down to wait. Not much else I could do. To pass the time, I started to devise an exercise routine I could follow in the cramped space.

Before I got started on it, the door slid open.

"Pack out," the CO told me. That meant for me to gather my things.

"I don't got nothing but a blanket."

"Well, then, pack out your blanket."

He stood aside for me to step out, but didn't put on any restraints, so I could be pretty sure we weren't going too far.

Sure enough, he escorted me to booking. They took the blanket away from me.

I knew the routine. Fingerprints, mug shots, on to medical for a physical and a shower. I had to hand over all my clothes.

No one told me whether I was getting new charges or a parole violation, but I should be finding out soon enough, when they gave me a copy of the charging papers. I'd waited this long. I could wait a while longer. The shower was welcome. The jumpsuit they issued was way oversized, and since I didn't get a tee shirt or socks, I was cold. Eventually, though, they'd have to assign me to a cell. Then I'd be issued bedding and I could wrap the blanket around myself.

I did get an ID, a wristband with my name, picture and a commitment number on it. "Don't lose that," the intake officer warned as she slipped it on my wrist. "It'll cost you twenty bucks for a replacement."

Instead of being handed a pile of bedding and given a cell assignment, though, I was taken to a bigger holding cage where a few other men sat despondently on the bench.

"What's this for?" I asked as the door opened for me to step through.

"I dunno." The CO shrugged. "Maybe you're on the list for a bail hearing?"

That meant it couldn't be a parole violation. Had to be new charges.

"They didn't give me charging papers," I said.

"That right?" The CO didn't look like he cared much. "You should have them. I'll ask."

He might. Or he might not. I hoped he would. It would be nice to know what I was charged with if I was going to have a bail hearing.

As if a bail hearing would do me any good. The charges had to be something fairly serious, or they wouldn't have bothered to lock me up. They'd just have contacted my parole officer and asked him to take care of things.

The charges had to stem from that girl's ID of me. But I still had no idea what had been done to her. Obviously she hadn't been abducted.

I did know, though, that whatever it was, I hadn't been the one to do it.

Most people involved in the criminal justice system know just how unreliable eyewitness identification is. But it still could be used in court.

I glanced at the men already occupying the cell. In the corner, an older white man dozed with his head leaning against the wall and his mouth hanging open. Three guys, all in their late teens or early twenties, two white and one black, argued loudly among themselves, casting unfriendly looks at the remaining occupant, a thin nervous white man. He was seated at one end of the bench, his shoulders squared and his blond hair slicked back. Despite wearing a jumpsuit like the rest of us, he somehow managed to look well put together. His jumpsuit actually seemed to fit, and on him, it looked more like some kind of misguided effort at leisure attire than a jail uniform. His cheek jerked repeatedly. A tic.

He glanced at me, his face rigid and his hand clutching his paperwork. I nodded a greeting and sat down between him and the threesome. I suspected that, sooner or later, they would try some mischief, if only out of boredom. It never pays to be in a cell when there's a problem. Everybody gets blamed. Maybe if I sat between them it would head it off.

The man licked his lips and nodded back at me. Then he held out his hand. "Kyle Staten."

I took his hand and shook it. "Jesse," I said, not giving a last name. Under the circumstances, adding "Pleased to meet you" didn't seem appropriate.

"My lawyer says this may take a while," he said.

"Oh?" I answered.

"Yes. The judge isn't the regular one. It's a visiting judge or something."

"You don't say?"

"And my lawyer has no idea whether he'll be reasonable or not. It could even be a woman."

Why would it make any difference if the judge turned out to be a woman?

I didn't see how any of that would matter to me anyhow. My representation would be an overworked public defender who was handling all the bail reviews assigned to the office today. He would have taken a cursory glance at my record, and he would request a bail. Probably half-heartedly, since he'd privately agree with the state's attorney that there was no way I should be released on bail.

No one, reasonable or not, was going to set a bail for me anywhere near where I could meet it. All I had was the six dollars. I tried to put the idea of Steb's three thousand out of my mind. After all, it wasn't my money.

On the other hand, Steb wasn't getting it back until I either got sprung or talked to somebody who could come get it. So maybe...

But even the whole three thousand would only cover a bail of thirty thousand. Assuming there was a bail bondsman out there who was willing to assume the risk. Big assumption.

Kyle was rambling on. "I just talked to my attorney before they put me in here. They didn't find out until this morning that the scheduled judge was not going to be in. So they had to call in a substitute, but it might be afternoon before they hold the bail reviews." He shifted in his seat. "Do they feed us even if we're not in the cellblock? I didn't eat the breakfast."

"Yeah. A bag lunch. Prob'ly a bologna and cheese sandwich and an apple. Milk, or maybe coffee."

He wrinkled his nose. "Bologna? I don't like bologna."

I shrugged. "They won't care whether you like it or not. Take it, though. If you don't want to eat it, somebody else will."

Kyle looked over at the teenagers, who were once again huddled in a group. "Should I give it to them? Boys that age are always hungry."

"If you want. But then they might expect you to hand over all your food," I said.

"What do you mean?"

I shrugged. "Depends on how long we're in here. Then we either get bailed out or put in the jail population. If you end up in the population, and anybody thinks they can get away with it, they'll take all your food."

He frowned. "If I gave it to you, would you eat it?"

"Sure. It's food. Hard to get enough to eat in here."

He leaned close and lowered his voice. "Those kids kind of scare me."

A sensible reaction. "So just leave them alone," I said.

"Suppose they don't leave me alone?"

"Ignore them if you can. If you have to fight, give good account of yourself. Even if it's three against one and you know you're going to lose."

"What?"

This guy was going to have problems if he didn't get bailed out.

"In jail, you don't mix it up unless you have to. But if you do have to, make sure everybody knows you'll go down fighting. And do some damage. That way they'll think twice about attacking you again."

"But I might get hurt."

"Well, yeah, but you'd get hurt anyhow. So make the best of it."

He looked at the teens and moved closer to the wall. "They better hurry up with those bail hearings."

"They generally have twenty four hours to hold it." Not that they had followed that in my case. "When did you get arrested?"

"Last night, around seven."

"So they'll have it today."

He glanced at his wrist. The only thing there was his ID. Of course they'd taken his watch, if he had one. "Are you going to have a bail hearing, too?"

"I would think so."

"Is someone going to post bail for you?" he asked.

"I doubt it. I don't know too many people with that much money. And it's likely to be set fairly high."

Kyle raised his eyebrows. "Really? What have they charged you with?"

"I'm not sure. They haven't given me the charging papers yet. But I'm on parole. Violent offenses. So the judge is likely to set bail so high I can't make it."

"How can they keep you in here if you don't know what the charges are?"

"Not a problem. Just hold me for parole violation. Getting arrested is a violation itself. And I'm sure they have the paperwork somewhere. I'll get a copy eventually."

But he wasn't paying attention. "This whole thing is a misunderstanding," he said. "As soon as they set bail, my secretary will get the money and be down to get me out."

"Good for you."

"Yes. Embezzlement! Can you believe that? Okay, I played a little fast and free with a client's money. But embezzlement? They can't prove that. And the money will be repaid. I'd bet it's already been transferred back into his account."

Embezzlement was way out of my area. I tuned him out as he ranted about intent, accounting irregularities and audits.

He finally wound down and took a deep breath. "So you're on parole? For what?"

No reason to hide the truth here. "Murder."

His eyes opened wide and he inched away. "Murder? Who did you kill?"

"Well, I didn't actually kill anybody myself. I was just a dumb kid, acting lookout for my older brothers. I thought they were making a drug buy. Maybe they were, or maybe they planned to rip off the dealer. At any rate, somebody got shot. And died."

"Who got shot and died?"

"The dealer."

"And a jury convicted you?"

"Didn't go to jury trial. I copped an Alford plea. Didn't admit guilt, but agreed that the state had enough evidence to convict me if it went to trial."

"But you didn't kill anyone."

"No. But there's this charge called felony murder. It's when you're involved in a felony, and somebody dies as a result of it. For sure they had grounds for that."

"Even if it wasn't you who killed him?" He asked.

"Even if I wasn't even there. I was outside."

"That seems harsh. How old were you?"

"Sixteen." I tended to agree with him about it being harsh, but that didn't make much difference. "Before the whole thing started, my brothers made me agree that I'd take responsibility if it went wrong. We figured I'd just pick up juvenile charges. Worst that would happen was I'd end up with a slap on the wrist. Few months in juvie hall. So I didn't deny that I was part of it. But I didn't know anybody'd been killed."

"Sounds like you got more than a few months in…" He frowned. "Juvie hall, did you say?"

"Sure did. I didn't know murder charges could end up in adult court when you're sixteen."

"Did they?"

"Sure did," I said.

"So you got sent to adult prison?"

"Yep."

"At age sixteen?"

"Well, I was seventeen by the time I actually got there."

He frowned. "How long were you there?"

"Almost twenty years. I got paroled, just before Christmas."

"And now you've been arrested again?"

"Yep."

Kyle shook his head. "What do you think's gonna happen to you now?"

Not something I liked to dwell on. "Depends," I said. "But I'm not likely to be happy about it."

He lapsed into silence.

The kids continued their arguing. The other guy snored lightly.

We got lunches. The predicted sandwiches, apples and milk.

The bologna had a chemical smell. The cheese was rubbery. The bread was stale. The apples were bruised. And the milk was warm.

The kids complained, but they ate theirs. Kyle gave me his. The other guy woke up briefly, took a look in his bag, and gave it to the kids.

A CO showed up. "Staten. Time for your bail hearing."

Kyle stood up and looked at me, panic in his eyes. He licked his lips yet again.

"Nothing to worry about," I told him. "Just go and watch on the screen. Don't try to hide from the camera. If you can't understand something, ask them to repeat it. They know the sound's bad. Answer questions, but don't say nothing you don't have to. Let your lawyer do the talking."

I made it sound easy. Keep emotions under control and not say much. But I knew it wasn't really like that. When my turn came, I'd likely be panicky, too. And maybe say something stupid.

CHAPTER 4

A woman in civilian clothes stopped by the holding cage. She looked at the paperwork in her hands and frowned. "Jesse Damon?" she asked.

I got up. "That's me."

"Here are your charging papers," she said, passing a few folded sheets of paper through the bars and wrinkling her nose as if something smelled bad.

"Thank you," I said.

She didn't say, "You're welcome." Or look at me. She just turned and walked away.

I took them back to the bench. They were carbonless copy forms, and they had that distinctive odor. I sat down and took a deep breath before I unfolded them. The printing on them was faint and I had to turn it to the light to make it out.

When I started reading, my mind went blank. Assault. Attempted carjacking. Assault with intent to rape or defile. Attempted murder.

What the hell had that girl told them? And why did she think I was the one who did it?

Well, the answer to the second question was easy. Very few people were out on the street at three o'clock in the morning. If I bore any resemblance whatsoever to the perpetrator, she'd be likely to say it was me.

Biting my bottom lip, I tried to get a handle on my emotions. This wasn't the time or the place to cry. It might be hours, even days, before I found a corner to myself. Unless I ended up in an isolation cell. Jails didn't exactly specialize in privacy, and they were no place to break down in tears. Not if I wanted to survive.

Although it did occur to me maybe survival wasn't all that important an issue, if I was headed back to prison.

My mind wandered to the marvelous things I'd been able to do in the last few months since my release. Take long walks. Go out and look at the stars. Fix dinner in a real kitchen with Kelly. Read stories to her two kids. Snuggle down with her in her warm soft bed. Work a decent job among regular people. Take a shower when I felt like it. Cash a paycheck.

Choose my own food. My thoughts swirled. Was all that really over for me? I rubbed my nose and choked back a sob.

Kyle reappeared, his face more relaxed. "Not too bad. Ten thousand bail. And I have to turn in my passport. Do they really think I'd leave the country over this nonsense?"

I couldn't answer that.

The CO looked at his clipboard. "Damon," he said.

I stood up and jammed my feet into the shower shoes. They were too big and threatened to slip off my feet, so I had to shuffle along.

Since there was no way I could afford an attorney myself, I expected to be represented by a public defender. Who had skipped the usual step of coming to the jail to talk to me before the bail hearing.

Not surprising. The booking had been very last-minute, so maybe he—or she—hadn't had a chance. One look at my record and he probably figured there was no way the judge was going to set a reasonable bail. Or for me to make it if he did.

Even though it was his job to represent me, I'd take bets that he wasn't too enthusiastic about it.

I stood in a small booth-like room, a camera above and a video monitor to the side. It smelled like unwashed feet. The monitor screen was divided into two sections, one with the judge and the other with the rest of the courtroom.

The judge had a lined face and fluffy white hair. A visiting judge, they'd said. Probably someone called out of retirement to help with the overwhelming caseload, which was made worse by having the regular judge call in sick or whatever happened. I hoped this guy hadn't been called away from a golf game or some birthday party for his grandchild or something else he wanted to do. That would put him in a lousy mood.

They could see me, and I knew I looked a wreck. Since I'd been relieved of the elastic that had held my ponytail, the wiry brown curls of my shoulder-length hair stood up around my head like some kind of wildman. I needed a shave. The orange jumpsuit was too big, and I had to keep hitching it up on my shoulder.

Was the judge experienced enough in criminal cases that he realized jail inmates didn't have much of a chance to spruce up for bail hearings? I knew I looked more than a little demented.

The air in the little room was close, and I felt like I could hardly breathe. I suppressed a cough. If I had to say much, I wasn't sure I'd be able to form the words I needed.

I looked down at the charging papers in my hand. They were barely legible, but that might have been because my eyes were blurring up.

The picture on the monitor was grainy. Someone started talking. I couldn't see who, but it must have been the bailiff.

"State vs. Damon. Case number…"

I couldn't understand all of what he said. I missed the case number, but it would be on the charging papers.

"Counsel, please identify yourself for the record."

The state's attorney mumbled something, but I didn't worry about it.

The other attorney spoke more clearly. "John Billings for the defendant."

I knew all the local public defenders by name and reputation. John Billings was not one of them.

The state's attorney's voice came through in a crackly whisper. "Your Honor. We recommend no bail. The defendant is a convicted felon on parole, and the charges against him are quite serious. He represents a clear threat to the public. He has few connections to the community and is a flight risk."

Well, that was probably that. They'd hold me until the state's attorney came up with the best plea bargain the public defender could negotiate, and then I'd end up agreeing to it. It was unlikely I'd ever see the outside of a prison again in this lifetime. I choked back the vomit that rose in my throat.

The minor fact that I wasn't the person who had tried to carjack the girls wouldn't matter much. They had positively identified me.

Another man stepped up. He wore a well-cut dark suit. The video was not in color, so it looked gray. Surprisingly snazzy suit for a public defender. His hair wasn't just cut, it was styled. I was sure I'd never seen him before. He wasn't young, but he might be a new hire. Great. An inexperienced public defender.

Or a panel attorney, a private attorney assigned by the court. That could be either the best possible situation or a total disaster, depending upon how much experience he had and how much work he was willing to put in.

And an unknown, visiting judge.

This was very unlikely to go in my favor. But then, I hadn't really expected it to.

"Your Honor," the lawyer said. "I realize the charges are serious. But there is little evidence that my client is the perpetrator of the crimes of which he is accused. Only an identification, on the street at night, connects my client with them. He is gainfully employed and has been compliant with supervision since his release from prison."

Was I hearing right? "My client?" Had he somehow already been assigned to the case? And actually showed up at the bail hearing?

The state's attorney interrupted. "Eyewitness identification is hardly 'little evidence,' Your Honor."

The other attorney spoke again. "The victim was under duress. She said that a man tried to open the door of her car and pull her out, so she drove off. She was so upset she ended up crashing the car into a utility pole a few blocks away. My client happened to be in the area, and she identified him as the person she thought had attacked her. It was not a line-up; he was the only possibility presented. I propose, Your Honor, that under the circumstances, it would be difficult to make an accurate identification. It was dark. The victim has been hospitalized with a head injury, which may very well have impaired her abilities."

"The time frame is important, Your Honor," the state's attorney said. "At this hour of the morning—shortly after 3 a.m.—very few people are out and about. The defendant was definitely out on the street in the area where the crimes were committed when he was picked up. And he fit the general description the victim gave of the suspect."

"My client was picked up just outside his place of employment. He had just gotten off work."

"Your Honor," the state's attorney said, "it's common knowledge that we have recently had a spate of kidnappings, which have led to several sexual assaults and murder. None of these incidents occurred prior to this defendant's release from state prison in December of last year. This defendant is not being charged with those crimes at this time, but he is a person of interest. It would be a disservice to the community to permit this person to be free on bail while the investigation is ongoing. And he has little incentive to remain in the area."

"As the state's attorney has noted," said this amazing guy who apparently was my attorney, "the defendant is a convicted felon. DNA evidence has been recovered from at least two victims, one alive and one dead. As a convicted felon, my client's DNA is on file and readily accessible. If a match could be made with the evidence from these crimes, he would have been in jail, awaiting trial, not getting out of work at three in the morning."

The judge looked from one lawyer to the other. "You say he is gainfully employed?"

"Yes, Your Honor. Since his release he has been working at Quality Steel Fabrications, on an overnight shift."

The judge peered at the state's attorney. "These kidnappings have occurred during the early morning hours in the middle of the workweek, haven't they?"

"Yes, Your Honor."

"When the defendant should have been at work?" the judge asked.

"We have not yet checked the defendant's absences from work against the dates of the crimes. The investigation is ongoing. That is definitely on our list."

"You can do that whether he's incarcerated or out on bail, can't you?"

"Yes, Your Honor. But…" the state's attorney protested.

"And," the judge turned toward my lawyer. "There is no record of parole violations?"

"No, Your Honor. Not one. He's made it on time to all his appointments. And Mr. Ramirez, the parole officer, took him off house arrest a few weeks ago."

"Any FTA's?"

Those were failure to appear when summoned by the court. I hadn't ever had a chance to fail to appear—pretty much every time I was summoned, I'd been escorted to court in shackles from a jail or a prison. Like now.

"No," the lawyer answered, as if I'd had a choice. "None at all."

"Has the defendant got anything to add?" the judge asked, gesturing toward the camera. His hand filled the whole screen in front of me.

I swallowed hard. "No, sir."

The judge nodded. "Twenty five thousand dollars bail."

"Your Honor." The state's attorney shook his head. "This could be a high profile case. Just this morning, in the newspaper…"

The judge frowned. "We handle these things in court, not in the newspaper." He turned to my lawyer. "However, I will request that the defendant be fitted with a GPS tracking device if he is released."

Twenty five thousand dollars bail. Amazingly low. But still out of reach. If a bail bondsman would take it, I'd have to come up with two thousand five hundred dollars. That was impossible.

Unless I used Steb's money…

CHAPTER 5

When I returned to the holding cell, Kyle was pacing its short length, bouncing on the balls of his feet. He seemed to have forgotten that anyone else was present. There wasn't much room, and he was coming uncomfortably close to stepping on other people's feet. The shower shoes we'd all been issued offered little protection from a stomping, inadvertent or not.

Kyle stood still as the CO approached again with his clipboard, rousing the old man and hauling him off for his bail hearing.

I folded my charging papers and tucked them between snaps of the jumpsuit. The distinctive odor tickled my nose.

Muttering to himself, Kyle resumed his pacing.

Annoyed, one of the kids glared at him. "Why the hell don't you sit down?" he snarled.

A scowl on his face, Kyle swung around, his fists clenched. "Now you just look here…"

What was the matter with him? We were all much better off an hour ago, when he admitted he was "kind of scared" of them.

As one, the three teens stood, their heads jutted forward and their arms hanging loose by their sides. "What did you say?"

If there was a fight, we all stood to get a good dose of pepper spray. And even if I wasn't part of it, it would notch my security level up one when I got put in population at the jail. I was likely to be assigned to a fairly restrictive level as it was.

I got to my feet and stepped between Kyle and the kids. "I'll take care of it," I told them. They didn't move.

"None of us needs more trouble," I said. "And you don't want your bail hearing postponed because you got into a fight. Judge won't be happy to hear that."

I put my hands on Kyle's shoulders and shoved him down on the bench. "Sit down, dude. You're driving everybody crazy."

He set his jaw firmly and I thought he was going to argue, but he sat. I plunked down next to him and took his arm. I shook it until he looked at me, then I kept a grip on it so he couldn't get up.

The kids stood there, staring. I ignored them.

I gave his arm a little squeeze. "Not enough space in here for you to walk like that. Look at everybody else. Nobody's bothering anybody, just minding their own business." That wasn't entirely true. The three teens were paying close attention to Kyle. To judge by the way they were glaring, any minute they might be doing a lot worse than bothering him.

Kyle shook his head and turned to look at them. His eyes opened wide. They were wiry, street-smart kids with tattoos on their necks and scarred hands. Probably gang members.

Sweat glistened on Kyle's forehead.

"Sorry," he muttered. "My bad."

I deliberately didn't look straight at them, but from the corner of my eye, I saw them relax. Crisis averted.

"How long will it be before we get out of here?" Kyle asked.

I chuckled mirthlessly. "You? Couple of hours, at the most. If somebody arranges bail. Me, I dunno. Maybe never."

"My wife is already pretty mad at me," he said. "I've been thinking that maybe I don't want to go home for a while. Show her. Maybe I should just find someplace else to stay for the time being. I don't suppose you know of anyone who might have a place for rent?"

I thought about my landlord, Jumbo George, and the buildings he was renovating.

A number of the apartments were empty. Not luxury units, but they might do.

Jumbo George had inherited some money recently, and had bought all the buildings on the block where he had his shop. It was only one street away from a sprawling condo development that had been built across from the new riverfront park. The whole surrounding area showed signs of coming up in the world.

I rented a few crumby rooms over his shop. He was charging me way below market rate, even for the shape it was in. In exchange, I was supposed to help him with the massive renovations he envisioned. I knew he had some money, but I was afraid he may have bitten off more than he could chew.

He envisioned cutesy storefronts with trendy tenants below, funky but updated apartments above. A few of the storefronts were already done, and he'd rented some of them out.

The storefronts were his first priority. The apartments were mostly vacant, and in various states of disrepair. They were all on the second floor above the storefronts. Some of them were such total wrecks they were unlivable, with exposed wiring or no running water. A few of them, like the one I was living in, were inhabitable. Assuming the tenant's standards weren't too high.

Kyle looked like he was going to be good for the rent. Although if he were an embezzler, would he be likely to try to pull some kind of funny business? Jumbo George could make him pay upfront.

If I got locked up, Jumbo George might have to find somebody else to help him with the renovations. I tried to push that thought to the back of my mind.

"Yeah," I said. "I know a guy might have a place. Over on Second Street, where they're fixing up some of those old stores."

"Down by the river?"

"A block or two in. He owns a couple of those buildings. Storefronts downstairs, apartments up. Nothing fancy."

"I don't need fancy. Do you think he'd rent month to month? I really don't want to commit myself to a year's lease right now."

"Prob'ly."

"What's his name?"

"George Stenski."

"Do you have his cell phone number?"

"No." I'd never seen Jumbo George with a cell phone. I sure didn't have one. He did have a land line, but I didn't know the number. "He runs a head shop down there. Usually you can find him there during business hours." I wasn't going to tell him that Jumbo George lived in the back room.

The old man came back from his bail hearing surprisingly quickly. He sat back in his corner, laid his head against the wall, and promptly dozed off again.

Kyle didn't say anything else, but he sat right next to me, away from the teenagers. His leg jiggled non-stop, and every few minutes he sniffed and wiped his eyes.

Maybe he had his problems, but it looked like he was going to be bailed out soon. Unlike someone else I could mention.

A CO showed up at the door, clipboard in his hand. "Staten?" he asked.

Kyle glanced up hopefully. I gave him a nudge. "That's probably your bail posting. Get up."

He stood.

"Let me see your ID," the CO said.

Kyle looked confused.

"Show him your wristband," I said.

He held up his arm, shoving it through the bars. The CO checked it and nodded.

Then he looked down at his clipboard again. "Damon."

What was this? I got up and went over, holding out my wrist for him to check. Maybe Kyle was wrong that someone would be right down to bail him out. Maybe we were both going to get cell assignments.

The CO radioed for the door to be opened. We stepped out. He nodded in the direction we should go and stood back so we could precede him.

We stopped by a counter where a clerk was shuffling papers and forms. He checked our IDs and handed us property bags. "Make sure everything's there. And sign the receipt."

The bags were stapled shut. I opened mine. My clothes were there, laundered. I appreciated that. They were neatly folded on top of my boots and belt. Wallet, keychain and Steb's empty money clip were in the bottom.

The clerk shoved sealed envelopes across the counter to us. "Here's your cash." I checked the one he gave me. Three thousand six dollars and change.

Maybe they assumed I wanted to take the money and post bail? Was that fair to Steb? I could arrange for him to get back the ninety percent when the bail was refunded, whether I was convicted or not. If I was working, I could eventually pay back the ten percent the bail bondsman would keep.

Frowning, Kyle opened the briefcase they'd handed him, and unfolded a suit jacket and pants. It didn't look like his shirt or underwear had been washed, but then, they probably weren't dirty and sweaty like mine were when they were confiscated.

"Change into your clothes and put the jumpsuits in that laundry hamper," the officer said, pointing toward a cart on wheels in the corner.

I wasn't sure what was going on, but I didn't need much convincing to strip off the jail clothes and put my own on. I sat down on a bench and tied my bootlaces.

Kyle got dressed, too, and tried to smooth the wrinkles out of his pants. He flipped open his briefcase and put his wallet in there.

The officer handed us each a few sheets of paperwork. "You understand you're on bail," he said. "All the information you need is on those papers. You have to report when summoned to court, or your bail will be revoked and a bench warrant issued. Any questions?"

I had plenty of questions, but I wasn't about to ask this guy any of them. "No, sir."

"There may be additional conditions of bail," he said. "Your attorney can clarify them, or you can check the paperwork. You'll be assigned a supervision officer, if you don't have a parole officer. Failure to comply may result in revocation of bail."

"Yes, sir."

"Sign here."

We signed. I wanted to see if the paperwork explained what was happening, but it would have to wait.

Nothing compared to walking out the front door of a jail or prison, free, after a period of incarceration. The first time I'd done it, I'd been locked up for nearly twenty years. I was so ecstatic I had to keep myself from cheering. A few times since, I'd been locked up for a little while, and I found the thrill of stepping out that door to freedom never diminished.

The heavy door in front of us opened and we stepped into the sally port. The first door clanged shut and I could hear the lock engage. Then the other door, the door to the rest of the world, slid open.

I was tempted to run screaming through the lobby, out the front door, down the steps and across the street to put as much distance as I could between me and the jail.

But I didn't, of course. Kyle and I stepped sedately out into the lobby.

Mr. Billings, the lawyer who'd represented me at the bail hearing stood there. He wore dark designer shades and he carried a leather briefcase. The suit was even snazzier in person than it had seemed on the monitor from the courtroom. It was a pale blue-gray with pinstripes, much fancier than I'd expect for a public defender.

He frowned when he saw me.

"So they did spring you, I see," he said. "I figured I'd better wait around and make sure they didn't try to play any more games."

"Yes, sir. But I'm not sure I understand what happened here."

He shook his head. "I think they were just trying to hold you, which they aren't supposed to do without charging you. Probably looking for enough evidence so they could tell the media they have a viable 'person of interest' in those missing women cases. But they certainly should have gotten a DNA match by now if they were ever going to get it."

"Thank you for checking on that," I said. I didn't add I hadn't expected that much effort.

He laughed. "I took a real chance there. By the time they told me you were scheduled for a bail hearing, I had to rush over to the courthouse and I didn't have time to look at that or anything else. That'd be one of the first things they check. I just couldn't see how, if there was any kind of a match, you would have been out on the street."

I rubbed my wrists, still finding it hard to believe there were no handcuffs there. "I thought DNA results took a long time to come in."

"They usually do," Mr. Billings said. "But they can get the results expedited if they push for it. Which they would here, with a potential serial rapist and murderer on the prowl."

"Well, thanks," I said, wondering how this whole thing had come together.

"That was the best bet," he said, "If the judge still didn't want to set bail, I was prepared to challenge the way they did the ID. Not standard at all. For one thing, the victim is supposed to be transported to the suspect to make the ID, not the other way around."

In my experience, they could, and did, do whatever they wanted. "I don't think that'd make much difference. I'm on parole, so they can do pretty much whatever they want."

"There's always that. And a flawed ID is not nearly as compelling an argument as lack of a DNA match. Just as well we didn't have to go there."

"Are you a public defender?"

He snorted. "No way. I don't think they'd even informed the public defender's office you needed representation. The powers-that-be didn't expect to have an attorney looking into what was happening with you. The jail personnel wouldn't even confirm that you were being held, and were not happy when I inquired as to what your charges were and when the bail hearing would be."

I wiped my sweaty palms on my pants. "I don't know how I can pay you," I said. "I know I had some cash on me, but it's not mine."

"Not to worry," he said. "I've done a lot of work for the Stenski family. George asked me to handle this. I'll bill him. You can figure out how to pay him back, or whatever."

"Jumbo George?" The light came on in my brain. "Did he post bail, too?"

"Yep. Or he had me do it. You'll have to work that out with him, too."

"Why'd he do that for me?"

The attorney shrugged. "I don't ask why. I just do my job."

"How'd he even know I was locked up?"

"I take it you haven't seen today's newspaper." He looked at the paperwork in my hand. "Just a few things—the way George wanted it set up, he lent you the money and you've posted your own bail. Through a bail bondsman. That means if you abscond, it's you, not George, who is responsible for the rest of it. You need to report to your parole officer on time. You'll be fitted with a GPS monitor. Otherwise, your bail and parole conditions are pretty much the same. Don't miss a court appearance."

I was totally blown away. Jumbo George had done that for me?

Mr. Billings turned to go, then stopped. "Oh, and one more thing."

"Yes?"

"I'm not a criminal defense lawyer. If you go to trial for whatever that girl ID'd you for, don't come looking for me to defend you."

I suppose that shouldn't have surprised me. He had no reason to care whether I was guilty or not. He was just doing his job.

"Okay," I said.

"And if you do pick up any kidnapping and sex charges, you'll need an experienced criminal defense attorney."

CHAPTER 6

Mr. Billings nodded a terse goodbye and left. I looked around.

Kyle, dressed in his suit and despite the wrinkles, looking very presentable for someone who'd just been released from jail, was arguing with a neatly dressed young woman. She was wearing heels and her hair was pulled back in a sleek bun.

She folded her arms across her chest. "I'm sure I don't know, Mr. Staten."

"But you must know something!"

"It's not my decision." She backed up a step. "I'm just conveying a message. Mr. Richmond says to tell you to take the rest of the week off and not come near the office. Here." She tried to hand him an envelope and some folded pieces of paper. "He sent you instructions in writing. And here's a note."

Kyle didn't take them. "But what about my clients?"

"He said to tell you someone will take care of them."

"Are they bringing in an outside auditor?"

"He didn't tell me." She held out the envelope and papers again.

"But they are, aren't they?" He took what she was trying to give him and unfolded one of the papers. "This is from my wife!"

The woman nodded. "Mr. Richmond said for me to give it to you."

Kyle waved the note. "Did you read it?"

"Of course not. It's for you."

"I'm married to Mr. Richmond's daughter, you know," he said.

She gave a tight smile. "I'm aware of that. I think most of the office is."

I expected her to say something like, "And everybody knows that's how you got as far as you did." But she just kept the smile pasted on her face, her eyes blank.

Kyle scanned the note. "It says she's pretty upset and doesn't want to see me."

"You don't say," she said.

Kyle wiped his hand over his eyes. "If I'm not supposed to go to the office, where am I supposed to go?"

"I don't know. Home?"

"I can't go home." He waved the paper in the air. He seemed to have forgotten his intention to "show her" by moving out. "My wife says so. Her father bought the house for a wedding present. But it's just in her name. What am I supposed to do?"

"I'm sure I don't know, Mr. Staten," the young woman said. "Mr. Richmond just told me to bail you out and give you the car keys. And deliver the message and the paperwork. Now I have to get back to the office. Theo is out in the parking lot, waiting for me."

Kyle's face hardened and his nostrils flared. He took a step toward her. She took one backward. Alarm flickered across her face.

I stepped closer to them. The scent of an expensive perfume filled my nostrils.

He was scaring her. Right here in the lobby of the jail. If she screamed, there'd be real trouble.

Grabbing his arm, I said, "Come on, dude. It's not her fault. She's just doing what she was told. You got to get a grip."

Kyle tried to shake my hand off. I gripped tighter and pulled him back. "You're not thinking straight, buddy. You're lucky she's bailed you out. Say thank you, take your car keys, and let her get back to work."

He turned to face me, his jaw set.

I had his attention, so I kept talking to distract him. "Getting arrested and locked up does something to a guy. It messes with your mind. Don't do nothing you're gonna be sorry for later. And don't take it out on her."

Kyle relaxed. His eyes teared up. He took out a cloth handkerchief and wiped his nose.

"You prob'ly ought to get going," I said to the young lady. "He'll be okay."

Giving me that tight smile, she muttered, "As if I cared," under her breath.

Kyle wasn't paying attention.

She looked me over, taking in the hoodie, the blue jeans, the work boots. She wasn't used to taking directions from someone like me. Kyle wasn't, either.

But she said, "Thanks," and hurried off.

"You got a car here?" I asked Kyle.

He nodded, holding up the key. "She said she parked it over by the courthouse."

"Well, come on." I gave him a little shove toward the sidewalk. "Let's go find it. For sure we don't want to hang around here."

We circled the building, around to the parking lot between the county building and the courthouse. The parking lot was pretty full. I stopped at the edge, and looked out over the rows of parked cars. "What's it look like?"

"An Audi RS 5 Cabriolet," he said. "Red."

My tastes ran more to the used Chevy pickup I hoped to someday afford. I'd never even heard of an Audi RS 5 Cabriolet, but it sounded expensive. And small. And luxurious. "That's a little convertible?" I guessed.

He nodded.

I let my gaze skim over the lot. Most of the vehicles were good sized, SUVs and pickup trucks. A few sedans. There, at the end of one row, was a small car. It sat in the shade of a tree, and it looked maroon, but it could be red.

Kyle stood dumbly, wiping his nose once more with the handkerchief. I grabbed his arm again and pulled him over toward the car. "This it?"

It looked like it cost a fortune. And would be a target for thieves.

He stood next to it, his hand on the fabric roof. "Yes."

"And you got the key?"

"Yes."

"So take the key and unlock the door and get in," I said.

"It's a keyless entry."

I closed my eyes and took a deep breath. Why was I wasting my time with this clueless guy? "So open it however you open a keyless entry door. But get in."

He punched a few numbers on a keypad on the door. The locks clicked. He just stood there.

I opened the driver's side door and held it for him. The rich scent of new leather wafted up and tickled my nose. I sneezed.

He slid into the driver's seat. "Where'm I going to go? I can't go home. And I can't go to work."

"Away from here," I said. "You got any money?"

"Just a few hundred dollars. But I have my credit cards."

That was more than I'd ever had at one time. "Okay. Go get a motel room. Take a shower. Order a pizza. Catch a nap. You'll feel better when you wake up."

"Didn't you say you knew somebody who had a place I could rent for a month?"

"Yeah. But he don't want no crazy person living there. Get a motel room."

Kyle looked up at me with wild eyes. "I'm not crazy."

"You're acting like it."

"Let's go to a bar. I need a drink."

"No, you don't. That won't help. Besides, I don't know about you, but I'm not supposed to have any alcohol."

"I'm buying," he said.

"And I'm not even supposed to be in a bar, much less drinking. You might not be, either. I'm not sure what the usual conditions of bail are. I never been bailed out before."

He just sat there.

"Start the car."

He did that.

I went to shut the door.

"You need a ride anywhere?" he asked.

That gave me pause. As usual, I was walking. A ride would be nice.

"You don't mind taking me home?"

He snorted. "Home. What's that? Get in."

I relented a bit on the "crazy" designation. "If you wanted, maybe you could talk to my landlord about an apartment. But it's not much." I went around to the passenger side and opened the door. I ran my hand over the smooth gray seat. It felt like real leather. My jeans had been laundered, so I didn't have to worry about the oil and grease that were usually all over my clothes when I got off from work. I got in and closed the door.

The gear shift was on the center console. He put it into reverse. "Where to?"

I patted the pocket with Steb's money, now safely in the clip. I'd come much too close to using it to pay my bail. I'd better get it back to Steb before the next temptation came along. Who knows what I'd do then? "Actually, would you mind going to where I work and letting me run in for a minute or two? I got something I need to drop off. And I want to tell them I'm available for work the rest of the week if they need me."

By now, though, they'd have filled the limited positions available.

He backed out of the parking space and headed out to the street. The engine on that little car purred as we rounded a corner too fast. But it hugged the road.

Kyle pulled up next to the curb in front of Quality Steel Fabrications' main entrance. He peered at the grimy building. "You work *here*?"

"Yeah. Night shift."

"Doing what?"

"Laborer. Mostly drive a forklift, these days."

He shook his head. "How long are you gonna be?"

"I'm not sure. You don't have to wait if you don't want to. I can walk home from here."

He shut off the ignition. "I'll wait. And you can introduce me to your friend with the place for rent."

"Okay." I hoped I wouldn't be sorry I'd told him about Jumbo George's apartments.

I went through the front door of Quality Steel Fabrications, stopping at the receptionist's desk. She glanced at me, took in the work clothes, and her eyes went back to her computer screen. "Yes?"

"I found something that belongs to somebody who works here. I'd like to turn it in so he can pick it up."

"Whose is it?"

"Stebril Jenkins. He works nights."

"The shop is closed down nights this week. Retooling."

"He'll be working. He's a watchman."

"Okay." She pointed to a door. "You know where personnel is?"

"Yes."

"They have a lost and found."

She hit a button. The door buzzed like an annoyed hornet. Beyond the door, the plush carpet changed to worn wood flooring. Halfway down the hallway was a narrow table and a window in the wall.

I went to the window and waited for the secretary to acknowledge me.

"We're not taking applications," she said. "You can try next week, after we're back in production."

"I already work here," I said. "I wanted to turn in something I found that belongs to a guy who works here."

She sighed. "Why don't you give it to him yourself?"

"I'm not working, but he is. Midnight to eight."

"Nobody's working midnight to eight this week. Shut down for re-tooling."

"Stebril Jenkins, the watchman. He'll still work that shift."

"Oh. I guess you're right. He hasn't reported anything lost."

Steb wouldn't. He'd be secretive about it. "Well," I said. "I found it just outside. So he didn't lose it in the plant."

"Will it fit in here?" she said, handing me a large manila envelope.

"Yes, that should work fine." I slipped the money clip with its three thousand dollars inside.

"You want to write him a note?" she asked, offering me a pen and a piece of paper.

"That's okay. It don't matter who found it."

"Well, seal the envelope and put his name on it. I'll see that he gets it when I come in tomorrow morning."

I handed the envelope back. "Thank you. If they need any lift drivers for the rest of this week, could you tell John I'm available?"

"Okay, but I think they've got everybody they need. Your name?"

"Jesse Damon. He knows how to contact me."

She scribbled something down. "I'll let him know."

I went back out through the main office. The receptionist had pushed her chair back from her computer. She held the phone to her ear and had a newspaper spread on her desk. She was looking at the first page.

As I passed, she looked from me to the paper and back again, her lips pursed. She watched me until I got out the door.

CHAPTER 7

I half expected the Audi to be gone when I got outside, but there it sat at the curb, Kyle still in the driver's seat. His head leaned back against the headrest and his eyes were closed.

When I opened the passenger door, a musky odor of whiskey overwhelmed the new-leather smell. The glove box gaped open.

Kyle had a half-empty bottle clutched against his chest. The screw cap lay on the passenger seat.

"Hey, dude. What're you doing?" I asked.

He didn't respond or open his eyes, but he did lift the bottle to his lips and took a huge gulp.

How much could he have downed in the brief period of time I was gone? Surely the bottle couldn't have been full. At least it was a pint, not a fifth. Or whatever it came in now that the contents were measured in milliliters.

Sitting up, he wiped his mouth with his sleeve, and handed the bottle to me. "Have a drink, dude." His words were a little slurred.

I took the bottle and screwed the top back on it tightly. "You can't be drinking like that and driving. Get where you're going to. Then drink if you want to." I stowed the bottle in the glove compartment and closed it.

His eyes bleary, he looked at me. "I got no place to go. Unless your friend lets me stay in that apartment he's got for rent."

With a sigh, I slipped into the passenger seat. Quality Steel had security cameras all around. For sure I didn't want them to pick me up talking to somebody who was later found dead drunk outside the plant. I hoped he could drive well enough to at least get away from here.

"Let's get going," I said. "Left at the corner. Head over to Second Street. We'll figure out whether he's got a place you can rent when we get there." It wasn't far, but I held my breath the whole way. His driving seemed to be all right, but he took a railroad crossing without slowing down, skimming the oil pan on the tracks, and swung way wide on a left turn.

He parked crookedly down the street from Jumbo George's head shop.

A flood had devastated the area recently. But the city's riverfront renewal program, two blocks over, was well in progress, and the city had stepped in and repaired the sidewalks and pavement in the neighborhood.

The old rotting wharves on the river had been replaced by a riverfront walk and an extensive park. The flood control levee looked like an elevated walkway beside the park.

The underused warehouses had been replaced with a high-priced condo complex of townhouses and apartments.

The sturdy old brick buildings on the block where we were parked were from early in the last century, many of them vacant, withstood the flood, but suffered water damage. Most of the owners didn't have the interest or the funds to bring them up to code. Jumbo George, newly flush with his inheritance, had seen an opportunity and bought out the entire block. A few of the storefronts were already renovated and rented out.

Jumbo George was a long-time resident. He'd bought the building and opened his head shop back in the late 80's and seen the neighborhood deteriorate from working class to slum. Now it was on the upswing again, but it was skipping the working class and going straight for well-paid white collar workers and professionals.

Pricey shops catering to the new residents were sure to open up, and Jumbo George envisioned some moving into his picturesque storefronts. So far, a coffee shop, a pizza place and a women's clothing boutique had moved in.

Using emergency loan funds available to property owners in the flood zone, Jumbo George had hired a company that specialized in cleaning up disaster areas.

The brickwork had been tuck pointed. I was planning to start painting the trim. The exterior should look pretty good at that point.

The company had also cleared out the basements, which had been completely flooded. The dark cavernous spaces were now clean, reasonably dry and very empty. Another of my projects was supposed to be installing shelving for storage under the head shop Jumbo George ran.

The apartments above were another story. They had been above the flood line, but they all needed extensive work.

Two were still rented to old tenants, and Jumbo George had no intention of tossing anyone out on the street. Some guy had come in last week, looking for a short-term lease. Jumbo George talked to him about renting the front apartment right over the head shop.

He'd hired a contractor to work on them, but not much progress was being made, and the contractor was full of excuses.

Since Jumbo George couldn't make it up the stairs, he wanted me to help with the work and keep an eye on the progress—or lack thereof.

All this development was so new Jumbo George figured he had some time to work out his plans. Quite a few of the condos in the riverfront development weren't sold yet, and they were being offered with incentives like three months' free rent.

From my vantage point in Kyle's car, I looked at the block of buildings. I could see where Jumbo George saw potential. I also saw lots of work and expenses.

I climbed out of the car, looked over at Kyle and said, "I'll be back in a few minutes."

Maybe he'd take off this time. That would answer the question of whether Jumbo George should rent him a place or not.

The head shop had a model of a castle in the window. It was decked out with miniature knights and archers. Classier than the display of bongs and rolling papers he used to have there.

A big poster was taped to the glass in a corner. "Street Fair!" it announced, and gave details about an event planned for Saturday in the riverfront park.

Behind it were models of two civil war cannons pointed at the castle.

I frowned. If the forces that came to attack had cannons, the castle would be no good as a fortress. Something I'd have to discuss with Jumbo George at a later time. Although maybe he didn't care about being authentic. I pushed open the door to the head shop. The poignant scent of patchouli greeted me.

"Jumbo George!" I looked around the dim interior of the shop.

"Hey, there, dude," he said, lurching out from the back room.

He was enormous. His shirt hung loose over his jeans, which were so big that what was supposed to be the back pockets were around on the sides. His feet were shoved into dilapidated bedroom slippers. I knew he couldn't reach to tie regular shoes, or even see to get his feet in them.

He scratched his neck under his full beard. "Your girlfriend called up, looking for you. She sounded pissed."

"Yeah, well, I wasn't in any position to call her. Did you tell her I was locked up?"

"Nah. She called before I knew that. I figured she'd find out soon enough one way or the other."

"How'd you find out?" I asked him.

"You see this morning's newspaper?" He shoved it across the counter.

I looked at it and winced. There was one of the pictures Carissa had taken the other night. No mistaking that it was me. Handcuffed, arms held firmly by two burly cops, and looking more than moderately deranged. "Convicted Murderer Arrested in Attempted Carjacking" the headline screamed. Under it, "Person of Interest in Riverfront Rapes?" I guess the question mark was supposed to mean she wasn't sure, but it didn't come across that way.

The article wasn't a surprise. But it still was not something I was happy to see. I didn't read the whole thing now. I'd wait until I had a minute to myself. I was pretty sure I was going to be upset with what she had written, and that wasn't something I'd want anyone to see.

"Thanks for sending Mr. Billings over," I said to Jumbo George. "I'll pay you back as soon as I can."

He chuckled. "Coldhearted bastard, that Billings guy. But he knows what he's doing. Never seen him make a mistake. Thinks everybody else should be like that, too. He checked with the jail and the sheriff's office. They said they didn't have a record of you in the jail."

"Well, they didn't book me right away. Just locked me in a holding cell."

"When he found out you hadn't even been formally arrested, it kind of frosted his shorts. Said he was going to court and file a *habeas corpus* or something, make them admit they were holding you and explain it."

That must have been when they decided to process me instead of just keeping me in a holding cell.

"He got a bail set. I was surprised. And then you posted it. I don't know when I can pay you back, both the bail and the attorney fees, but I will."

"I only had to come up with twenty five hundred dollars for the bail. When you get the 90% back"—Jumbo George aimed a pointed look at me—"you are going to show up for the court date, aren't you?"

"Of course. Don't pay not to. Puts a FTA on your record, and they issue a bench warrant right away. How far could I get? I'd be picked up within a few hours."

He nodded. "Then you can give that much back to me."

"Mr. Billings said you fixed it so you lent me the money and I bailed myself out."

"Yep. I always say, think good thoughts about people and trust them. But keep the till locked."

"True, that." I nodded.

"So if you did abscond, I wouldn't be out any more than that." He scratched his beard. "You sure you don't plan to abscond?"

I laughed. "Nope."

"Even if it looks like you're gonna get locked up again? For a long time?"

My stomach twisted. "Yeah. Even then." The words stuck in my throat, but I choked them out. "I can't see that being a fugitive is that much better than being in prison. Always looking over your shoulder. You can't have any kind of a life."

"A lot of people wouldn't agree with you."

I shrugged. "That's how I see it. I'll get you the 10% of the bail soon as I can. Just in case I do end up back in prison."

"That's only two hundred fifty."

Two fifty was a lot for me, but when he put it like that, it didn't sound too terrible.

"I got a taste for some fried chicken," Jumbo George said. "You wanna go pick some up for us?"

"Okay. But first I got to do something about this guy I met who needs a place to stay. He gave me a ride over here."

He frowned. "Somebody you met in jail?"

"Yeah. He bailed out at the same time I did."

"You thinking he might move into one of the apartments?"

"Well, yeah. But I think he's got money to pay for it."

"What kind of charges did he pick up?"

"Embezzlement, I think."

Jumbo George scratched his head. "Embezzlement?"

"That's what he said. He's kind of a white collar type. And he says he's got some cash on him. Did that other guy take the front one over the shop?"

"Yep. Name's Paydon Norris. Works as a security guard in that new condo development. Moved in yesterday. Ever hear of him?"

"No."

"Well, he said he'd always lived with family, so he didn't have any references from other landlords, but he gave me a security deposit and first and last month's rent. And he does have a job. I tried to run him through one of those background checks on the computer, but I couldn't quite figure it out. I guess he's probably okay."

It was hard to see what would make Jumbo George decide someone didn't meet his standards for a tenant. After all, he rented to me. And I'm a murderer on parole.

"Any other places you might want to rent?" I asked him.

"I'd love to rent all of them. From what that contractor said, though, only two more are livable at all. The ones over the coffee shop. One's even supposed to have furniture. I haven't been able to get up there. But you could check them out and see."

"Okay. Can I bring this guy in for you to meet? He's been drinking since we bailed out."

"Sure. Bring him in."

CHAPTER 8

I went to get Kyle out of the car. He'd gotten hold of the bottle again, and the level was considerably reduced.

"Come on. I want you to meet somebody."

Kyle looked at me with bleary eyes. "Who is it?"

"My landlord."

"You think he's got a place for me to stay?" His words were even more slurred.

"I dunno. He might. You got to go in and talk to him."

Holding tight to the bottle, Kyle stumbled as he tried to stand. I grabbed his arm and shoved him, none too gently, toward the head shop. When I got him inside, I steered him past the merchandise to the back room, where Jumbo George was sitting, and deposited him in a chair at the table.

"Kyle, this is Jumbo George."

Jumbo George looked at him in amusement. Kyle blinked rapidly and held onto his bottle.

"Get us some chicken for supper," Jumbo George said to me, slapping a fifty on the table. "And some root beer."

I hurried down the street to the chicken place on the next block. Jumbo George had an enormous appetite, and would expect me to spend most of the fifty. I got two buckets of fried chicken, two dozen biscuits, a side of green salad and a side of red beans and rice. Jumbo George would grumble about the vegetables, but he would eat them. The only thing faintly resembling a vegetable that he ate on a regular basis was tomato sauce on pizzas. Time to introduce him to other options.

Then I stopped at the corner convenience store and got a twelve pack of root beer from the cooler.

It would be gone by tomorrow.

When I got back, Jumbo George was reading the newspaper. Kyle was still sitting in the chair, the now-empty bottle in front of him. He was crying.

I handed Jumbo George his change.

Nodding at Kyle, he said, "He wants more booze, but I told him I don't have any. He says we're his best friends, the only ones in the whole world he can trust."

I shook my head. Alcohol can put funny thoughts in a person's mind. "What'd you think about letting him stay in one of the apartments?"

Jumbo George stroked his beard. "I'm not real fussy about tenants right now," he said.

True. He'd just rented the front one to a security guard with no references. And he'd rented the back one to me. The only way to get to mine was by using the stairs that went up from inside the back room where we were sitting, which meant there was no way Jumbo George could lock me out of his place. My references weren't exactly stellar.

"On the other hand," he said, "this guy's in no shape to agree to anything. If he's got money, I don't want to take advantage of him. By tomorrow morning, he might decide he needs to go home and think I've cheated him out of the rent."

"How about renting a place for a week?" I said. "Say a hundred and fifty? I don't think that'll put a dent in his wallet. Seems fair to both of you."

"Sounds like a plan. See if you can get him to understand it. And if he wants to do it."

I put the food on the table and got three plates out of the cupboard. Jumbo George opened the chicken buckets, taking six pieces and putting them on his plate.

Then he opened the other containers and looked at the green salad and the rice and beans. "You trying to poison me?" he asked, but he dumped a huge portion of each on his plate. "You ever hear of fries?"

I grabbed a drumstick and put it on a plate in front of Kyle. Then I opened a can of root beer and handed it to him. "You got to eat something, dude. You might feel better if you do." Or he might just vomit.

He stared at the plate for a few minutes, as if he had no idea what to do with food, but then he picked up the drumstick and gnawed on it.

I sat down and filled my plate. The scent of the spiced chicken wafted up. After nearly twenty years of prison chow, I savored every bite of recognizable, tasty food like fried chicken.

Kyle put down his chicken and wiped his eyes. "You guys are the best friends in the whole world!" It was hard to make out what he was saying. "Ev'rybody telling me, go away. Go away. But you let me stay here. And you even feed me!"

Jumbo George raised his eyebrows and gestured toward Kyle. "See what I mean?"

"Yeah."

I reached over and tapped Kyle's hand, making him look at me. "You wanna rent a place upstairs from Jumbo George? For a week, to start with? Where you could maybe stay while you figure out what you're gonna do next?"

"Would he really let me stay?" He wiped his nose with his sleeve.

"I think so. It'd cost you a hundred fifty, though."

Kyle pulled out his wallet and dropped it on the table. "A hundred fifty?" He coughed, then hiccupped. He leaned over the table, trying to pull money out of his wallet. "That's a bit steep."

I glanced at Jumbo George. Even I didn't think a hundred fifty a week was all that bad.

"But I can do it," Kyle said. "You're my buddies. Giving me a place to stay. Nobody else wants me."

A credit card and money spilled onto the table. "Let me see. A week. That's seven nights. At a hundred fifty each—that's what, a little over a thousand?"

Jumbo George chuckled. "No. A hundred and fifty for the week. Not for a night. This ain't no high-priced hotel."

"A hundred fifty for the whole week?" Kyle fumbled with the money. "You guys are saints! Princes! Men among men!"

I reached over and took a hundred and a fifty from the pile of bills and handed them to Jumbo George.

He took a pad of numbered receipts from a corner of the table and filled out the top one. "One week's rent, a hundred and fifty. From today to…" he counted out seven on his fingers…"the sixteenth." He put the receipt on top of the money Kyle had left on the table.

"Now put the rest of that money and the other stuff back in your wallet," I said. "And put your wallet back in your pocket."

Kyle tried to stuff it back into the wallet, but it was too messy to fit. I took it and straightened everything out, slipping it in.

Between that and Steb's money clip, I'd never seen so much money in one place at one time.

"I think," Jumbo George said to me, "you'd better get him up to the apartment. Maybe stop in the coffee shop and pick him up a big cup of black coffee on the way."

He lumbered to his feet and rummaged in a cabinet. "Here's some aspirin. Maybe you can get him to take some before he goes to sleep. He's gonna need it in the morning. And here's the keys to both the apartments over the coffee shop. Choose one. One's supposed to have some furniture. And let me know what kind of shape it's in."

I tugged at Kyle's arm, but he didn't budge. "Come on. Put your wallet back in your pocket. Then come with me."

"You said he drove. What'd he do with his car?"

"Out front. Lousy parking job."

"You best be getting the keys from him, in case he takes it in his mind to go somewhere tonight. He's definitely in no shape to drive."

"Kyle, where are your car keys?" I asked.

He fumbled in his pocket and took out a key ring, with considerably more keys than just the one to his car. He dangled them on one finger.

I took them and tossed them on the table.

"It's kind of a fancy car," I said to Jumbo George. "I'm a little worried about leaving it on the street."

"You know them garages behind the coffee shop and the pizza place? I haven't decided what to do with them yet, but they're empty. They don't lock. You could put his car in one. At least that way, nobody would see it to mess with it."

I tugged at Kyle's arm again, and this time he staggered to his feet. "Come on, buddy," I said. "We're gonna get you to bed."

"Don't forget to get him the big cup of coffee," Jumbo George said, easing back into his chair.

"Kyle, gimme some money to buy you a cup of coffee." I was mindful of my six dollars, which had to last me until the end of the week. I wasn't about to spend it on coffee for a drunken rich guy who had more money in his pocket than I'd earn in a month.

"Don't want coffee," Kyle said, making no move to reach for his wallet again.

Jumbo George handed me a five. "I think he'll be good for it. And if he ain't, I got the rent money."

I took the bill and steered Kyle out through the storefront, down the sidewalk and to the coffee shop.

It was late in the day, and the shop was no busier than the head shop had been. I opened the door and maneuvered Kyle to a table, where he collapsed in a chair.

Stanley, who ran the coffee shop, was standing behind the counter. He had a clean white apron over his worn jeans and faded sweatshirt, his graying ponytail tucked under a net. "Is that guy as out of it as he looks?"

"'Fraid so," I said, laying the five dollars on the counter. "Big cup of coffee. Black. To go."

"You want any donuts or a piece of pie to go with that? I'm closing soon, and I could give you a deal on something," he said, taking out a big cardboard cup and filling it.

"No thanks."

A cellphone rang in Kyle's pocket. He sat up straighter and searched his pockets, but didn't find a phone.

"You gonna help him with that?" Stanley asked me.

"No." I didn't have a cell phone myself, and I wasn't about to let on that I had no idea how to work one. But even if I did, what would I say to somebody on Kyle's phone?

It stopped ringing, and Kyle stopped groping through his clothes.

I pulled Kyle to his feet again and grabbed the cup of coffee. "Jumbo George just rented him one of the upstairs apartments," I told Stanley.

"Yikes. So he's gonna live up there? He get drunk like this a lot?"

"I don't think so. And it's just for a week. He's got to get a few things straightened out with his wife." I didn't see much point in telling Stanley that Kyle had just bailed out of jail. Or, for that matter, that I had, too. Although Stanley got some newspapers for his customers and had undoubtedly seen my picture on the front page.

Out on the sidewalk, I stopped at the door between the coffee shop and the unoccupied storefront next door. It led to a staircase to the apartments above. I had to lean Kyle against the wall while I figured out which key unlocked it. He listed to the right, but caught himself before he fell.

I reached inside and hit the light switch. It didn't work. I shoved him through the door and up the stairs ahead of me, juggling the huge cup of coffee. Some of it spilled on my hand. It was hot.

The stairwell smelled musty, but it was dry and I didn't see any roaches or rodent droppings.

We lurched up the stairs, me behind him to give him a push whenever he stalled.

A door opened off either side of the landing at the top of the stairs. Weak sunlight shone through the grimy glass of a skylight. The door on the right opened without a key. I looked in.

It was furnished, after a fashion. A sagging old couch angled out from the far wall. On the back wall, against what would be the alley, was a kitchenette with a tiny window over the even tinier sink. Next to that was the open door to a bathroom with fixtures so old the toilet had a pull chain.

A rickety table with three chairs took up the center of the room.

Another door was across the room. I dragged Kyle over and opened it. The bedroom.

I sat him down on the stained bare mattress and handed him the coffee, which was half spilled by now. Reaching into my pocket for the aspirin, I put two in his other hand and said, "Take these. And drink some of the coffee."

Obediently, he tossed the aspirin is his mouth and took a big drink of the coffee.

Choking and sputtering, he said, "Hot! Hot!" But the aspirin seemed to have gone down.

"You need to get some sleep," I told him. "You wanna go to the bathroom first?"

He staggered up and walked unsteadily to the tiny bathroom.

"Hey," he said. "There's no handle to flush it. Gotta be one of those fancy motion sensitive ones or something, huh?"

I doubted that.

He came out, weaving, with his zipper down.

I reached in and pulled the chain, hoping that the old fixture still worked. It did.

"Lie down on the bed," I said. "Get some sleep."

He lay down on the bare mattress. I opened the closet. Two pillows and a few blankets were on the shelf. I took a pillow and put it under his head, then I took off his shoes and covered him with a blanket.

"I'm putting the aspirin and the coffee on the table in the other room," I said. "It'll be cold in the morning, but you might want it when you wake up anyhow."

"I'm not going to sleep," he said, his eyes closed.

A few seconds later he was snoring.

The light switch in the other room was the outdated push button kind. I turned on the overhead light. He'd probably wake up in the middle of the night, and it would be dark. I didn't want him to stumble around in an unfamiliar place and maybe fall.

CHAPTER 9

Back at Jumbo George's place, I picked up the keys to the Audi. "Guess I better move this off the street."

Jumbo George was spreading butter and honey on the last of the biscuits. "Yeah. The neighborhood's getting better, but I wouldn't want to leave something like that parked out there over night."

I looked at the keys. I hoped I'd be able to deal with the keyless entry. And hadn't Kyle just pushed a button on the dash rather than insert a key to start it? "I don't have a driver's license."

"Well, I do." Jumbo George laughed. "I took a look at the car, and I don't think I could even fit in it. Just check to make sure no cops are around before you move it. And don't hit anything."

"It's got a manual transmission."

"'Course it does. No point in having a car like that with an automatic. Takes most of the fun out of it. You shouldn't have to get it beyond second. You could maybe even manage in first. You ever drive a manual?"

"Yeah. Years ago. A few times, my brothers got hold of cars and then got so high I had to drive home. I was pretty naïve. It wasn't until I got stopped driving one I realized they were all stolen."

"Well, cars don't change that much. And you drive the forklift at work. Just ease it around the corner and into the alley, then put it in one of the garages. Should be plenty of room."

First I went around back to take a look at the garages. Six of them sat in a row. The doors were the old swing-open kind, not the overhead ones everybody has these days.

I yanked open the doors to one on the end. It was good-sized. I hoped I wouldn't have any trouble getting the car into it.

The Audi started right up, roaring eagerly. I depressed the clutch and gingerly moved the gear shift, letting up on the clutch.

It jerked forward. And stalled.

I tried again. This time I managed to get it into first gear and inched along next to the curb. I hit the turn signal to pull out and glanced in the rear view mirror.

A car was approaching. A patrol car.

My hands frozen to the wheel, I hit the brakes and stalled again.

The patrol car crept by. I watched it until it turned a corner a few blocks down.

Once again, I started the engine and eased it into gear. The street was empty. I tapped the accelerator. The car lunged forward.

I hit the brakes and of course stalled again.

Finally I got it going smoothly. This time I eased my foot down on the accelerator gingerly and let up on the clutch. I decided trying to move into second gear would just make me stall it out again, so I inched down the street, around the corner and into the alley.

The steering was as sensitive as the accelerator, but I managed to get it into the garage without hitting anything or scraping the sides. I got out, locked it and shut the doors.

Jumbo George was sitting in his recliner, the TV flickering but the sound muted. He grinned. "Make it?"

"Yeah."

He chuckled. "I heard you stall it a few times."

"That I did. But it's off the street and out of sight." I tossed the keys on the table and poured the last of the stale coffee into a mug.

"You wanna call your girlfriend, you can do it in the shop," he said, reaching for the remote and turning up the sound on the TV.

Carrying the mug into the shop, I called Kelly's house. She had a cheapie cell phone for emergencies, but she had to buy minutes for it, and she wouldn't appreciate me using them up. If she even had the phone turned on.

Her eight-year-old son Chris answered.

"Hey, dude," I said. "What's up?"

"Jesse! What're you doing? Where have you been?"

"I hit a bit of a problem there," I said. "I couldn't call. But now I'm over at Jumbo George's place."

"Did you get arrested again?"

I winced. I didn't care too much about what most people thought, but the kids were different. "Yeah."

"We did a newspaper project in school, and I saw your picture. On the front page."

"Did you read about it?"

"Not really. We were supposed to be finding an article about sports. But it did say you were arrested or something."

I hadn't read the entire article myself yet, so I wasn't sure what it said. "I'm out now," I said. "Did you tell your mom?"

"About you getting arrested? No—she's been real busy lately. Are you gonna come over?" Chris asked.

"That's one thing I want to talk to your mom about. Is she there?"

"Yeah. Hang on." I heard him drop the phone. "Mom! It's Jesse! He wants to talk to you!"

She picked up the phone. "Jesse?"

"Sorry I been out of touch," I said.

"You could of at least called."

"Well, actually, I couldn't."

"I asked around, but nobody knew where you were. Jumbo George said he hadn't seen you, and I checked with the jail, but they said you weren't there."

I listened for any trace of slurring in her voice. Kelly had an alcohol problem. She'd joined AA and was trying to stay sober, but I knew it was an uphill battle. She sounded okay, though.

"I even talked to John at Quality Steel," she said. "But the last thing he knew, he'd sent you home early 'cause the power went out."

I wished she hadn't called our foreman. That job was a major break for me, and if I lost it, I'd never get another one anywhere near as good again. I tried to be a responsible employee. John didn't need to know nobody could find me.

He'd probably seen the newspaper, though. Anyhow, it was too late to worry about it.

"I was locked up," I said.

"Where?"

"County jail."

"I called." She sounded incredulous. "They didn't have any record of you."

"They didn't process me for a while."

She coughed. "They can't hold you for more than twenty four hours without processing you."

"Yeah, well, they did. Just in a holding cell, not in the jail population."

"Parole violation?"

"Partly, I guess." I really didn't want to tell her all the new charges I was facing.

"But they released you?"

"I'm out on bail."

"Bail? They set bail for you?" I could hear the disbelief in her voice.

"I was surprised, too. But they did." I lifted the coffee to my mouth. It smelled burnt. I put it down on the counter.

"How'd you come up with it?"

"Jumbo George. He sent a lawyer over, too."

"A real private lawyer? Not a public defender?" she asked.

"A real private lawyer. I don't think I'd have ended up with any bail set otherwise. That guy's something else. He knocked the wind out of some of the charges they're trying to bring."

"New charges?"

If I didn't want her to find out about them, I should have kept my mouth shut. Too late now. "Unfortunately."

"What were they? Serious?"

"Well…you might say they're serious." I wrapped my hand around the mug. Despite the heat, I clutched it tightly.

"Come on. What did they charge you with?"

"Attempted carjacking."

"Attempted carjacking?" she repeated.

"Yeah. And assault with intent."

"To murder?"

"Yeah. And rape."

Her voice rose. "What the hell were you doing?"

"Walking down the street."

She snorted. "Oh, come on. You must have been doing *something*."

"No. Strictly the wrong place at the wrong time. Then this girl ID'd me."

"What girl? You were with a girl?"

"No!" I wasn't saying this very well. "She was in a car that crashed into a utility pole. She said I tried to carjack her."

Kelly sighed. "That's not good. They think it was part of that Riverfront Rapist thing? Those women who went missing?"

"That's what the district attorney tried to say."

"They couldn't have charged you with those or for sure you'd still be locked up."

"True, that. But if it hadn't been for Jumbo George's lawyer, I'd never have been released." I peered into the mug. The contents looked thick and tarry. What would stuff like that do to my stomach?

"So you're a suspect?"

"'Person of interest.' Pretty much the same thing."

"Weren't they mostly hookers? And those girls disappeared in the early morning hours. When you were at work." Kelly would know. She worked the same shift as I did.

"I know that. And you know that. But I'd just gotten out of work when they were looking for the carjacker. I was out on the street. So that's what I've got hanging over my head right now."

"If they thought that, I can't believe they set bail."

"That's where the private lawyer comes in. He pointed out that I'm a convicted felon, and my DNA is on file. Of course they ran the DNA on the body they found. So if there wasn't a match, I couldn't be the one they're looking for. At least not the only one."

"That kind of thing isn't usually a group activity," she noted.

"You're right."

"But they didn't drop the charges?" Her voice was uncertain.

"Not the ones to do with the carjacking. The girl ID'd me, and they're gonna look into that. They're gonna put an ankle box back on." I felt my ankle itch at the thought of it.

I didn't want to tell her that, but better I should tell her now than have her discover it when we were in her warm, soft bed. If she ever let me back there again.

"You're gonna be on house arrest?"

"Not house arrest. This is one of those GPS tracking thingies. But I don't have a schedule when I have to be home." That was a big break.

"Those are some pretty serious charges." Her voice was distant, like she was holding the phone away from her mouth.

"Yeah. The lawyer made it sound like a hysterical girl would have ID'd anybody they'd shown her. But I'm worried about those charges sticking. I'm gonna try to figure out what happened there." I didn't look forward to that, and I didn't know how to begin, but I had to do *something*.

"Sounds like they think it might have been the Riverfront Rapist. They should be able to find him pretty soon."

"You'd think so. But so far, they haven't made much progress that I can see." Of course, they wouldn't be telling me if they had. I'd have to read about it in the paper with everyone else.

"How come," Kelly's voice turned steely, "when I called the jail, they told me they didn't have a record of you?"

Back to that. I couldn't blame her for doubting me. "Prob'ly because they were trying to hold me without formally arresting me. They know I'm not going to really object, not as long as I'm on parole. No point in it."

"Even so, they can't do that."

I swallowed hard. Was there any possibility the lawyer would talk to her if I asked? He probably would, but he'd charge for it. Heaven knows how much he got per hour. "I know they're not supposed to. But they *can* do whatever they want. It was Jumbo George's private lawyer showing up and asking questions that got the process started. Otherwise I'd probably still be in a holding cell wondering what the hell was going on."

"So now what?"

"Now I owe Jumbo George big time. And next time I go see Mr. Ramirez, I'm gonna be fitted with the box."

"When's that?"

"I have a parole appointment tomorrow. He's not gonna be happy."

She was quiet for a little bit. I let the silence grow.

"What're you doing the rest of this week?" she finally asked.

"Mostly working on Jumbo George's stuff. Putting together some shelving in the basement so he can use it for storage. Stuff like that."

"Even if you're doing some of the work as part of your rent, the whole project has to be costing a fortune."

"Yeah. I know his father left a fair amount when he died," I said. "I don't know exactly how it worked, but there were three sons, and the money went to them. Aaron is dead. And his other brother Nick's in prison. I think Jumbo George is handling all the money."

"And he's spent it on those decrepit buildings."

"He's looking at it as an investment. If the neighborhood continues to turn around, he might make a lot of money."

"And you're working for him?"

"Helping him out. But not like an employee or anything. He gave me a good deal on the apartment if I'd keep an eye out and handle some chores. You know he has trouble getting around."

"Are those buildings as old as they look?" Kelly asked.

"Well, when was the last time you ran into a toilet with an overhead tank and a pull chain?"

She laughed. "That old, huh?"

"Yeah. He's got a good contractor, when he shows up. He's almost done with the storefronts. Then he's gonna start working on the apartments, says he's gonna make them retro chic, whatever that is. In a year or two, he figures he ought to be able to get a decent rent for them."

"Sounds like you got a busy week planned."

"Well, I got some stuff I got to do. But I was wondering when we could get together."

"I'm pretty busy myself. A couple of things came up that I got to take care of. And when I didn't hear from you…" She took a deep breath. "I'll give you a call when I get some free time."

That stung. We didn't have to go out anywhere. The kids were in school, but she had to be home for them afterwards. She knew I'd love to come over, fix dinner, help them with their homework. Even if we didn't end up in bed.

Unless she was seeing someone new. I tried to put that possibility out of my mind.

"Look." I tried not to sound as desperate as I felt. Didn't she want to see me? "There's a street fair in the park on Saturday. You wanna bring the kids over and we can take them?"

"Saturday?"

"Yeah. The kids'll love it."

"*This* Saturday?"

"Yeah. It'll be fun."

"Okay, I guess."

CHAPTER 10

The next morning, Jumbo George was puttering around when I got downstairs. I grabbed a cup of coffee and sat down at the table.

"I got an appointment with my parole officer this morning." I grimaced. "Mr. Ramirez isn't gonna be happy."

Jumbo George took a gulp of coffee from his oversized mug. "I don't imagine you're gonna be real happy, either. Especially not when he straps that box on your ankle.

"True, that. But it don't matter much what I think. What Mr. Ramirez thinks matters a whole lot."

"You got any other plans for the rest of the day?"

"Not really. Kelly says she's busy."

He snorted. "Some girlfriend."

I felt compelled to defend her. "She's not really my girlfriend. She wants to give the whole relationship thing more time. She's just gotten out of a bad marriage. You can't blame her if she wants to take it slow, especially with some guy who's out on parole and might get locked up again any time. She's got to think of the kids…"

"Nice kids." He'd met them a few times.

"Yeah. But they've had a rough time. The marriage turned into a mess, and the divorce was even worse. All kinds of custody and visitation and child support fights. Their dad drinks a lot."

Jumbo George glanced at me. "So does their mother."

That was true. He'd only met Kelly a few times, and then briefly. I didn't realize it was that obvious.

I changed the subject. "I got to see if I can figure anything out about that carjacking. I mean, I didn't do it, but with that girl IDing me, I'm in for a rough time of it."

"Didn't you say you got out of work early because the electric power went out?"

"Yeah."

"And what made the power go out?" Jumbo George peered into his coffee mug. It was empty.

"She hit a utility pole. The wires were down."

"Why'd she hit the pole?"

I thought for a minute. "Driving erratically 'cause someone had just tried to carjack her, maybe?"

"So if you were at work when she hit the pole, and she hit the pole 'cause someone tried to carjack her, it should be pretty clear that it wasn't you who tried to carjack her. Can't your foreman vouch for you?"

I stopped and stared at him. It was so obvious. "If that's what happened. Do you think something else could have knocked out the power?"

"I suppose that's always possible. But if it turns out the crash was what made the power go out, you have an alibi. They'd have to drop the charges."

"You'd think. But they're still looking at me for those other women who disappeared." I shivered.

"I suppose. Although weren't they looking at that because they thought you tried to carjack that girl?"

"Yeah. But once they get an idea in their heads, it tends to stay there."

Jumbo George stroked his beard. "It don't help that those women were all somewhere around here when they disappeared. And the car that was recovered was a few blocks away. They found it in a truck yard to a vacant warehouse on Washington St."

"Must have been looking pretty hard for it."

"Yeah. But the yard was walled in. You couldn't see it from the street."

That should have made it hard to find. "Really? How'd they know to look there?"

"Lojack."

"That anti-theft device you can put on your car? How'd you know that?"

Jumbo George leaned back. "You got to start reading the newspaper, son. That lady reporter's doing a whole series on those women who've gone missing. She has a fair amount to say about you, too. You're not gonna like what she says, but you should be aware of it."

He was right. "You save the papers?" I asked.

"Yeah. I thought you might want to read them sometime." He reached over to open a cabinet door. A pile of newspapers sat on the shelf. "You'd think anyone would realize that no one in their right mind would kidnap anybody or ditch a car anywhere around where they lived, wouldn't you?"

"Nobody in their right mind would be going around snatching women, either. So we're prob'ly dealing with some crazy person. Some crazy person who knows how to act normal most of the time. Some of those guys like to taunt the cops. Kind of a 'you can't catch me' game."

"You got a point there." He looked forlornly into his empty mug.

I got up and poured him the rest of the coffee.

"Well, you best go check on that guy you dumped upstairs before you leave for your appointment," he said. "Make sure he didn't die from alcohol poisoning or something overnight."

In spite of myself, I laughed. "Yeah. If he did, I don't know whether that takes care of some problems or just makes more."

"Dead body in one of my apartments? That'd make more problems for sure." Jumbo George belched. "And they'd think one of us had killed him."

"Me, I'm sure," I said glumly.

He grinned and nodded. "He was out of it, but he wasn't *that* drunk last night. I mean, he could walk. In fact, he might have gotten up and wandered away by now."

I grabbed the key ring off the table. "At least he couldn't drive away. Even if he can open the door without a key, I don't think he could find the car."

Jumbo George pulled a ten from his pocket and pushed it across the table. "Bring back some donuts."

"Okay."

Outside, I opened the door to where I'd left Kyle and climbed the stairs to the second floor landing. It was no less depressing in the morning brightness than it had been yesterday afternoon. If Jumbo George wanted to make these apartments desirable to the young professionals moving into the neighborhood there was a lot of work to be done. Expensive work.

No sound was coming from inside the apartment. I knocked and waited a few minutes. When no one answered, I unlocked the door and went in.

The main room was empty. Sunlight streamed through the grimy windows. The doors to the bedroom and the tiny bathroom were shut.

Easing open the one to the bedroom, I looked in.

Kyle lay on his stomach on the bed, one arm hanging off the side. The blanket was bunched up under him. The pillow was on the floor.

"Hey, dude. Kyle." I nudged him.

"Huh?" He opened his eyes and shut them immediately. "Where the hell am I?"

"You don't remember?"

"No." He moaned and rolled over. "The last thing I remember was walking out of the jail. And giving this guy a ride. And taking my emergency stash bottle out of the glove compartment. And then I woke up in this hell hole…"

He opened his eyes again and looked at me. "Was that you?"

"Yeah. You pretty much drank the whole damn bottle. How do you feel now?"

"Terrible. My head hurts." He looked at the stained mattress underneath him and frowned. "Where're the sheets?"

"You can get some if you're gonna stick around. Last night, I just had to get you to bed."

His face took on a greenish tinge. He choked and swallowed. "I'm gonna throw up." He stumbled out of the bed and into the other room. "There's gotta be a bathroom here. I found it before. At least I think I did. I pissed somewhere."

He vomited into the kitchen sink.

I shoved open the bathroom door. "Here you go. Right next to the kitchen."

He turned on the water in the sink. It ran rusty. When it cleared, he rinsed his mouth, then wiped it with the back of his hand. "Now I got to piss again."

I stood back and let him stagger into the bathroom.

"What kind of toilet is this?" he asked. "How do you flush it?"

"It's an old one. You pull the chain."

He did. Water rushed into the bowl. At least the plumbing seemed to be working.

Unsteady on his feet, Kyle reeled over to the table and slumped in a chair. He picked up the cardboard cup of cold coffee from last night and sniffed at it. "I need some hot coffee. And some aspirin."

"Here's the aspirin," I said, shoving the bottle toward him. "And maybe there's a kettle or something to heat the coffee."

He looked around. "Where's the microwave?"

I laughed. "No microwave here."

He frowned. "Anywhere to buy a fresh cup of coffee?"

"There's a coffee shop downstairs."

"Downstairs?" He held his head, then looked up at me. "Could you run down and get me some?"

"I suppose," I said. But I still wasn't about to spend my limited money on coffee for him, so I just stood there.

He looked around. "Where's my wallet?"

"On the dresser."

"Could you get it for me?"

I went into the bedroom and retrieved it.

Looking at me suspiciously, he opened it and counted the money. "It's pretty much all still here," he said, surprise evident in his voice.

"Of course it's still there. You gave Jumbo George a hundred and fifty rent for the week. Otherwise I don't think you've spent anything since you got out of jail."

He grabbed his head and moaned. "Jail! It was all real, wasn't it? I was in jail. It wasn't just a nightmare."

"Well, it might be a nightmare all right. But it was real enough."

I went downstairs and got him his coffee and a donut. He took a swig of the coffee, then picked up the donut. He brought it up to his nose and sniffed its cinnamony sweetness. He turned greenish again and put it down quickly.

"I looked out the window," he said, "and I didn't see where I parked my car. Do you have any idea where it is?"

"Your car's in a garage in the back alley. We were a little worried about leaving it out on the street." I pulled the keys out of my pocket and put them on the table.

"We?"

"Me and Jumbo George. The landlord." I watched Kyle take another gulp of coffee. "You prob'ly want to drink the coffee, take a few aspirin. If you're not slept out, get a good nap."

"How long was I out for?"

"Well, I left you here about seven last night. And now it's eight. The next morning."

He moaned. "I shouldn't need to sleep any more. But I don't feel well enough to do anything else."

"Best bet's try to get some more sleep. When you wake up again, you might feel a little better. Then get a shower." I realized belatedly I didn't know if the shower worked. Or if there was any hot water.

"I don't have any clean clothes. Or even a toothbrush."

"You could go buy some stuff. There's a drugstore on the next block that'll have a toothbrush and prob'ly some underwear. And a Goodwill down a bit further."

"Goodwill?" Kyle didn't look like someone who would shop at Goodwill.

I shrugged. "I'm sure there are other places to buy clothes. But that's what's around here."

"So you think I should just stay here?"

"I don't think nothing. It's your life. You could stay here for the time being. Until you feel better. Unless there's other things you should be doing. From what you were saying last night, though, I don't know that you should go home until you get your act together."

He rubbed his eyes. "You got that right. Although I could get some of my clothes and things. My whole life is a mess."

"Well," I said, "you're not gonna solve that going home with that headache, looking like you do. Get it together a little more first." I got up to go.

"Where are you going?" he asked.

"I got to go see my parole officer. I have an appointment every week."

"Your parole officer?" He looked surprised. "Are you a criminal or something?"

I gave him a withering look. "Yes. You shouldn't be surprised. For one thing, you met me in jail. A lot of the people you meet in jail tend to be criminals."

"What did you do?"

I didn't have time to go into it now. "We discussed this yesterday. I caught a murder charge, among other things. Now I got to get downtown. What with being arrested again and all, I'm in enough trouble without being late for the appointment."

CHAPTER 11

The waiting room for the parole office was deserted when I got there for my weekly appointment. It was in the basement of the county building, down a worn flight of stairs from the sidewalk. Although it was a warm morning, the air in the waiting room was chilly and damp. Moisture condensed on the grimy windows set high on the wall. The whole place smelled like a clogged drain.

I was a bit early, and the only person in sight. No one sat at the reception desk behind a window in the wall, but a clipboard with a single sheet of paper lay on a ledge. A pencil was tied to the clipboard with a piece of dirty string. I signed in on the clipboard, making sure my name was legible. The molded plastic chairs were damp. I found one without too many cracks in it and wiped off the seat with the sleeve of my hoodie.

And waited.

A few more people drifted in, signed in on the clipboard, and sat down. None of us looked at each other.

A heavy woman with a bright gold sweater stretched over her ample bosom and cat's eye glasses appeared in the office window. She picked up the clipboard. She snapped her gum as she scanned the list. Then she gazed out over us, frowned, put down the clipboard, and disappeared back into the offices.

There wasn't much to do but wait. More people arrived, including a man wearing at least five layers of sweaters and jackets. Apparently none of them had been washed in weeks. He smelled like he hadn't been washed in weeks, either. He sat down unfortunately close to me.

I was debating moving when the woman showed up again, picking up the clipboard and adjusting her glasses. "Damon," she said.

"Yes?" I got to my feet and went to the window.

She sat down at the desk. Her fingers ran over the computer keyboard.

"Mr. Ramirez will see you now. Have you got your fees?"

Of course I did. The parole fees ate up an uncomfortable part of my income. They were especially a problem in a week like this when Quality Steel was shut down and I wasn't working. The GPS monitor was likely to come with its own set of fees.

But no matter how much it cost, it was better than sitting in jail, I reminded myself. I pulled out my wallet and gave her the forty dollars I'd removed from my little savings stash that morning.

She sat at the computer, chewing her gum. The printer sprang to life. "Drug test?" she asked.

"No, ma'am," I said. "I don't think there's one ordered." Thank goodness. That would be another chunk of change.

She peered at the computer screen. "Looks like that's right," she said. She handed me the receipt from the printer and got up to open the door that led to the offices. "You know where you're going?"

"Yes." I'd been back there every week since my release a few months ago. I slipped through and down the hallway, where the door to Mr. Ramirez's tiny office stood open.

He sat at his desk, holding an open file folder and a pencil in his pudgy fingers. He was short, but he was every bit as wide as he was tall.

I stopped at the doorway and stood there, waiting for him to tell me to come in.

Glancing up, he gestured at the worn wooden chair in front of his desk, and went back to the file, frowning as he read.

I sat down and waited.

Finally he looked up. "So." He put the file down on his desk. "I don't know how you manage to get yourself in so much trouble.

"Just lucky, I guess." I stared at the scarred surface of his desk.

"You realize this could be pretty serious?"

"Yes, sir."

He tapped the file folder with his pencil. "You're out on bail? Twenty five thousand dollars?"

"Yep."

"I had to reread it to make sure that was really what was going on. Almost couldn't believe it. They set bail for you? And somebody came up with the money?"

"Yes, sir. My landlord. He sent his lawyer. And paid the ten per cent."

Mr. Ramirez shook his head. "Your landlord? The guy who runs the head shop you live over? Why'd he do that?"

"He's bought a couple of buildings, and he's trying to get them fixed up. I'm doing some of the work."

"What kind of buildings?"

"Storefronts on Second Street. With apartments above."

"That's down by where they built those fancy new condos and things? Right on the riverfront?"

"Well, Jumbo…" My voice trailed off. Maybe I should skip his nickname. "George's buildings are two blocks over. But yeah, that's the neighborhood."

"What's that got to do with bailing you out?"

"He can't get around real well. So I'm doing some of the little stuff and keeping an eye on the work he's hired a contractor to do."

Mr. Ramirez snorted. "Bet the contractor loves having you hover over his work."

"Not like that. I just report to George what needs to be done and how it's coming along."

"How is it coming along?"

"What's been done is pretty good. But the contractor's busy and right now he's working on another project. A couple of the storefronts are finished and they're rented out. People are living in a few of the apartments. But they really need a lot of work."

"How about the one you're in?"

"It's not in great shape. But it's livable."

"Any roommates?"

I hesitated. Mr. Ramirez was a government official. He was the wrong person to let know that Jumbo George was undoubtedly violating zoning by actually living in the back room of the store. Technically he lived upstairs with me. "I really just rent a bedroom. The apartment's got two. George uses the other one. Nothing fancy."

"He lives there, too?"

"Yeah. But he spends most of his time in the store. The stairs are hard for him."

"How's the head shop business?"

"Not real good, to tell the truth. The area's changing. George figures the head shop has to change with it. He's making it into more of a gift shop-type place."

"A gift shop with bongs and rolling papers?"

It sounded a little crazy. "He's getting other stuff to sell. These little collectable figures. Real expensive. Civil War soldiers and knights and such. Plus a whole line of trail mix and gluten-free snacks. Trying to appeal to a more upscale crowd."

"Why are stairs hard for him? Is he disabled?"

"Not officially, I don't think. But he weighs over three hundred pounds. And he uses a cane. Just hard for him to get around."

"So you're basically a go-for?"

"Well, yeah." I'd been seeing myself more as a trusted assistant and possibly even a friend, but go-for might be a more accurate assessment.

"And do you get paid for this?"

"Nah. But I don't pay much rent." And Jumbo George bought most of the food. It was a good deal for me.

Mr. Ramirez held up the file folder. "Now, what have you got to say about this other stuff?"

I took a deep breath. "Not a whole lot. I mean, I'm not even sure what's going on."

"Tell me what happened."

"I was at work. They weren't running a production shift. We were just setting up for retooling. They do that twice a year or so. Moving machinery, emptying plating tanks—stuff like that. The electric power went out, and the foreman sent us home. He said it wasn't safe to work with just the emergency lights. So I put my lift in a recharging bay and ran through the checklist. Then I left."

"Did the foreman see you go?"

"Yeah. He had to let me out and lock the door behind me."

"How many people got sent home?"

"Maybe ten. Setup men, mostly."

"Where were the others when you got picked up?"

"They'd already left. I had to put the forklift back in the charging bay and run the checklist, so they were gone by the time I got out."

"How about the foreman?"

"He stayed."

"Did you go home?"

"I was headed there. Then these cops picked me up. They took me a few blocks away and made me get out of the car for this girl to look at. She said it was me tried to do something to her. But I didn't."

"Tried to do what to her?"

I shrugged. "Carjack, I guess. That's what the charges were. And they added assault and attempted rape and murder charges."

"Why would she say it was you if you didn't do it?"

"I dunno. It was dark. She'd hit a utility pole and she was kind of messed up. So maybe she just couldn't see all that well. Or remember."

"And the judge set bail?"

"Yeah."

"Why should I believe you when you say you didn't try to carjack her?"

Thank goodness Jumbo George had laid it out so well for me. "Well, for one thing, she hit the pole 'cause she was upset that somebody tried to carjack her. That's what made the power at work go out. And I didn't get sent home until then. So I was still at work when the guy tried to carjack her. John, my foreman, will say that when they ask him about it." At least I hoped he would.

Mr. Ramirez tapped the pencil on his lower lip. "Can you tell me what connection that has with a front page newspaper article on you being a 'person of interest' in these abductions of women lately?"

"I dunno. Maybe they were carjacked?"

"Maybe. Some of them had cars. One got away. And one body was found."

"Yeah. I think that's what got me bail set. They got DNA. Mine's on file. If there was a match, you know I wouldn't be sitting here now."

"You know they can trace these disappearances to the neighborhood where you're living?"

I nodded.

He put the pencil down and leaned back in his desk chair. I was afraid it was going to tip over backwards. If anything happened to him, I knew I'd be blamed, probably for attacking him. "You know you're supposed to get an ankle monitor?" he asked.

I sighed. "Yeah."

"But the judge didn't say anything about house arrest. Are you still working nights?"

"We're off for retooling this week. But yeah, I still work midnight to eight."

"So I see no point in giving you a curfew," he said.

No curfew and no house arrest were definite steps in the right direction.

Mr. Ramirez adjusted his glasses. "Says a GPS monitor. We don't have too many of those. They're expensive. Mostly use them for sex offenders. But this court order puts you right at the top of the list."

Great. "How much is this gonna cost me?"

He grinned. "You're in luck there. We got a grant to buy a new kind, and we're evaluating them. So right now there's no charge. I'm sure there will be when the grant funding runs out."

He didn't volunteer when that would be. "Do I need a phone line?" I asked.

When I'd first been released from prison, I'd been fitted with another type of ankle monitor that read through the phone line. I'd had to get a line installed in my apartment for it. It had taken up most of my available funds. If I hadn't found a soup kitchen, I would have starved those first two weeks until I got a paycheck.

I didn't think Jumbo George would appreciate having something like that set up on his phone.

Mr. Ramirez was scanning a brochure with a picture of an ankle monitoring box. "I wasn't assigned to the initial project, so this is the first one of these that I'm issuing. I'm not even scheduled for training for another month. They don't work the same way as the one you had last time. You don't need a phone. They transmit a signal themselves."

"So how do they read?"

"To a computer. But I know one of the problems—one of the reasons they're doing this on an experimental basis—is that they don't know if it'll work well around here. If you get a hill in between you and the computer, it might lose track of you. And I wouldn't be surprised if the welding equipment and such at your job is going to interfere."

"What do I have to do?"

"Keep it charged and don't worry about it unless you hear from me."

"What happens if it loses track of me?"

He shook his head. "Not much, I imagine. The computer'll track where you've gone unless it loses the signal. Then it'll keep looking until it picks it up again. It keeps a record the whole time."

"So if there's a problem, they'd be able to tell if I was right there or not?"

"Assuming we're getting the signal, pretty much."

I pondered that. "It should work to show I didn't do stuff as much as it does to show anything I did."

"Doesn't show what you're *doing*. Just shows where you *were*. Or, rather, where the box was. If it's on your ankle, it works. If you remove it, you're in trouble."

He pulled open a desk drawer and pulled out a sealed bag holding a plastic box with a strap attached. When he ripped the bag open, a strong plastic smell filled the air.

"It looks pretty much like the other one," I said.

"Yeah. You have to recharge it every day, which you didn't with the other one. Takes between an hour and two hours. You got to plug it in somewhere. Most people do it when they're watching TV or something."

I didn't watch much TV. I'd never owned one. But I read a lot. Maybe I could charge it then.

"It's pretty water resistant," Mr. Ramirez said. "But I'd suggest showers instead of baths. And don't go swimming."

He handed me the brochure. "Here's the information you need. And here—" he shoved a sheet of paper across the desk "you need to sign that you got the box and the instructions."

Taking the pen he handed me, I scrawled my name on the paper.

Monitor in hand, Mr. Ramirez heaved himself to his feet. "Put your foot up on the chair. I can't bend down."

I got up, put my foot on the chair and pulled up the leg of my blue jeans.

"Over the sock?" he asked.

"Yeah." I was wearing good heavy work socks. Even with them, the box was going to rub my leg raw until the skin toughened up. And I'd better get some baby powder or something. My leg would sweat under it and develop a real sore spot.

"I'm gonna put this on loose," Mr. Ramirez said. "Good thing you don't have regular work boots."

When I started at Quality Steel, I'd had to buy a pair of steel-toed boots. They were expensive. Because I'd had a monitor then, too, I'd had to get ankle boots instead of the high ones most of my coworkers wore.

Mr. Ramirez cinched the plastic strap around my ankle.

"I always tell everybody, the monitor costs over three hundred dollars. This one's probably a good bit more. You decide you're gonna abscond, cut the strap with a pair of scissors and turn the monitor in. Or dump it in a mail box—it's got an address on it. That way you won't have to pay for it."

I nodded.

"But…" he looked up at me, his dark eyes deceptively bland. "Don't do that. Your parole gets violated, you're locked up again for years. Maybe the rest of your life."

CHAPTER 12

Kyle sat at the table in the back room of Jumbo George's shop, a humongous cardboard cup of coffee in his hand. It was more like a carton.

His eyes were bloodshot and his clothes looked like he'd slept in them. Which, of course, he had.

An open laptop computer sat on the table. Both of them stared at the screen.

"I dunno," Jumbo George said. "Seems like a lot of trouble for a long shot."

"It's *not* a long shot." Kyle took a gulp of the coffee. "You have better than a 50-50 chance of getting it."

Jumbo George looked up as I walked in. "Kyle thinks I should apply for this here city grant for historic renovation. He thinks there's a chance I could get some money."

"More than a chance," Kyle said, pushing the donut boxes aside.

A few crushed donuts lay in the bottom. I hadn't had any breakfast, so I reached in and took one. I wondered if I'd have any luck converting Jumbo George over to oatmeal for breakfast. I could try.

"It looks like a complicated process." Jumbo George pushed back from the table. "And it says I need a 'narrative statement' on how the project would benefit Rothsburg. It'd benefit me, all right, but I'm not sure about the rest of the city. And I'm not even sure what a 'narrative statement' is."

Kyle sighed in exasperation. "All you need is a couple of paragraphs on fixing this block up. Something like it would enhance the area. And you'd need to cite the neighboring developments, how close you are to them. The city's already poured a ton of money into the riverfront park." He flipped to another image on the computer screen. "And they gave huge tax breaks to the condo complex. Your project is in exactly the right location. You'd just have to apply. And keep your renovation authentic-looking for the period."

"How the hell am I gonna fix up the apartments into any kind of decent shape if they have to be authentic-looking?"

"Just the exterior."

Jumbo George frowned. "I'm not sure I could write a couple of decent paragraphs."

"Well, *I'll* write the narrative statement if you want." Kyle leaned back in his chair.

"How will you know what to say?" Jumbo George stroked his beard thoughtfully. "And there's all those questions in that application we'd have to answer. How could anyone ever figure out what they should be saying?"

"I know what they want. Any questions I don't know the answer to, I'll ask you and you can tell me. Or get the information."

"Some of those questions are pretty tricky. How can you figure out what they even mean?"

"Look." Kyle ran his fingers through his hair. "I can answer them. I know what they all mean. For the love of all that's holy, man, *I* wrote the whole grant application myself."

We both looked at him. Jumbo George finally said, "You did?"

"Yes. My father-in-law—the great Henry Richmond—bought a block of vacant warehouses further back from the river. He had me write up a grant proposal to present to the city council so they'd hand over a big chunk of money to him to do most of the renovations."

"The city's gonna pay him to fix up his property?" Jumbo George asked.

"That's what he thinks. Up to two hundred and fifty thousand dollars." Kyle pointed to something on the computer screen. "But whole procedure has to be open to anyone who wants to apply. He had me write it so it'd be hard for any other project to fit the criteria. And the timeframe's short."

Jumbo George shook his head. "So how could this work?"

"The trickiest part we put in there is that it has to be a whole city block. It can't be one or two buildings, or even a bunch. It has to be an entire block. We didn't know of anybody else who owned a whole block in the right area. But you do."

Jumbo George looked at me over Kyle's head. "There must be other people who'd want that money. How are people supposed to find out about these things?"

"They're not supposed to find out. That's the beauty of it. There's requirements that the grant be advertised, and applications solicited. But in this case, all they had to do was put a legal notice in the paper. Most people don't read them. A few people do make it their business to read the legal notices—usually people who are thinking about contracts with the city—but the deadline is coming up so fast, it's doubtful anybody would be able to get the property bought and all that by the application deadline. Which is midnight tomorrow."

"So your Mr. Richmond is going to put in an application?"

Kyle frowned. "He'll probably have somebody do it. If he thinks of it. The whole project was my baby. So he might forget. In which case you'd have no competition at all. It's not that big a deal to him."

Jumbo George shifted in his chair. It creaked ominously. "Two hundred and fifty thousand dollars and it's not a big deal to him?"

"He's got a lot going on," Kyle said. "I mean, if he remembers, he'll get somebody to handle it. But he's just getting into real estate development. I was moving in to run that part of the business."

I reached down and moved the box on my ankle a bit to the side. The spot where it rubbed was already tender.

How trustworthy was Kyle? Probably not very. "How'd you end up with embezzlement charges?" I asked him.

He drummed his fingers on the table. "Took some money from one account for the down payment on the warehouse property. And a little extra to cover some gambling debts."

Jumbo George raised his eyebrows. "You had gambling debts?"

"Not much, next to the amount for the down payment. Just a few thousand. We do it all the time—switch money around to cover expenses. Usually we get it back before anyone notices. Or say it was a misposting and fix it right away."

"You do that with *clients'* money?" Jumbo George had been talking about investing with a broker. I could see that this was raising alarm flags in his mind.

"Doesn't hurt the client. And saves us a fortune in interest. This time, though, the guy whose account it was—he's this old fart, never pays any attention to his money—decided it was time to rewrite his will. Called and asked for a statement. The secretary sent it out without checking with senior management. The guy almost had a heart attack—called his lawyer. And the district attorney. Who hates Henry Richmond's guts. And, since I work for Henry Richmond…"

"And *you* got arrested for that?" I asked.

"Yes. Richmond was pissed that I'd taken some for the gambling debts. And I've been having trouble with the wife lately. Don't ever marry the boss's daughter."

"Not something I think we got to worry about," Jumbo George said.

"So when someone had to take the fall," Kyle continued, "they dumped it on me. It didn't have to go anywhere near that far."

"What's gonna happen to those charges?" I asked.

"The money'll get put back right away. Say it was an accounting error. But the arrest—that may have ruined my career. At least around here. Nobody else'll ever hire me." He sniffed and lifted the coffee to his lips. "I got to get the best possible severance deal. Shouldn't be hard—I know where a lot of the bodies are buried."

He saw me wince.

"Not real bodies. That's just an expression," he said. "And I guess I got to get a divorce. Then move away and see if I can make it on my own. Open a financial consulting business." He sniffed and wiped his eye.

"Back to the grant application," Jumbo George said. "If all this stuff is politically connected—and I bet it is—what makes you think I have any chance of getting it?"

"Your project fits the guidelines a lot better than Richmond's. He's planning to tear down the old warehouses and build a restaurant and some housing. He'd build a fake façade. Your project is renovating the actual old buildings. And your location is much better. Should be no contest."

"What do you mean, no contest?"

"Well, yours should win, hands down. The committee that evaluates the applications should see that. But like I say, the whole process is political. My father-in-law is connected. So we can't be sure he wouldn't have a hand in appointing the committee members."

"That'd mean it was a foregone conclusion that he'd get the money, not me."

"Not foregone. He thinks it's a wrap, so he's not paying much attention. And there probably are a couple of genuine historic preservation people on that committee. They'll be thrilled to see your project."

"Why do you want to help me with this?" Jumbo George asked. "What's in it for you?"

"What's in it for me?" Kyle laughed. "If you get the grant, I get to imagine the look on the old man's face when, for once, somebody else comes out ahead of him. And know I had a hand in making that happen."

Jumbo George shrugged. "Guess it's worth a try. Save me a ton of money if I got it. You sure it's not some kind of a loan? I wouldn't have to pay it back?"

"No, no. It's an outright grant. Okay. First I need some pictures of the place before you had any work done."

"I don't got any pictures," Jumbo George said. "What would I have taken pictures for?"

"Well, can you take some now?"

"Pictures?"

"Yes. We need them for the grant application."

Jumbo George rubbed the side of his face. "I knew this would be too complicated. I don't got a camera."

"Use your phone."

"My phone don't take pictures."

"Yes, it does. All phones take pictures these days. Let me see it."

Jumbo George pointed at the old black desk phone on top of a display case out in the store.

"You don't have a smart phone or a cell phone or anything?"

"Just the dumb one."

Kyle looked at me. "How about you?"

"I don't even got a dumb one. I just use Jumbo George's if I need a phone."

Kyle shook his head in disbelief, but he pulled out his own phone. "Can Jesse show me where the work's gonna be done?"

I looked at Jumbo George, who nodded yes and asked me, "You get fitted with that box?"

"Yeah." I put my boot up on a chair and lifted the leg of my jeans to reveal the black plastic device.

"House arrest?"

"No. Just monitoring."

"How's it work?"

I covered the box and put my foot back on the floor. "I'm not really sure. I have to read all this paperwork Mr. Ramirez gave me, I guess. But it's a GPS thing—a computer keeps track of where you are. I got to recharge the battery every night. It don't run off of a phone. At least I won't have to pay to have another line installed."

Kyle stared at my leg. "You have to wear that thing all the time?"

"Yeah. Until either the court or my PO says I don't."

"Is it hard to get off?"

"Nah. Just got to cut it with scissors. But if I did that, it'd break the circuit and set off an alarm right away."

He shook his head. "What would happen then?"

"I get locked up again."

I didn't want to think about that, so I grabbed the master set of keys Jumbo George kept on a hook in the cabinet and said to Kyle, "You wanna take a look around? Maybe get some pictures?"

"Okay. We need to concentrate on the exterior. That's what gives the neighborhood its ambience, so that's where we need to get the most pictures."

As I showed him around the buildings, Kyle took pictures with his phone. He took a few shots of the whole block, but mostly he zeroed in on what he called "architectural detail." That was things like the stained glass in the transoms over the outside doors and little carvings in the trim around the display windows.

We went around back. Once again, he took a few pictures. "I don't think we should make a big deal about the garages and such," he said. "They look pretty rickety. Jumbo George might want to pull them down and put something else in their place."

I pointed out the garage where his car was stowed.

"Can I keep it there until I figure out a better place?"

"As long as you're staying here, yeah. I don't think it's real smart to park a car like that out on the street overnight."

He put the phone in his pocket. "I think I'm gonna run by the house, see if I can pick up some of my clothes and things."

"Is that smart? Your wife told you to stay away."

"My wife plays cards and golf and goes out to lunch most days. If I time it right, she'll be out of the house and I won't have to see her."

As we left the back alley, a patrol car drove by. I felt dampness gather at the back of my neck.

We rounded the corner onto Second Street. The car had pulled in at the fire hydrant just down from Jumbo George's shop.

A trickle of sweat made its way down my back.

I turned to Kyle. "Maybe you ought to just take off for a while, until we see what they want."

"Why? I didn't do anything."

"Maybe so. But you're out on bail. It's easy to get caught up in something."

I should know.

CHAPTER 13

But Kyle stayed right with me. "I got to get my computer. I left it on the table."

The cops were still in the patrol car as we went into the store.

Jumbo George was sitting on a stool behind the store's counter, sorting some astrological postcards. He hadn't given up hope that he'd get some customers. The patrol car would take care of that possibility for now.

"Cops." I nodded toward the door.

"Coming in here?"

I shrugged. "Don't see why they would. But they're out there." I turned to Kyle. "Get your computer shut down and put it away."

"Why?"

"'Cause if they do come in here, you don't want something like that in plain sight. They might confiscate it."

"Why would they do that?"

"'Cause they can. If it was my computer, I wouldn't take a chance on it."

Dragging his feet, Kyle went into the back room, shut the computer, and put it in a cabinet over the sink.

Just in time for the door to open.

Two cops came in, a man and a woman. They paused as the strong patchouli scent hit their nostrils. The woman wrinkled her nose. The man sneezed.

Jumbo George put the postcards down and laid his hands on the counter. I let mine hang by my side. Kyle stuffed his in his pockets.

"Can I help you?" Jumbo George asked.

"Maybe." The female cop was wiry and fidgety. She eased around behind the counter and looked at the shelves. I took a step closer so I could read her name tag. I always tried to get the names of cops if I could do it without making a big deal about it. I'd learned the hard way it was better not to ask.

"Fulton."

As soon as I took that step, the male cop moved right up next to me. I glanced at his name tag. "Jerentolski." Harder to remember, but I would.

He looked at Kyle. "Get your hands out of your pockets," he said.

Kyle blinked. "What?"

The cop put his hand on his holster flap. "I said, get your hands out of your pockets. And keep them where I can see them."

"Now just see here…" Kyle started to say.

"Do what he says," I said to Kyle.

"Huh?"

"Get your hands out of your pockets," I said. "And shut up."

Officer Fulton looked around. "What is this? Some kind of a head shop?"

"Yes." Jumbo George sat up a bit straighter. "That's exactly what it is."

"And you have drug paraphernalia?"

"Just legal stuff. Rolling papers and hookahs and such. Novelties. Also trail mix and incense and astrological postcards. Some miniatures, like soldiers and knights. You interested in buying any?"

Fulton laughed. "Not really. You selling spice?" she asked, naming a popular—and illegal—synthetic marijuana.

"Hell no."

"Bath salts?" she asked. Another manufactured drug.

Jumbo George shook his head. "Nope. Nothing like that."

She inched down the counter, continuing to look at the shelves. "You got any weapons here? A gun under the counter, maybe?"

"No, he said. "Slow as I move, I figure having a gun would just be an invitation to someone else to grab it before I could get to it. Then I'd be one of those statistics of people shot with their own guns. What are you here for, anyhow?"

Jerentolski roused himself. "Welfare check."

"Welfare check?" Jumbo George snorted. "Who the hell asked for a welfare check?"

"I don't know. We were told to check on the welfare of one—" he pulled a notebook out of his pocket and glanced at it—"George Stenski."

"Well, that's me. And I'm fine. So you can go."

Kyle threw his shoulders back and ran a hand through his already disheveled hair. "You can't just come barging in like this."

Jerentolski glanced up from his notebook. "Oh? We can't?"

"No." Kyle rubbed his forehead. "You need a warrant or something. You got one?"

The cops just looked at him.

"Kyle," I said. "They don't need a warrant. This is a store. It's a public place. Anybody can come in here."

"Well…" Kyle looked confused.

"So just shut up, okay?" I said.

Fulton was grinning. She turned to Jumbo George and said, "Can I talk to you outside for a minute?" She came around the far end of the counter to the front and started looking at the merchandise in the display cases. Pipes, rolling papers, an assortment of tobacco in pouches.

Jumbo George heaved himself to his feet. "Could somebody get me my cane?"

I remembered someone who'd been shot because he'd reached for a cane and a cop thought it was a rifle. A chill ran down my back. "Can I get it for him?" I asked Jerentolski.

He nodded.

I reached through the doorway into the back room and got the cane from its hook on the wall.

Jerentolski held out his hand for it.

I gave it to him. He examined it and gave it to Jumbo George.

We watched in silence as Jumbo George inched toward the end of the counter and grabbed the cane. Fulton stood aside and let him exit the store ahead of her.

Turning to me, Jerentolski asked "Your name?"

"Jesse."

"Jesse what?"

"Damon."

"On probation or parole?"

"Yes."

"Which?"

"Parole."

He raised his eyebrows and glanced toward my leg. I was sure he already knew all about me. "Where do you live?"

"Here."

"Here?" He looked around.

"Apartment upstairs."

"And George Stenski—where does he live?"

I wasn't about to point out the potential zoning violation, so I said, "Upstairs."

"You share an apartment?"

"Yeah. It's got two bedrooms."

"Domestic partners?"

I shrugged. No point addressing that issue.

He took a few quick notes and turned to Kyle.

"Your name?"

"Kyle Staten."

"Probation or parole?"

"Neither." He should have stopped there. But he didn't. "I'm out on bail, though."

Jerentolski scribbled in his notebook. "And do you live upstairs, too?"

"No. I live across town. In a house. But I'm having some personal problems. So for now, I'm staying in an apartment down the block. Over the coffee shop."

"Mind if I look around here?" Jerentolski asked no one in particular.

Kyle started to object. "Why the hell…"

I nudged him. "Shop's not ours. We can't give permission. You'll have to ask George Stenski."

"But you work here?"

"No."

"Why don't you two sit down at the table." Jerentolski gestured toward the back room. It wasn't a suggestion. I gave Kyle another nudge in that direction. We both sat down.

Jerentolski looked around, but he didn't open the doors to the bathroom or the alley or the stairs leading up to the apartment. He stayed where he could keep an eye on us, his hand again resting on his holster flap.

A few minutes later, Jumbo George lurched in, leaning heavily on his cane. His expression was unreadable. Fulton was right behind.

"That guy's the owner," Jerentolski nodded at Jumbo George. "Did you get permission to do a search?"

"It'll have to wait," she said. "We got a call. Urgent."

Jerentolski shoved his notebook into his pocket and they hurried out. A few seconds later, we heard the siren wail as the patrol car peeled away from the curb.

Jumbo George plopped into a chair and sighed.

"What was that all about?" I asked.

He shrugged. "Who knows? She wanted to know if I really wanted you to stay here, or if you were forcing me to let you stay."

"Forcing you?"

"Yeah. And were you trying to control what I did and where I went."

"You mean, like holding you against your will?" I laughed, trying to imagine anyone bossing Jumbo George around.

"More like domestic abuse, I think." He pulled a handkerchief from his pocket and mopped his forehead.

"That other cop wanted to know if we were 'domestic partners,'" I said.

"What'd you tell him?"

"I didn't answer. Figured it was none of his business."

"I'm not sure what they think's going on. Or who put them up to it."

I frowned. "Wouldn't be Mr. Ramirez. I mean, I know he's not thrilled I'm living over a head shop. But he'd stop by himself if he wanted to see what the situation looked like."

"They wanted to search," Jumbo George said. "They didn't say what for. Do they think I've got some illegal merchandise?"

"I dunno. If they'd really wanted to search, they'd have done it. They could always claim they thought I was in control of the premises and it was a parole search. Don't need permission for that." I reached down and pushed the monitor over to the side a little. The sharp edge of the band was cutting right through the thick sock and making a sore spot on my ankle.

Jumbo George rested his hands on the cane. "Yeah. But if they seized anything, there'd be a good chance the evidence would be thrown out of court, since it wouldn't have been properly obtained."

"True, that. But if you ask me, it's just harassment. Meant to keep us on our toes."

Jumbo George reached for his coffee mug. "Us?"

"Well, more likely me," I said.

"Who'd do that?" he asked. "And why?"

I had a pretty good idea. "Belkins. He's mad 'cause I'm not sitting in a holding cell like he wanted. So he's taking his petty revenge."

Jumbo George wiped his forehead again. "Any coffee left?"

I reached over, grabbed the pot and sniffed it. "A little bit. But it's pretty bitter."

"Make another pot, will ya?" Jumbo George said.

I got to my feet. "Sure."

Kyle had been following the conversation closely. Now he got his computer from the cabinet and said, "I don't believe they thought they could just come in and look around like that. If I'd left it out, would they have taken my computer?"

"Might of," Jumbo George said. "Good thing you got it put away."

"They shouldn't be allowed to do things like that and get away with it."

I shrugged. There were a lot worse things I could think of that they got away with.

Kyle sat down and started the computer again. "I'm gonna e-mail my wife. Maybe she's not so mad anymore."

I made the coffee. We sat in silence, broken only by the dripping of the coffee maker. The rich coffee scent overwhelmed the patchouli, at least in the back room.

After a few minutes, Kyle looked up from the computer. "The bitch wrote back, 'If you come around here, I'm going to call the police.' She can't do that, can she?"

"Of course she can do that." Jumbo George handed me his empty mug. "So don't go over there."

"She says that since I've been staying out overnight so much anyhow, I might as well just stay away altogether." Kyle put his head in his hands. "What am I going to do?"

"Well, first thing is get in touch with your lawyer." Jumbo George took the mug of coffee I handed him. "Find out where you stand. Both with the criminal charges and the marriage. 'Specially if you got a lot of stuff at your wife's place. She might decide to throw it all away or sell it or something."

"I doubt it," Kyle said. "She'll try to be what she thinks is reasonable. But I got to find a lawyer."

"How about the guy who represented you for the bail hearing?" I asked.

"That guy's not really *my* lawyer. He works for the company. He told me I'm going to need a criminal attorney for the embezzlement charges. Someone who specializes in white collar crime. And now it looks like I'll need a divorce lawyer, too."

"Then call him up and ask if he knows anybody who's good. I bet he does. And the better your lawyer, the better your outcome." Jumbo George blew across the top of the coffee.

"That'll cost a ton of money," Kyle said.

"I imagine it will."

"But they told me not to come into work! Do I still have a job?"

Jumbo George cradled the mug in his hands. "One way to find out. Call them."

"And say what?"

"Ask if you still work there. Or, if you want to be tricky, ask to speak to yourself and see what they have to say."

Kyle perked up. "They might recognize my voice. Jesse, would you call and ask for me?"

I didn't say no fast enough. Kyle dialed a number on his cell phone and handed it to me.

I took it and put it to my ear. It rang. "What'm I supposed to do?"

"Ask for me," Kyle said.

A polished female voice answered. "Richmond, Wellington and Masters. How may I direct your call?"

Phone skills aren't my strong point. I could count on my fingers the number of times I'd been on the phone in the last twenty years. And most of those calls had been from Mr. Ramirez, checking up on me. "Uh... Could I please speak to Kyle Staten?"

"I'm sorry," the woman purred. "Mr. Staten is not available at the present time. Would you like to speak to another representative?"

"No, thanks."

"Ask when he'll be in," Kyle whispered to me.

"Could you...could you tell me what would be a good time for me to call back and talk to Mr. Staten?" I asked.

"I'm afraid I don't have that information," she said. "Let me transfer your call to Mr. Lyons. I'm sure he can help you."

"Mr. Lyons?" I asked.

"Hang up," Kyle said, making a stabbing motion with his finger. When I didn't respond, he grabbed the phone out of my hand and pushed the "end" button.

Jumbo George chuckled. "That don't sound promising to me."

"Damn Lyons. Usurping my clients. Suppose this whole thing doesn't get cleared up?" Kyle said.

"What's the whole thing?" Jumbo George took a small sip of the coffee.

"This embezzlement charge. It's bogus! Lots of people borrow money from one account to pay something off or finance an investment. I bet they already have the funds back in the stupid account."

"How about the gambling debts?" Jumbo George asked.

"Well, that is a little different. But I'd get it back." Kyle slammed the phone down on the table.

I hoped it was sturdier than it looked.

"I'm not all that sure what it takes for embezzlement," Jumbo George said, "but taking money out of one account for something that has nothing to do with it sure sounds to me like it might be embezzlement." Jumbo George took a big gulp of the coffee and coughed.

"Well, technically, I suppose it is." Kyle frowned. "What'll I do if I really get convicted of it?"

Jumbo George looked over at me. "You tell 'em, Jesse. Your conviction was kind of a technicality, wasn't it?"

I took a mug and filled it with coffee. "Yeah. What you do, Kyle, is you go to prison."

"I can't go to jail!" he said.

"Not jail." I shook my head. "Not unless you only pick up a short bit. Prison."

"There's a difference?"

"Sure is. Prison is long term. After you're convicted. Actually, I'd take prison over jail any day. You can have a life in prison. Not a great life, but still a life."

"What happens in jail?" he asked.

"In jail, nothing's settled. You never know from one day to the next what's going on. Your cell buddy could be a scared kid, or a crazed murderer. Very unstable existence."

"I'll lose everything!"

"Pretty much," I agreed. "You start over when you're released."

He drummed his fingers nervously on the table. "I need a drink. You got anything here besides coffee?"

"Prob'ly some root beer left," Jumbo George said. "And I think there's most of a gallon of milk."

Kyle took a deep breath. "I mean anything to drink? Like alcohol?"

"Not here," Jumbo George said. "Don't keep it."

"Why not? Don't you ever want to offer anybody a drink?"

"Nope."

"Everybody I know drinks," Kyle said.

Jumbo George nodded knowingly. "And when things get tough, I bet a lot of them drink too much. I suppose you can go that route. I don't recommend it, though. Just makes things worse. But you can do it if you want."

Kyle looked at the full coffee mug I'd set in front of him. "What route?"

"The alcohol route. A lot of people do that. Or get into drugs. You don't strike me as a druggie type. But I could see you getting mixed up with cocaine. Or crystal meth."

"What do you mean, I don't strike you as the type?"

Jumbo George laughed, his shoulders heaving.

Kyle's eyebrows knit close together. He scowled. "I've smoked pot. You don't know the half of it. Neither does my wife. If she knew what I did some nights when I didn't come home…"

Alarm bells went off in my head. I wasn't sure I wanted to know, but I asked, "What do you do when you're out late?"

"Oh, you know. See other women. Go slumming. That kind of stuff."

I exchanged looks with Jumbo George. Was Kyle "slumming" now, hanging out with us? Probably. And did his "seeing other women" include snatching them off the street?

Kyle was ignoring us. "First thing, I need to figure out how to get some money."

He already had a pile of money in his wallet. But lawyers are expensive.

"Sell that fancy car?" George suggested.

Kyle frowned. "Wish I could. It's a company car. I'll swing by the bank and see how much is in our checking account. Get some out. But not enough so she thinks I'm trying to empty it."

"You don't think she's already taken everything out of it?"

"Nah. That wouldn't be fair. She's got this thing about *fair*. So she wouldn't do it." He got to his feet. "I've got to get some decent clothes. Either stop by the house or buy some." He shivered. "And some sheets for that bed. You say I've got the apartment for a week?"

"Yeah."

"Longer, if I want it?"

"Maybe." Jumbo George didn't promise.

"Okay. And I'll get to work on that grant. Show old Mr. Henry Richmond he's not the only one who can play games."

CHAPTER 14

I hadn't heard from Kelly by Friday night. We'd left it that she and I would take the kids to the street fair in the park Saturday. Were they still planning to come? I wanted to see her so badly I found it hard to breathe whenever I thought about it. Like there was a stone in my chest. The sensible thing would have been to call and ask if we were still on, but I was afraid to, as if giving her an opportunity to cancel would make her do just that.

Wouldn't she have called if she'd changed her mind? Or was it more likely she'd call to confirm the arrangements if she was coming? It didn't bear thinking about. So I tried to ignore it.

Restless, I woke up early. With a few hours to go before I could expect Kelly to show up—or not show up—I snuck down the stairs and out the back door into the alley, trying not to disturb Jumbo George. He was snoring heavily in his recliner, and there was no reason for him to have to get up now.

The pavement in the alley was old and worn, with grass growing in the cracks. The rotting garbage dumpster smell wasn't prominent, but it was noticeable. A few plastic bags and some fast food wrappers were wedged in corners where they'd blown.

The door at the top of the basement stairs gaped open. I was sure I'd locked it behind me yesterday, but the wood was warped, and a solid shove would push it open. Maybe even a strong wind.

Jumbo George didn't have any merchandise stored down there to worry about yet. He'd told me where to find some tools in one of the garages, and I'd moved them down there, but they were undisturbed. The only other thing anybody could take would be the parts for the shelving. I had half of them moved down there, but the rest of the boxes were still sitting on the loading dock. If anybody was going to take them, they'd be gone by now.

Leaving the basement accessible like that wasn't a good idea, though. A squatter might move in, looking for a place to sleep. Or shoot up. I'd have to say something to Jumbo George about getting a hasp and padlock to put on the door for now. It really needed a whole new door, but so did a number of other entrances. It would make more sense to get them all at once.

I schlepped the rest of the boxes of shelving parts down to the basement, stacking them on cinderblocks against the wall. They should have a little time to sit down there and acclimate to conditions before I assembled them.

The whole place smelled musty.

I made sure to lock the door as I left, for what good it would do.

Jumbo George wasn't in his recliner when I got back inside. The coffee was brewing and I heard water running in the shower.

"Jesse?" he called from the tiny bathroom.

"Yeah?"

"There's a ten on the table. Go down and get some donuts."

I took the money and headed for the coffee shop.

The street fair didn't start until ten o'clock, but parked cars already lined the curb.

I got two dozen donuts at the coffee shop and brought them back. I poured myself a cup of coffee and had one donut. George was dressed. He ate a dozen right away and put the half-empty box on the counter.

A car horn honked outside. I got up and peered out the front window. It was Kelly. I felt my shoulder muscles relax. I hadn't realized how tense I'd been.

She was driving her bright red RAV 4. Although whether it was hers or not was open to question. Someone she knew had bought it for her, and she was supposed to be making payments to him, but he was dead. Until someone asked about it, she figured she might as well drive it. Lord knows cars are expensive, and Kelly was chronically short of money. When she first got the car, she had scraped up a hefty down payment, and she'd made another payment or two, so she felt she had some rights to it.

Replacing the car would be difficult, perhaps impossible, for Kelly. But she needed a car. She not only had the kids to worry about, she lived too far away from work to walk.

The car was double parked. The traffic wasn't that heavy, so she wasn't holding things up, but she couldn't leave it there.

"There's no parking." Kelly stood next to the driver's door, looking up and down the block.

She was right. "You can park back in the alley," I said. "Behind Jumbo George's place. It says 'Loading Zone. Cars Will Be Towed,' but it's Saturday. No shipments are coming in."

"Sometimes they tow anyhow."

"It's not one of those towing services with spotters and all. He'd have to call to have it towed. He won't."

She leaned back on the car and closed her eyes. Her ample bosom pushed against her sweatshirt. My hands itched to pull her warm bulk close to me. She smelled faintly of lavender shampoo. I wanted to bury my face in her long dark hair.

Not the time or the place. I shoved my hands in my pockets.

"Look." She opened her eyes. They were cloudy and troubled. "I got a lot of stuff I should be doing today. And I been with the kids all week. By myself."

I considered saying I would have been happy to spend some time at her place, and I would have helped with the kids. But that might just make her mad.

"Do you think you could take them to the street fair by yourself?" she asked. "I'll come and pick everybody up later, and we can go to the house and fix supper."

The stone began to settle in my chest again. We hadn't seen each other in a week, and here she didn't want to spend the day with me.

And she wasn't making sense. "Didn't the kids have school?" I asked.

"Yeah, but you know what I mean. I've been real busy."

I didn't know what she meant, but I just shrugged.

When she paid attention, Kelly could read me like a book. She was paying attention now. She tossed me that little suggestive smirk and raised her eyebrows. "And after we get the kids to bed…" She grinned.

Of course she knew that would get to me. She had introduced me to sex. And she was the only woman I'd ever slept with. I wanted nothing more than to spend the evening in her warm bed, holding her close. I took a deep breath.

But if the sex was to be any good, she had to want it, too. If it was payment for taking the kids off her hands for a few hours, I could live without it. Not happily, but I wasn't about to start making bargains for sex.

I looked at the kids, strapped in the back seat. They were staring straight ahead, pretending not to hear.

Those kids hadn't had a life that provided a whole lot in the line of treats and adventures. And they'd been promised a street fair.

"Sure, I'll take them," I said. "But you don't have to pay me back."

"It's not like that…" she started to say, her lips pouty, but then she just shook her head. "Thanks. We'll talk about it when I get back."

She ducked her head into the open car window and said, "Go with Jesse now, okay? Best behavior!"

Chris opened the back door and held it for Brianna.

Kelly handed me a five dollar bill. "Get them some ice cream or something."

I hesitated, but then I took the money. I'd raided my pathetic savings stash for twenty bucks spending money, but I had a feeling that wouldn't go very far.

The kids scrambled up on the sidewalk and went to look in the window of the head shop. They were dressed in worn jeans and sneakers. Chris's jeans were too short, what we used to call "floods."

Chris pointed. "The castle! He put it in the window." On a previous visit, Chris had helped Jumbo George assemble parts of the model. Some of the harder parts that had stumped Jumbo George.

Kelly gave me a half-hearted peck on the cheek and got back in the car. "Be back around four. Or I'll call."

She'd have to call the store phone, since that was the only one I ever used.

I shepherded the kids into the store. "You guys have breakfast?" I asked.

They looked at each other.

"No," Brianna said.

Chris looked down. "Well, we split a banana. But it was pretty mushy."

Brianna's nose wrinkled. "I didn't eat my half."

I sighed. What did Kelly have to do that was so much more important than making sure her kids had a decent breakfast?

As I ushered them into the store, Brianna stopped and inhaled deeply. "I love that perfume!" she said.

Patchouli.

I asked Jumbo George, "Can they each have a donut?"

He scratched his chin under his beard. "Sure. There's that almost full gallon of milk, too." He looked past us. "Kelly parking the car? You tell her she could use the loading dock space?"

"Kelly's got some stuff to do," I said.

Jumbo George snorted. "So you're taking the kids to the street fair by yourself?"

I poured milk in two glasses and set them on the table. "I guess so."

"She takes advantage of you."

Brianna's face crumpled. Chris suddenly found his sneakers to be fascinating enough that he had to stare at them.

I said, "I suppose you could look at it like that. But the street fair is gonna be fun. Even more fun if I go with the kids. So maybe it's more like she's doing *me* a favor, letting me take them."

The kids brightened up a little.

I held the donut box for them to each choose one. I hoped there would be some kind of reasonably nutritious food available at the street fair we could get for lunch. Cheap, reasonably nutritious food.

"The castle looks real good in the window, Mr. Jumbo," Chris said. "When did you finish it?"

Jumbo George grinned. "About two weeks ago. I got some knights and stuff to put on it. You like it?"

"I 'specially like the knights."

The kids finished their donuts and milk. Brianna looked into her empty glass and frowned.

I filled their glasses again.

"You gonna come with us, Mr. Jumbo?" Chris asked. "Jesse says it's gonna be fun."

Jumbo George stroked his beard. "I got to stay here and keep the store open."

We both knew that, as the neighborhood gentrified, fewer and fewer customers made their way into the shop. He'd hoped some of the new riverfront residents, who had lots of money, would shop there, but they were mostly young professionals, far too clean-cut to buy much in the line of incense and rolling papers and astrological sign postcards. At least in broad daylight when someone might see them.

"You could leave your 'Closed' sign on the door," Chris suggested.

"I suppose I could." Jumbo George looked past the kids to the sunlight shining through the display window.

I put in my two cents worth. "It'd do you good to get out."

He didn't need much convincing. "Okay. Let me get my cane."

We walked slowly because of George's immense bulk, but it wasn't far. Around the corner and down to the next block, and we were across the street from the newly established and very trendy Riverfront Park.

Brianna stopped and stared, shrinking back against my legs.

It looked magical. Bunches of colorful balloons were tied to either side of the gate. Tinny music danced through the air. A few rides, including a carousel, swirled, their lights flashing. The tantalizing scent of popcorn drifted on the breeze blowing off the river.

Popcorn, I reminded myself, was one of those things that smelled much better than it ever tasted. We wouldn't spend our limited money on popcorn.

"Well, come on," Jumbo George said gruffly, limping into the crosswalk and heading for the gate.

The posted prices were higher than I'd hoped they would be. I should have taken more money out of my stash. We'd have to be making careful choices about where we decided to spend our money.

Brianna stood watching the carousel with wide eyes, clutching my hand tight. I wondered how much one ride would be.

A girl just about Brianna's size sidled up to us. She was wearing a bright yellow jacket with a cartoon princess on the back.

Brianna had a navy blue hoodie with frayed cuffs and a zipper that stuck.

"Do you live around here, Brianna?" the girl asked.

Brianna shook her head.

"Oh. I live right over there." The girl pointed to the fancy new condo development. "So we decided to come see about the fair. My mom and me." She glanced over her shoulder at a trim woman in a fitted gray tracksuit with fuchsia stripes on the legs. Her hair and makeup were impeccable.

"And my big brother's supposed to meet us here," the girl said.

The woman was looking at us and frowning.

I glanced around. Almost everybody was wearing fashionably casual clothes. We looked a bit out of place.

"You have a big brother, don't you?" the girl said to Brianna. "But he's not much bigger than you. *My* big brother is out of high school already."

Brianna held onto my hand and rubbed her cheek against my sleeve.

"Are you going to go on the carousel?" the girl asked, a smug smile on her face. "I told my mom I was going to ride it five times. At least."

Brianna shrugged. "I dunno."

I spoke up. "Yes, Brianna's going to go on the carousel."

Her fragile hand tightened its grip on mine.

"Sophia!" the woman called to the girl. "I have the tickets. Let's catch this next ride."

"Well," Sophia said, tossing her hair. "I have to go. See you around. Or in school on Monday."

Brianna leaned against my leg and watched her go. "Sophia's mean," she said. "She says I'm a dummy."

"Just 'cause she says it don't make it so," I said.

"Maybe. But I *am* a dummy. I have to go to the resource room on Friday afternoon. Sophia's really smart."

Jumbo George led us to the enclosure with the rides. They were street carnival rides, and probably wouldn't have impressed anybody who'd ever been to a real amusement park. But that didn't include Chris and Brianna. Or me, for that matter.

Tickets were fifty cents each. Some of the rides took five tickets. We'd run through money fast there.

George waddled up to the booth, slapped down a twenty dollar bill and reeled in the string of tickets the attendant gave him. He turned to the kids. "What do you want to go on first?"

Brianna's smile lit up her peaked little face. "Carousel!"

Chris cocked his head. "Okay. But I'd like to go on some of the other stuff. The big kid rides. You know, the Zipper and things like that."

"Oh, no," Brianna said. "I'm not going on anything that turns you upside down."

I turned to Jumbo George. "Suppose I stay here with Brianna, and you take Chris over to the 'big kid rides.'"

Jumbo George looked at me in alarm. "I'm not going on any damn rides."

"You don't have to actually go on any of them," I said. "I'm just gonna stand here and keep an eye on Brianna. That's all you need to do with Chris."

"Well, okay." The two of them headed for the Zipper.

Sophia and her mother were at the carousel eying several mounts and arguing. "How about the camel? Or the elephant?" Sophia's mother suggested.

"They just stand there. I want one that goes up and down," Sophia insisted, looking at a prancing silver horse with a red saddle that was at the height of its ascent.

Brianna ran over to the silver horse. "This one!"

This wasn't good. I said, "Sophia was here first. If she wants that horse, she's got it. There's lots of others."

A pained expression I couldn't decipher came over the mother's face. She pulled Sophia back. "Oh, no," she said. "You may certainly have that one if you'd like."

No sense giving Sophia something to be mad about. I pointed to a big black charger, poised to leap, nostrils flaring red and sporting gold and green tack. Also at the height of its ascent. "This one's bigger. And it goes up and down, too."

Brianna looked over her shoulder at Sophia and smirked.

I lifted her onto the horse's molded saddle. "Now you got to hold on tight to the pole," I told her. "The horse is going to move up and down, and the whole thing's going around. You can't get down until it stops. Understand?"

She nodded, her slender hands grasping the pole.

I gave her the two tickets she'd need and went to lean on the fence surrounding the ride.

Sophia seemed to have won the discussion with her mother, although by that time a young boy in a red jacket was on the silver horse. Pushing her mother's helping hand away, Sophia climbed onto a bay horse with a flying mane.

The mother came over and stood next to me. "How do you know my daughter?" she demanded.

I blinked. "I don't, really."

"You know her name."

"Well, yeah." The woman had said the kid's name within my hearing just a few minutes ago. But I didn't think she'd appreciate me pointing that out. "Brianna's in her class. Brianna knows her." I left it at that.

"Are you Brianna's father?"

"No." This was a little awkward. "Her mother's boyfriend." Kelly might not like me claiming boyfriend status, but otherwise it got too complicated to try to explain.

The woman looked me over. I resisted the temptation to glance down at my ankle and make sure the box wasn't visible.

She pulled the jacket of her tracksuit protectively tighter. "Do you live around here?"

"Yeah. Two blocks over. On Second Street."

"Oh." Her face relaxed. At least I wasn't contaminating the immediate area of her residence. "I didn't realize there was housing over there that was appropriate for children."

What kind of housing was "appropriate for children?" Most kids lived wherever their parents could afford to live. But I said, "Brianna lives across town. In a house. With her mom and her brother."

"I see." The woman surveyed the area. "And is her mother here?"

"She had to work." That wasn't exactly what she'd told me, but it beat the real explanation that I had no idea why she wasn't here with us.

"And she let you take Brianna to the street fair without her?"

This conversation was going in a direction that I didn't like. She seemed like she was being pretty judgmental. Bordering on rude.

I was tempted to say something that might shock her. Like that the judge hadn't put me on the sex offender registry yet, so what was the problem? But that would just make the situation worse. Besides, it sounded to me like Brianna was having a tough enough time of it in school without having parents telling their kids to stay away from her.

So I just said, "Yes."

A young man in his late teens or early twenties stepped up beside Sophia's mother. "Mom! I've been looking all over for you," he whined. "You should have waited for me."

Sophia's big brother, who was out of high school?

"How was I supposed to know when you were getting home?" Her voice had a sharp edge to it, like controlled anger.

Maybe she just always sounded like that. Just as well I hadn't given into the temptation to egg her on by saying something about the sex offender registry.

She said to the young man, "Edmond. You were out all night—again—and I'm supposed to wait for you to take Sophia to the street fair?"

"You knew I'd be coming. I told you. You know my band is gonna play on the stage at noon." He gestured across the park.

She shook her head. "No, I didn't know that."

"I told you."

"I don't remember that."

"Well," he said. "If you'd get me a car, I could maybe make it home more easily. As it is, I have to wait until somebody'll give me a ride. Or stay where I am."

"I hope you didn't bring anything illegal into the house again."

"No. I told you and Dad I wouldn't do that anymore, and I haven't."

I glanced at the brother, then took a closer look. He was my height and skinny. His brown hair was pulled back away from his pale face in a pony tail. He was wearing blue jeans and a gray hoodie. Designer jeans, maybe, and a brand name hoodie, but not all that different from what I was wearing. And on his feet were hiking boots. They may not have been the steel-toed work boots I wore, but they looked somewhat similar. He looked as out of place here as I did.

He was a lot younger than me. If it was dark out, I wasn't sure that would be obvious. And he was out at night a lot? Could he possibly have been the guy who tried to carjack those girls?

CHAPTER 15

The kid didn't have a car of his own, which might mean that he walked a lot. And he was out at night.

And that might be a reason to steal a car to use for a while, but stealing a car wasn't the question here. Carjacking was something else altogether. It was about the excitement, the adrenalin flow, the fear in the eyes of the driver. Not about transportation.

At my bail hearing, the prosecutor made it plain that he thought that the incident was the beginning of an intended sexual assault and murder, and that these girls had just managed to get away. There were two of them, which would have to make it harder for the guy. Had he not realized there were two people in the car?

I tried to examine Edmond out of the corner of my eye, not looking directly at him. Was he capable of that type of crime?

Who was I fooling? Under the right circumstances, anybody was capable of all sorts of heinous crimes. Appearances had little to do with it. Serial sex offenders, in particular, were likely to look normal, whatever normal was.

I turned away to keep an eye on Brianna, but I overheard their continuing conversation.

"I need some money, Mom," Edmond said. "To get something to eat."

"And are you coming home after you play?"

"Maybe. I got to go with the guys to drop the amplifiers off."

"I'd like you to have dinner with the family, at least once this weekend."

"Is Dad going to be there?"

"Yes."

"Are you sure he wants me there? He's really been getting on my case about getting a job or taking some classes or something. He doesn't believe in me. He doesn't think we can make a go of this band."

Sophia's mom sighed. "It's not so much that he doesn't think you can make a go of it. It's more that he thinks you need to start supporting yourself if you're not going to go to college."

"What does eating dinner with the family have to do with anything?" he asked.

She turned to face him. "It would make me happy if you did. Can't you do something once in a while to make your mother happy?"

Edmond shuffled his feet. "Okay. What time are you eating tonight?"

"Seven thirty."

"I'll be there."

She handed over a few bills and he left.

When the carousel came around, Brianna was holding on tight, a frightened grimace on her face. She didn't look like she was enjoying this at all. Not much I could do until the ride stopped.

A high-pitched and familiar voice came out of the crowd. "Jesse!"

Carissa. I closed my eyes. Not exactly a welcome encounter. I still hadn't read the articles she'd written about the missing women. Or what she'd said about me.

Perfectly reasonable, I guess, for a reporter for the local paper to be visiting the street fair. She was probably going to be writing a story about it. Complete with pictures. But for sure I didn't want to give her any more ammunition for her feature series on the kidnappings. And she would manage to turn anything I said into a damaging misquote anyhow.

She pushed her way over to where we stood, ignoring Sophia's mom. "What're you doing here?"

"Seeing what's at the street fair," I said.

"When did they release you?"

Just what I needed. Carissa asking questions out in public. In front of somebody I'd hoped would forget about me.

"They had no reason to hold me," I said, turning away. Some reporter. She hadn't even followed up to know I'd made bail.

She raised her penciled-in eyebrows. "No reason to hold you? How about somebody identifying you as a carjacker?"

I sighed. "I wasn't involved."

"But that girl *identified* you. Right there. In person. And how about the other women who've gone missing? Didn't they charge you with any of that?"

Sophia's mom was staring, her mouth open.

The carousel stopped. With Brianna and Sophia right in front of us.

"Jesse!" Brianna called. "Can I ride again?"

After she'd been terrified the first time around? But I said, "Sure."

Carissa tossed her multi-layered blond hair. "Who's that little girl?" she asked. "And where did you get her?"

I took a deep breath. "Babysitting," I said. That wasn't entirely accurate, but it was close enough.

"And who," Carissa asked, "is letting a convicted murderer babysit for a little girl?"

Inwardly, I cringed.

"And possibly on the sex offenders list?"

Carissa of all people should know that stupid rumor wasn't true. Checking facts should be her stock in trade. But she never let facts mess up a great article.

So what if somebody thought I was a sex offender? I knew I wasn't. And so did the people I cared about. It didn't usually bother me.

But I did have the murder conviction.

I was doubly glad I hadn't made any sarcastic remarks about the sex offenders registry.

In this case, poor Brianna was the one who might have to live with the consequences.

The sounds of a band tuning up drifted across the park from the stage by the waterfront.

"Oh!" Carissa's head jerked up. "I have to go interview that band! I'll talk to you later, Jesse!"

She took off at a trot that I wouldn't have thought possible in the stiletto heeled shoes she wore.

Sophia's mother had extracted herself from her position leaning on the fence next to me and was dragging Sophia off the carousel.

Brianna clung tight to the pole and her horse. "I can ride again?"

"Sure," I said, giving her two more tickets. "Was it fun?"

"Uh huh."

Brianna used up all her tickets on the carousel, although I did get her to change horses a few times.

"Sophia said she was gonna ride the carousel five times," she said. "But she didn't. Her mom made her get off after only one time."

"Maybe she wanted to try a couple of different rides."

Brianna ignored me. "I rode lots more times than she did."

I didn't like the ugly smirk on her face, but I could understand why she felt that way.

When the tickets were gone, we found Chris and Jumbo George at a picnic table, eating lunch. Jumbo George couldn't fit his stomach between the bench and the table, so he was sitting sideways at the end, three plates in front of him.

As we came up, he nodded at two covered plates. "Pulled pork sandwiches. With sweet potatoes and baked beans." He shoveled a handful of fries in his mouth. "I know you worry about what the kids eat, but I figured there had to be some nutrition in that."

I slipped onto the bench and uncovered my plate. The pork was spicy and moist, the sweet potatoes smooth and creamy.

"This is really good," I said, taking a bite. "Thanks."

Even Brianna ate most of hers.

"How were the rides you went on?" I asked Chris.

His face lit up. "Great! I never had so much fun! And then Mr. Jumbo let me help pick out what we were gonna get for lunch."

"We got money for ice cream. Then do you wanna go listen to the band?" I asked him.

"No. But," Chris pointed at a table a few yards away. "They've got free face painting over there. Could we get our faces painted?"

"Sure. I'll clean up after lunch. Can you take Brianna with you?"

They set off and I finished the food Brianna had left.

Jumbo George stretched and reached a ham-sized hand out for a bottle of water. "I see what you mean."

"What?"

"When I told you that woman was taking advantage of you, and you said maybe she was doing you a favor."

"With the kids?"

"I kind of forgot how happy kids can be. And it's contagious."

"Yeah. Those two don't have an easy time of it, but they're great kids." I felt my face twist into a half-smile. "Wish there was some way I could make sure they get what they need."

Jumbo George shoved the trash toward me. "We can only do what we can. Don't remember the last time I felt this good. And all it took was forty bucks spent on a couple of kids."

I gathered up the plates and napkins. "They appreciate it. So do I."

"Best money I spent in years."

We sat and watched as the kids waited patiently in line until their turn came and the artists got to work on them.

They came running back to us.

"I'm a kitty cat!" Brianna beamed at us.

Sure enough, her face was painted like a kitten, with a black nose, whiskers and gray stripes.

Chris had similar markings, but his features were fierce, with orange and black stripes.

"A tiger?" Jumbo George guessed.

"Yep."

I stood up. "Let's get the ice cream and then go back to the shop. Wouldn't want your mom to get there and have to wait for us."

The kids agonized over the available flavors of ice cream. Chris chose something called Space Rocket Debris. Brianna ended up with vanilla.

As we left, they looked longingly back at the street fair. Jumbo George leaned heavily on his cane and huffed as we crossed the street in front of the big condo complex. I held onto Brianna's hand.

"Jesse! Wait! I didn't get a chance to talk to you!"

I glanced over my shoulder and saw Carissa rushing toward us.

"Keep going." I let go of Brianna's hand. "Even if I stop to talk to her, go back to the shop with Jumbo George. I'll be along in a few minutes."

Brianna stood frozen.

Carissa caught up and grabbed my arm. "Jesse!"

I stopped and turned to face her. "What?"

Her bright red lips formed a pout and she tossed her hair. "You act like you're mad at me or something."

"I'm not mad at you. I just don't want to talk to you."

"Why not?"

"Are you kidding? So I can show up on the front page of the paper again?"

"You could give your side of things," she said.

"Yeah, right. What am I supposed to say? I didn't do any of the stuff you say I done?" I tried to shake her hand off my arm, but she grasped tighter.

She changed tactics. Smiling at Brianna, she said, "Honey, what's your name?"

"You leave them kids alone," I said to her.

To Brianna, I said, "Go with Jumbo George. I'll be along as soon as I can."

Brianna didn't move. I gave her a little push toward Chris and Jumbo George. "Go on."

Reluctantly, she moved toward them.

Jumbo George took her by the hand and looked questioningly at me.

"Go ahead. I'll be right along."

"What's the matter?" Carissa tilted her head sideways and looked up at me, a simpering smile on her face.

"I got nothing to say." I tried again to pull my arm free.

She gripped tighter, her voice rising. "I want some answers here," she said. "And I'm not leaving until I have some."

I shook my arm, hard. "Let go!" I said.

Behind us, the gate to the courtyard of the condo complex opened. A security guard stepped out.

"This man bothering you, miss?" he said, his hand on something on his belt. It looked like some kind of holster. I didn't think security guards were usually armed. But I could be wrong. And I had no desire to find out the hard way.

"Not really," Carissa said with another toss of her head. "I can take care of myself."

"Is this your boyfriend?"

She laughed. "Jesse? Hell, no. He's not even supposed to be here. He's supposed to be in jail."

The guy reached for a radio on his belt. "You want me to call 911?" he said to Carissa.

"Paydon!" Jumbo George was waddling back toward us, the kids trailing behind him. "That's one of my tenants. He ain't done nothing!"

The security guard froze and regarded Jumbo George. "Seriously?"

"Yeah. I don't know who the broad is, but Jesse's been with me all morning."

"Really?"

"Yes. If you call the cops on anybody, it better be that bitch."

That'd be a waste of time. Last I knew, she was dating Detective Belkins. It seemed an unlikely match to me, but nobody asked my opinion.

Carissa's hand fell away from my arm. "Bitch? That's not nice."

I took the opportunity to pull free from her and step past Jumbo George, where I took Brianna's hand and hurried down the street with the kids in tow.

When I got to the corner, I stopped to wait for Jumbo George and looked to see what had happened to Carissa.

She had turned her attention to the security guard, tilting her head and aiming her hundred-watt smile at him.

He puffed out his chest and pushed his hat back a bit on his head. He returned the smile.

Grabbing his sleeve, Carissa moved in close beside him.

Better him than me.

CHAPTER 16

We got back to the shop.

Kelly was nowhere in sight. The message light on the phone's answering machine wasn't blinking.

Jumbo George swung the "closed" sign to "open." He shrugged. "You never know. Somebody might want to buy something." Exhausted, he slumped in a chair.

"Can I watch TV?" Brianna asked.

I frowned. She watched entirely too much TV as it was.

"I guess," Jumbo George said. He glanced at me, and seeing my face, said, "She's been out in the fresh air most of the day. She's got to be tired."

The TV was on the end of the counter in the store. I grabbed a cushion and a blanket and put them on the floor, then turned the TV so she could see it. I flipped through the channels until we came to a cartoon.

"That one!" Brianna said.

She curled up on the cushion, pulling the blanket around her, and stuck her thumb in her mouth. She stared at the TV, glassy-eyed. She looked really lonely. I wished I had a teddy bear or something to tuck in next to her, but I didn't.

"You gonna watch TV, too?" Jumbo George asked Chris.

He looked at the cartoon on the screen and shook his head. "No. I hate stupid cartoons." He went over to the ancient computer Jumbo George used for bookkeeping and ordering. "Does that have an internet connection?" he asked.

Jumbo George grinned. "Yeah. I got wifi for all the buildings. Good selling point, especially for the storefronts. The guy who runs the coffee shop said he needed it for his customers. So I just had it put in for everybody."

"Can I play some computer games?"

"If you know how."

In a few seconds, Chris was working on some kind of puzzle. Jumbo George looked over his shoulder. "Can you show me how to do that?" he asked.

"Sure. But this is kind of slow. If you had a new computer, it'd go much faster."

"You got a computer?" Jumbo George asked.

"Not at home. But I can use one at school. Mostly for school stuff. But if we get done with our work, we can play math games or something. That's fun. And sometimes I get to use one in the public library."

Still no sign of Kelly, but everybody seemed settled. Brianna's eyes were glazed over and her eyelids drooping. Soon she'd be asleep.

I picked up this morning's newspaper and carried it into the back room. It was still folded in its plastic bag. Nobody was paying any attention to me. I took it out and steeled myself for the latest of Carissa's feature stories.

For once, it wasn't on the front page, but there was a little blurb about it, directing me to the Local News and Events section. I turned to that.

Today's article analyzed the circumstances surrounding the disappearance of the women.

Each one had been out in the Riverfront Park area in the early morning hours. Three were known to have been driving, one was definitely on foot, and the other may have been in a car, but no one knew for sure.

Two were coming home from working the late shift at a bar or club, alone. One had been in a fight with her boyfriend and stormed out of the apartment, again alone. The others may have been soliciting or with a john.

Hours or even days had gone by before anyone was concerned enough to report any of them missing. No one had any idea where they had gone. The woman who survived, who worked as a bartender until closing, reported that she was stopped for a light near the park when someone opened the back door of her car and threw a large towel over her head.

She managed to get her hands under the towel and tried to push it off. When the assailant reached in front of her face to grab it, she bit down on his arm. Hard.

He loosened his grip. She accelerated away and he fell from the open rear door. She didn't slow down for ten blocks, at which point she called 911.

The now-bloody towel was from a local motel. Police scoured the registration records from the motel and questioned numerous people, but came up blank.

One body had been recovered, the one who got out of work at a club when it closed. It had been found in a dumpster not far from Quality Steel's factory.

She'd lived in one of the townhouses in the new condo complex, with a couple of roommates. One of them had called the police when her boss called, asking why she'd missed work for two days.

The DNA recovered from that body matched the DNA on the bloody towel.

The car one of the women had been driving was recovered from an unused shipping yard on Washington Street. Like most of the ones in the area, the yard was surrounded by a solid wall.

The car was hidden in the back, behind a couple of decrepit trailers. When the Lojack anti-theft device was activated, it brought authorities directly to the site.

The entire area was thoroughly searched, but it appeared that it had been driven there and abandoned.

The car that belonged to the woman who had argued with her boyfriend was recovered from long-term parking at the airport. There was no record of her having taken a flight anywhere, but the possibility remained that she had left voluntarily.

The third car had not been found.

Families and friends held out hope that the remaining women would turn up alive, but that seemed unlikely.

Some things were missing from the body that had been recovered, but the police were withholding many details. Whether the items were clothing, purse, jewelry or other things wasn't reported.

The article repeated that the police were not revealing all the details, and speculated that there were similarities that also were not being revealed.

The paper had pictures of all five women. That made them more real. I shivered. Three people, gone. Probably four lives snuffed out. I'd spent years in prison, and associated with some of the most depraved members of society, but I still couldn't get my mind around doing that to another person. Or treating a woman so callously.

The article ended with a reference to the attempted carjacking, identifying it as a potential sixth incident in the series.

At least in this article Carissa didn't have any ominous hints about a person of interest. Who had a prior conviction for murder.

I put down the paper and stared at nothing. Thank goodness for DNA testing. Had this all happened before that was available, I had no doubt I'd be locked up, looking at spending the rest of my life in prison. As a despised sex offender.

What I couldn't understand, though, was Detective Belkins continued insistence that I was involved. Wasn't the DNA evidence enough for him? Or was there more to it than I knew? Like, maybe a strong suspicion that they were dealing with two perpetrators, an original and a copycat.

The bell on the front door tinkled. I got up and slipped into the shop.

Kelly. Her dark hair was pulled back in a messy ponytail. Instead of the sweatshirt she'd had on when she dropped off the kids, she wore a nice blouse. And sparkly earrings. Her eyes were red and tired, as if she'd been crying.

I went to give her a hug, but she backed up a step. I leaned as close as I dared to see if I could catch a sniff of alcohol. No. But the patchouli tended to deaden my sense of smell, so it might have been there and I missed it.

She gave me a crooked half-smile. "Sorry I'm so late. I should have called." She didn't lean over to give me a kiss like she usually did.

I shrugged and shoved my hands deep in my pockets. I didn't entirely trust them not to wander over and touch her earring. "We're doing okay," I said.

She looked around. Brianna was asleep. Chris seemed to be concentrating on the computer, but I noticed his hands were still and he was biting his lower lip.

"How was the street fair, Chris?" she asked.

Chris hesitated for a minute. "Fine," he said, his voice wary.

Kelly shook her head at the face painting. "We'll have to get that cleaned off as soon as we get home."

Chris set his mouth in a stubborn line. "Why? We could leave it on 'til school Monday morning."

"You can't go to bed like that. You'll get it all over the sheets." She moved over and peered at Brianna. "She's got face paint, too?"

"Yeah. She's a kitten. I'm a tiger."

Kelly turned to me. "Did they behave?"

"Yeah. We had a good time. And we got lunch."

"Good."

"They're gonna need supper."

She bristled. "Don't you think I'm planning to give them supper?"

Maybe I should just have kept my mouth shut, but I said, "I don't think they had much breakfast."

"Are you trying to tell me how to raise my kids?"

"No." I was in too deep now to back out. And it was past time she faced the fact that she didn't exactly qualify for a Mother of the Year award. "But they do need to be fed."

She took a deep breath. "We were rushed this morning. They'll get a good supper."

I didn't say anything.

"Well," Kelly said. "Let's get going."

Reluctantly, Chris got to his feet.

Kelly reached down and picked Brianna up from her nest on the floor. "Come on, kiddo. Time to go home."

Brianna whined a bit, then settled her slender body against Kelly's sturdy one, her head resting on her mother's shoulder.

She turned her head toward me. "You coming?"

I was surprised. Usually when she went into the "don't tell me how to raise my kids" mode, she was mad at me and didn't want me around.

I looked at her ample curves. Although I kept them firmly in my pockets, my hands twitched with the effort to keep them from reaching out and touch the hair that brushed her shapely rear, to put my arm around her broad shoulders and pull her close to me so I could plant a kiss on her lips.

But she'd backed away from my hug. And she hadn't really even greeted me when she came in.

If I went along with her, I could make sure the kids got supper and had bedtime stories. But then we'd end up arguing. So I'd leave.

Tough on the kids. Tough on me. I wasn't sure about whether it was tough on Kelly or not, but I suspected it was.

I didn't have a lot of experience with women, but usually Kelly was just as eager as I was in bed. Or so it seemed to me.

Maybe Jumbo George was right. Maybe she was just using me. And I was too dumb and horny to realize it.

Maybe I should stop pretending I meant something to her.

"You look pretty tired," I said. "Might be best if you just went home and got some sleep."

She rolled her eyes. "Suit yourself." She shifted Brianna into a more secure position and held out her hand to Chris. "Let's go."

"Come back soon, Chris," Jumbo George said.

Chris looked back over his shoulder. "Hope so, Mr. Jumbo."

"Talk to you tomorrow night at work, Jesse," Kelly said as she dragged Chris toward the door.

It shut behind them. I stared at the closed door, my stomach in a knot. My mind froze and I couldn't make sense of what just happened. Or maybe I didn't want to.

"Took care of her kids all day, and you didn't even make it into the sack with her." Jumbo George chuckled.

I sank into a chair. "Well, I didn't take the kids to the fair to get laid. Although it would have been nice. Besides, it was you who spent the money on them."

"Yeah." He reached over and shut off the computer. "But she don't know that."

I nodded.

"But I do see what you mean about having them kids around. It's kind of fun."

"After you been locked up for years, you appreciate things like that," I said.

He nodded. "Years of living by myself and not getting out much may have done the same for me. She's got some great kids and a decent job. Sounds to me like the basis for a good life. What's her problem, anyhow?"

"She don't have it easy." I shook my head. "Her ex is an abusive alcoholic, and he's giving her a rough time over custody and child support."

"Is he trying to get custody?"

"Yeah."

"Does he have any family support? She drinks, too. Maybe they'd be better off with him."

"I don't think so. He's just got his mother, who's getting on in years. She's pretty much housebound, and she's got some kind of dementia. And their Aunt Louise, who I think is actually their father's aunt. She's not so healthy herself. The kids'd be more than she can handle."

"Doesn't Kelly have any family around?" Jumbo George heaved himself off his stool and headed for the back room.

"Not really. Her mom died when she was a kid, and her dad raised her. But he's in prison now. Even when he's not locked up, he's a biker, an officer with the Predators. Not exactly the ideal person to help with the grandkids. He stayed with her last time he was released, but it was a disaster."

"She's got a stable place to live, don't she?"

"Kind of. A house they bought when she was married." I closed my eyes and pictured it. A big house, in a nice neighborhood. With good schools. But expensive for one person at our pay scale. "She got it in the divorce settlement, and she's trying to hang onto it, but it's not easy. Just the mortgage payment takes up a good chunk of her salary."

"So where do you think she was today, that she couldn't go to the street fair with you and the kids?"

"I was hoping she'd gone to an AA meeting, and didn't want to say anything about it in front of you."

"An all day AA meeting?" Jumbo George filled the coffee pot and turned it on.

"I didn't say it was a particularly realistic hope," I admitted.

Jumbo George laughed. "So now what?"

"See what she has to say tomorrow night at work, I guess."

"Those poor kids. Both parents boozers. You think they do any drugs?"

"I don't think Kelly does. I don't know enough about her ex to tell."

"Know what I think?" Jumbo George rinsed out two coffee mugs and peered into the donut box on the counter.

"No." I wasn't sure I wanted to know.

"I think maybe those kids are lucky to have you in their lives right now."

Not good. I had another twenty years backup time on my sentence. Mr. Ramirez's signature on a piece of paper and I'd be returned to prison on a parole violation. The kids didn't need any more losses in their young lives.

With that thought in mind, I tried not to let them get too close to me. But my time with them was the best time I ever had. Made me feel like a regular person, not just a paroled convict.

Although with the way things were going, I might not be a *paroled* convict much longer.

Add that to the way Kelly was acting toward me. That didn't look like how a promising long term relationship was supposed to develop.

Jumbo George pulled a few donuts out of the box and put them on a paper towel on the table. "Let me eat these. Then we can decide what we're going to do for supper."

"I can make some fried egg sandwiches," I said. "And heat up some canned beans."

He snorted. "Seriously, though, Jesse. I think you may be the best thing those kids have going for them right now."

I closed my eyes. "I sure hope not. I'm nobody to count on here."

CHAPTER 17

"Trust me. It'll look great." Jumbo George stuffed a fried egg sandwich into his mouth. It was his fifth one. He washed it down with an entire can of root beer.

"Okay," I said. "It's your call. But do you want me to buy a quart of the paint first, and just do a little bit, so you can see for sure?"

"Nah. Get one of those big buckets. What are they, five gallons?"

"In red?"

"Not red. Scarlet. There's a difference. Scarlet is richer. Get semi-gloss. Top of the line." He held his plate below the edge of the table and brushed crumbs onto it.

"That's prob'ly going to be two hundred dollars. If they even sell them that big."

"Yeah. But it should do the front doors and the trim of most of the buildings."

"True, that. But scarlet?" I tried to picture it. The exteriors of all the buildings were weathered red brick. They'd been recently tuck pointed.

"Stand out. Make the buildings look fresh." He wiped his mouth with a paper towel. "It'll make a bold statement."

That it would. If I'd been choosing a color for the trim, I'd have chosen white. Or tan. Or, if making a bold statement was what I was aiming at, maybe dark green.

"When can you get started?" Jumbo George asked.

I took a bite of my own fried egg sandwich. "I'm not done with the shelving in the basement. I should finish that first."

"Okay.'

"And I have to take a look at the paint, see what kind of shape it's in. Any place that's flaking I'll have to scrape down. Then I'm gonna have to scrub it good. Let it dry good. And run masking tape all along the windows. We don't want paint on those big display windows."

"Okay."

"That's assuming the wood underneath the old paint is in good shape. If any of it is rotting, it'll have to be replaced."

"Okay." Jumbo George opened another can of root beer.

"So I won't buy the paint until I've got that done and are actually ready to paint."

"Okay."

"So you can change your mind, if you want."

He narrowed his eyes. "I'm not gonna change my mind. Scarlet. If we run out before you get all the buildings done, we can switch colors. Purple, maybe?"

That didn't sound much better, but he was the buildings' owner. If he wanted scarlet and purple trim, that's what he'd get.

What colors would he choose for the garages out back? I didn't even want to think about that. They were clapboard, and the entire structures needed to be painted. Or torn down.

I got to my feet. "I'll go out and take a look now, while the light's still good."

The storefronts all had recessed entrances flanked by big display windows. That protected them somewhat from the weather. Most of them had single wooden doors with glass panels, although a few had double doors. The trim and door to the head shop looked pretty good.

The solid wood doors that led to the apartments upstairs, though, were exposed to the weather. They might be in much worse shape.

The sidewalk sloped down toward the corner, so that each storefront was a foot lower than the previous one. I had a feeling the lower ones would need more work. After the recent flood, they'd been under water for a few days.

Between the storefronts were the doors that led to the apartments. I stopped at the one that led to Paydon's apartment over the head shop. The paint was faded and peeling. The numbers, 214 ½, were tarnished. Brass? The numbers over the head shop door, 214, were still shiny. So were the numbers 216 for the empty store next door.

Maybe the tarnished numbers would polish up. If not, they shouldn't be too hard to replace. They must sell ½ numbers, although I'd never seen any.

I reached up and ran my finger over the numbers. The surface was rough. I leaned in to peer at them.

The door swung inward, leaving me standing there with my hand raised.

Paydon Norris, the security guard from the condo complex, stood in front of me, just as surprised to see me as I was to see him. He wasn't wearing his uniform. Just what seemed to be the neighborhood standard—jeans and a hoodie.

He ducked and threw his arm up in front of his face. "You trying to hit me?"

"No, dude. I'm looking at the door. I'm gonna paint it. Looking to see if the numbers need replacing."

Looking over his shoulder at the stairs that rose steeply between walls with peeling paint, he said, "You gonna fix up the inside of the apartment, too?"

"Eventually," I said. "But that's pretty far down the list of stuff Jumbo George wants done."

Paydon frowned. "He's not gonna raise my rent, is he?"

"You just moved in. I don't think he's gonna raise your rent for a while."

"Good. I can afford this place. I lost my driver's license, and I need a place where I can walk to my job."

I didn't have a license, either, but I'd never had one. I knew most people did. I wondered why he'd lost it. Probably traffic violations. DWI's or something.

Jumbo George said Paydon didn't have references. He'd tried to run some kind of a check on the computer, but I was willing to bet Jumbo George didn't know how to do a thorough search.

It'd be nice to know if Paydon had issues in his background. The guy seemed a little dicey to me. But then, who was I to talk? If anybody ran a background check on me, they'd run the other way fast.

Maybe Chris would know how to find a site that did good background searches. Or at least be able to point us in the right direction. But I'd hate to get the kid involved in something like that.

Paydon stepped out the door, looking up and down the street. "You're the guy who was giving that lady reporter a hard time earlier, aren't you?"

If anybody was giving anybody a hard time, it was her giving it to me, not the other way around. But I was the guy he had in mind. "She was trying to talk to me, yeah. I try not to talk to her."

"'Cause she knows how much trouble you're in? She told me about it."

"'Cause she'll twist anything I say all around and make me sound bad. Things are tough enough. And 'cause she's dating a cop."

He raised his eyebrows. "She's dating a cop?"

"Yeah. One Detective Belkins. He's trouble. So is she."

"Are they, like, an *item*?"

"Seems like it."

He frowned. "Damn. I asked her if she wanted to go out on my day off, get a few drinks or something. See where that led. She said yes. She didn't say nothing about dating a cop."

"Yeah, well, she's prob'ly trying to get some kind of information out of you for her articles. Was I you, I'd be careful. Belkins isn't a cop you want pissed at you. You pay for that."

"I take it he's pissed at you."

I nodded. "You got that right."

"And here I thought she was impressed with my svelte physique." He laughed and ran his hand over his small paunch. "I don't think she could get much information out of me. I don't know much."

"You know she's doing a feature series on those women who've disappeared. You're working as a security guard right around where a lot of stuff happened. One of the victims lived in the complex where you work. I bet Carissa wants to pick your brains, find out if you know anything. Or if she can get you to say something she can use in a story."

"Is that what she was trying to talk to you about? The whole Riverfront Rapist thing?"

"Yeah. She already did one article about how I'm a 'person of interest.'"

He smiled. "I saw that one. Took me a minute to make the connection, but when I saw you arguing with her…"

"The cops got to be watching the park and the surrounding area pretty close."

"Yeah. And that's one of the reasons the property management hired a few more guards. They have us working 24-7 now. Used to only be evenings and Saturdays during the day." He grinned again. "Job security. They had me working twelve hour shifts last week, six at night to six in the morning."

"Did you see anything?" I asked. Although my arrest and the car hitting the utility pole were a few blocks away.

But it meant he couldn't have been the guy who did it, for what that's worth.

"Nah."

"At least one of the women was a hooker." I moved back from the door. "Many of them out in the park there?"

"Nah. Every once in a while I used to see a girl or two who might be on the game. Not often, though. And since the disappearances, I hardly see anybody out there at all at night."

"How long have you been working there?" I asked.

"A few months, on and off. I was working a couple of different places for the security company, but when they expanded the hours here, I asked if I could be there full time. Easier without a car. That's when I started looking for a place to live in the neighborhood." He frowned. "It was harder than I thought. Most places are pretty expensive. This apartment is pretty decrepit, but I can afford it. And it's right where I need to be."

"So you were working there when that hooker disappeared?"

"I worked the shift before, but not when she actually disappeared. So I don't know if she was working the park then." He scratched his head.

"How about the one who lived in the condo complex?"

"I'm not sure I'd even recognize her. But from what the paper said, she closed down the bar where she was working at three a.m. or so. She probably never made it back home."

"Anyhow." I looked down the street to where a car was pulling into a parking space. A red Audi. "I bet that's why Carissa wants to spend time with you. Even if you didn't see anything, she can probably squeeze a quote or two out of you."

He laughed. "Fat chance. But I'm not gonna turn down a broad like that. You think there's any possibility of getting her in the sack?"

"I dunno. Might be. But if Belkins found out, he'd be on your case."

"So? What could he do?"

"Who knows? But he's a cop. And he don't always play by the rules." I rubbed the side of my face. No bruises showed now, but I remembered some of his questioning in the past.

Paydon turned to go.

"Say," I said. "You know a guy who lives in the condo complex somewhere? Late teens, early twenties. Long brown hair, pulled back? Wears jeans and a hoodie? Got a little sister named Sophia. His name might be Edmond or something."

He nodded. "Gotta be Edmond Geer. Thinks he's gonna be a rock star. Ain't none of my business, but I don't think he works or goes to school or anything. His dad gives him money, but his mom is getting a little fed up. Might be a stepmom."

"Really?"

"Yeah. They live in the first townhouse, right by the gate. If you're sitting in the guardhouse, sometimes you hear all this arguing. People shouting at each other. If they have the windows open. And you know how it is—you're invisible if you're a security guard. They'll walk right by me, him yelling and her saying nasty things, and never blink."

"But he lives there?"

"I guess. He goes out a lot, late afternoon, early evening. I don't usually see him come back before I get off duty."

"You think he looks like me?"

Paydon let his gaze travel over me.

"Some. A lot younger than you, though."

"Well, yeah. But in the dark?"

"I guess. Why?"

"This girl said I'd tried to carjack her. Positive ID. But it wasn't me."

"Is that what you got picked up for?"

"Yeah. And then they said I was a 'person of interest' in the disappearances."

"Wow. No wonder Carissa's interested in you. But I'm surprised they cut you loose."

"Bailed out. They got some DNA and it didn't match."

"They could tell that fast?"

"I'm a convicted felon. They got my DNA in their data bases. If it'd been a match, I'd of been long gone."

"I guess." He looked at me, then at the door. "What did you say you were going to do to the door?"

"Paint. It and the trim."

"Yeah? What color?"

"Scarlet." I wrinkled my nose.

"Scarlet?"

"Yeah. That's, like, bright red."

"That's what I thought. Colorful, I guess." He sighed and continued on his way, toward the bus stop.

Down the block, Kyle was shoveling things from his car to the sidewalk. He had some boxes and a pile of clothes. Most of it looked like tailored suits, but on top was a grey hoodie.

When he saw me coming, he grinned. "Hey, Jesse, got a few minutes? Help me get some of this stuff upstairs?"

"Okay." I picked up the pile of clothes and carted it up to the apartment Kyle was renting. He followed me, carrying a suitcase and a gym bag.

"I went by my house. Or what used to be my house. Figured if she wasn't home, I could get a lot of things. If she was, maybe I could talk to her, too."

"Was she there?"

"I'll say."

"How'd it go?" I asked, looking at the expensive suits and shirts I had just dumped on the bed. I noticed the old mattress now had sheets.

"Terrible. She yelled the whole time. But I got enough clothes that I won't have to buy any for a little while, at least."

"So she's not gonna take you back any time soon, huh?"

"Doesn't look good," he agreed. "I stopped by the lawyer's office. He's referred me to a criminal defense lawyer for the embezzlement charges. And a divorce lawyer."

We went back downstairs. Kyle leaned into the car to reach a few boxes. He backed out quickly, wrinkling his nose.

"Pew. Smells like shit."

I took a whiff. It did smell like shit. I looked into the car.

There, on the back seat, a small creature huddled in the corner. It had pinkish skin with black blotches and a tuft of tan hair on its head. Its tongue lolled out of one side of its mouth, between crooked teeth that pointed every which way. It looked up at me with frightened eyes.

"What's *that*?" I asked.

"Stupid dog," Kyle said. "Shit all over the car seat."

"That's a dog?" It didn't look like any dog I had ever seen.

"Yeah. My wife insisted I take it. She says she doesn't want it. I sure don't, either."

"You guys have a dog, and neither one of you wants it?"

Kyle shook his head. "No. Couple years ago, she said she wanted a dog. So I got one for her for Christmas." He grinned. "Took me a while to find it. It's a Chinese Crested-Chihuahua mix. Ugliest puppy I ever saw."

"Why'd you get her an ugly puppy for a Christmas present?"

"It was a gag gift, okay? She wanted something little and cute. It's little, all right. And cute is in the eyes of the beholder. You should have seen her face when she saw it." Kyle laughed. "She wanted something she could show off to her friends."

"You got a dog as a gag gift?"

"Yeah."

I looked at the poor thing, cringing back into a corner of the seat. I thought about giving Kyle my opinion about a person who would use a living animal for a gag gift. But if that concept was something he could even begin to understand, he wouldn't have done it in the first place. "How long has it been since you put it in the car?"

He shrugged. "Few hours, I guess."

"You can't leave a dog in a car like that. No wonder it shit on the seat."

"Well, what am I supposed to do with it? Turn it loose on the street?"

"No. If you really don't want it, take it to the animal shelter."

"I drove by. They were closed."

I reached in to let the dog—if that's what it really was—sniff my hand.

It whined and tried to back further into the corner. It stared at me with bug eyes.

"It's scared. What'd you guys do to this dog?" I asked.

"Me? Nothing. It pretty much stayed out of my way. I don't know about Delores. I guess she fed it and things."

I slipped my hand under the dog's hairless belly and scooped it up. It felt like a bag of bones. It was a he.

He struggled in my grasp, so I brought him up against my chest and cradled him. He was trembling.

"Has he got a name?" I asked.

"Snaggletooth."

"Did you call him that?"

"Delores did."

The dog tried to crawl under my armpit. "It's okay, Snaggletooth," I said softly, stroking his side. "I'm not gonna hurt you."

Kyle brightened. "You want it? You can have it. It cost me a couple hundred bucks, but I'd be happy to just have it taken off my hands."

I didn't trust him to actually get the dog to the animal shelter. He just might really turn it loose on the street.

"I can't have a dog," I said. "I don't know if I'm gonna get locked up again or what. But I'll take him for now. Until you can get him to the shelter or something."

"Good. I'll give you its food and its bed."

"Just leave them on the sidewalk there. I'll come back for them."

I carried the little dog into the head shop. Jumbo George was sitting at the table, staring at his computer.

He looked up when I walked in. "What'ya got there?"

"A dog. At least, I think it's a dog. Can't really tell by looking." I set him down on the table, but held him so he couldn't jump off. He crouched down, still trembling. "Name's Snaggletooth."

Jumbo George squinted. "Good name for him. Where'd you get him?"

"Kyle's wife foisted the dog off on him. He went to get some clothes and things, and she gave him the dog."

"So why do you have him?"

"Kyle don't want him. His wife don't want him. Poor little thing's all scared. I bet they didn't treat him good."

Jumbo George reached over with a hand the size of a ham and lifted Snaggletooth, pulling him over. He rested the dog on his protruding belly and tickled his ears beneath the scanty tuft of hair on his head. The dog cowered. "See if there's not some of that chicken left. But take it off the bone—dogs shouldn't get chicken bones."

I got some chicken meat and skin and gave it to Jumbo George. He offered it to Snaggletooth, who sniffed at it, but trembled more violently and refused to take it from his hand.

He put it down on his tee shirt in front of the dog.

Snaggletooth eyed him warily, then scarfed it up.

"He's hungry," Jumbo George said. "Hate to see anything go hungry."

I grabbed a roll of paper towels and a spray bottle of cleaner. "Kyle left him in the car all afternoon, and he made a mess in the back seat." I went back outside.

Kyle had left a dog bed on the sidewalk, along with an unopened bag of dog food and a box. I looked in the box. It held a few dog toys, a harness and a leash. Leaning against the wall was a weird contraption. I picked it up and studied it.

"A pooper scooper," Kyle said. "Top of the line. Nothing too good for Delores's dog's shit."

He was taking a few more boxes out of the car. I handed him the cleaning supplies and took the boxes up to his apartment. The bottom of one of the boxes started to give way, so I hurried to get it to the kitchen counter before it completely fell apart.

Green ledger sheets fell to the floor. I picked them up and put them on top of the broken box. They looked like financial records of some kind.

That made sense. Whatever it was that Kyle did for a living, it had to do with accounts. And so did the embezzlement.

I came back downstairs. His nose wrinkled in disgust, Kyle held the soiled paper towels at arm's length. He carried them to the curb behind the car and dropped them.

Not the most responsible method of disposal, but I didn't say anything.

I closed the door to the stairwell and ran my fingers over the numbers. 220 ½. They had some kind of coating on them, but it was peeling off.

"Looks like these numbers'll have to be replaced," I said. "Can that go into the grant application?"

"Good idea. If you have to get replicas for these doors, that'll cost a fortune. I can price them out and put it in the application." He brushed an invisible piece of lint off his jacket and straightened his shirt collar.

"I need to see George about renting this place for another month or so," he said. "I've been working on a few things, but I do need a place of my own for a while."

"I think he'd rent it to you," I said. It needed a major renovation before Jumbo George would go looking for a tenant for it. In the meantime, anything it brought in was better than nothing. "You could talk to him about renting a garage space, too."

"Don't really need a garage. I have a new lady friend." He winked at me. "She lives in the condo complex two blocks over. Just broke up with a boyfriend. She has two parking spaces in the underground garage. She doesn't need the one the boyfriend was using. I'm keeping it there. And I'll rent a car to use most of the time."

"Why would you rent a car when you have that nice Audi?"

"The Audi's too conspicuous. For now, I want to fly under the radar."

He stepped back and looked at the building. "You'll give me a report on what work needs to be done on the building, won't you? Maybe in a few hours?"

I shifted uneasily from one foot to the other. "A report? Does it have to be written?"

"A list would work. Or, you could just tell me."

"Jumbo George wants me to get started on painting the trim."

"I suppose that could go in there. But I'd add something about replicating deteriorated pieces. That would be expensive. What color does he want it painted?

"Scarlet."

"Oh, no, no. The closer we can have the exterior to original, the better. Make him wait until we hear about the grant. And for goodness sake, keep him away from scarlet!"

"I'll do my best."

"You do that. Meanwhile," he grinned and gave his tie a tug, "I have big plans for tonight!"

I picked up the dog's equipment and went back to the head shop.

Jumbo George was leaning back in the chair, his eyes closed. Snaggletooth had crawled up his chest and buried his head under Jumbo George's scraggly beard. A pudgy finger stroked the smooth pink and black skin on the dog's back.

"You ever have a dog?" I asked him.

A sad smile played on Jumbo George's face. "Yeah. I had a pit bull mix of some kind. He was a great dog. Really good with the kids."

I was surprised. "I didn't know you had kids."

He blinked and stared at the scarred top of the table. His eyes were glassy.

"I don't, anymore. House fire. Took the kids. And the dog. And the wife." He wiped his nose with the back of his hand. "Sometimes I wish it took me, too. I was at work."

What could I possibly say to that? I bit my lower lip.

"But hey." Jumbo George reached down and gave the dog a gentle hug. "I think this little fella likes me."

CHAPTER 18

Snaggletooth jumped down and turned in small circles, sniffing anxiously.

"What d'you suppose is the matter with him?" Jumbo George asked.

"Prob'ly has to go out," I said, reaching for the harness and leash.

The dog sat in front of me, cringing warily but holding still.

I crouched down and slipped the harness over his comical head and around his naked belly. Then I snapped the leash on.

The pooper scooper sat in a corner near the door. "Guess we're gonna have to figure out how to use this thing," I said, examining it. It looked like oversized tongs with shovels on the ends. I also grabbed a plastic bag. If I was going to pick up the poop, I'd need something to put it in. Dropping it directly in the dumpster didn't seem like the best option.

When we got into the alley, Snaggletooth huddled back against my boots, his pink and black ears pressed down on his head. He stared at the dumpster, making a low sound in his throat.

A furtive movement behind the dumpster caught my eye. I strode over and looked.

Stanley, from the coffee shop, was shoving something into a cardboard box leaning against the dumpster. He looked up when he saw me.

"Just getting rid of some trash here," he said.

That was weird. Another dumpster was down the alley, right in back of his shop. Why would he be bringing trash down here to throw away?

As I watched, he picked up the box and hefted it into the dumpster. "Pickup's tomorrow," he said. "First thing."

He grinned and nodded, walking to the back door of the coffee shop. He didn't say anything about the dog.

Snaggletooth and I went to the end of the alley. He alternated between sniffing enthusiastically and keeping a cautious eye on me. Finally, he squatted. I cleaned up after him, struggling to make the jaws of the pooper scooper open and close properly.

If Jumbo George kept him, he'd have to start taking him out for some of his walks. Do him some good to get up and out a few times a day, even if it was just in the alley.

When we got back to the dumpster, I opened it. The box Stanley had tossed had landed on other trash, just below the edge of the dumpster. I pulled the top open.

A little stack of papers slipped out and down the side of the dumpster. I grabbed a few.

Pornography. And not high quality pornography. It looked like it had been printed off a computer. Although it was graphic, there was nothing particularly offensive about it. From their awkward positions, the women all smiled at the camera, and there were no children in sight.

Underneath that were little scraps of folded paper. I picked one up and flattened it out. The creases showed it had been in a druggist's fold, that old method of making a secure container for powder that was still used by some drug dealers. It was covered with a light dusting of powder.

I sniffed it. It had a slight chemical odor. What was Stanley up to? Had a customer left this behind? Or was he dealing and worried this would be traced back to him? Not my problem.

I put it back in the dumpster along with my plastic bag and slammed the lid.

Snaggletooth jumped at the sound.

He found the right back door and stood next to it. Juggling the pooper scooper, which chose that moment to open its jaws and catch the leash in its handles, I went to nudge the door open with my foot.

As soon as my boot got near him, Snaggletooth panicked, pulling on the leash and yipping.

I struggled to fold the scooper with one hand and picked up the dog with the other, holding him close to me and stroking him. He whined and hid his head in my armpit.

"What was he crying about?" Jumbo George asked when I got him inside.

"I tried to push the door open with my foot. I think he was afraid I was going to kick him."

Jumbo George held out his huge hand to take the dog. "Poor baby," he said. "You don't have to be afraid anymore." He turned his back on me as he sat at the table.

If I was planning to check into what Edmond did at night, I best be doing something about it now, before Jumbo George decided to send me for some food.

Tomorrow night I'd have to report to work at midnight, and it would be a whole week before I'd have a chance to look for him again.

"I think I'm gonna go out for a little while," I said. I tucked my key, wallet and a tiny flashlight in my pocket.

"You going over to the girlfriend's?" he asked.

"I dunno. Maybe." I didn't feel comfortable spying on Edmond, and I didn't want to give Jumbo George a chance to talk me out of it.

Leaving him comforting the wary dog, I went out the front door.

The evening air tickled my nose, bringing a fresh breeze off the river. The daylight was fading.

A siren sounded in the distance, approaching, and my stomach clenched.

I listened to it scream down by the riverfront, then turn up the hill toward where I stood.

An ambulance sped into view, then continued on its way past me toward the hospital.

I wiped the back of my neck. My hand came away damp from sweat.

Maybe I ought to just give this whole idea up and go home.

But if I didn't figure out who had tried to carjack those girls, who would?

Not the cops, if Belkins had anything to say about it. He was sure I'd done it, and he didn't think he needed to look any further.

He was sure I'd had a hand in the disappearances, and he was putting his efforts into trying to figure out how I'd managed to keep evidence of my participation out of it. The DNA didn't match. I must have found a way around that. He would be focused on that instead of trying to discover what really happened.

If I could find anything that indicated it might have been Edmond, not me, who had tried to carjack the girls, I might be able to get someone to listen to me. Maybe.

I had one major advantage over Belkins and the rest of the cops—I *knew* I didn't have anything to do with either the carjacking or the abductions.

What had Edmond said? That he'd be home for dinner. Which his mom said would be seven. Or was it seven thirty? So he would probably not be leaving until after eight. Maybe later.

Where did he go? What did he do? Did he have a regular routine? Did he meet up with friends? Did he regularly approach women, especially women in cars?

I knew of only one way I had any chance at all of finding out. Follow Edmond.

The ankle box would trace my whereabouts. So what? I would follow him for a while, see what he was up to.

Only a few people were in the park, and as darkness set in, they strolled towards the gates. The structures that had made the street fair such a magical place, the rides and booths and food stands just a few short hours ago were gone. A faint whiff of popcorn and cotton candy hung in the air. Paper napkins and cups overflowed from the trash barrels and drifted lazily across the ground whenever a current of air blew up from the river.

Overhead, clouds scuttled past an almost full moon. Away from the lighted paths, deep shadows formed in clumps of bushes.

I sat on the edge of a brick wall along a garden where I could see the gate to the condos across the street. Small animals rustled in the mulch and the river whispered as water rushed by the retaining wall.

Breathing deeply, I tried to concentrate on the peaceful sounds behind me. I felt the knot in my stomach ease. Think about good stuff, I told myself.

Kelly was probably home now. The kids would have been fed and maybe they were doing some of their weekend homework before she put them to bed.

Who was I kidding? They maybe got fed, but then they'd be watching TV. At least Brianna would. Chris might attempt some homework or read a book. But it wouldn't be because of anything Kelly did.

I peered at the security guard pacing near the pedestrian entry gate to the complex. A wrought iron-looking fence with vicious spikes on top extended over the whole front. I was sure it wasn't real wrought iron. It was in hinged sections which could be opened to let trucks into the courtyard. Right now, the gate was closed. The complex had an underground garage, but its entry was off an alley. That was where Kyle said he was keeping his fancy car.

I didn't recognize the guard. It wasn't Paydon. He'd worked an earlier shift today. Where had he gone?

Well, it was Saturday night. Normal people would go out to a bar. Or have a date. Not me, maybe, but a lot of people. I had to admit that what Paydon did was really none of my business.

The guard stood next to a narrow gate in a section of the fence near the guardhouse. He shook it, checking to see if it was latched. Then he went into the guardhouse and sat down for a while, keeping his head up and staring at the walls. I wondered if there were video screens he was watching.

Standing and stretching, he reached up and grabbed a cylinder at least a foot long. He got up and stepped through the pedestrian gate and out onto the sidewalk. The cylinder turned out to be a bright flashlight. He walked up and down in front of the complex a few times, shining his light behind the bushes planted in front of the wall and into the street, by the curb. Then he went back through the gate and I could see the flashlight beam roaming in the courtyard.

A couple walked up to the gate and paused. The gate buzzed. They pushed it open and went in.

Maybe Edmond hadn't stayed for dinner after all. Maybe he wasn't going out. Maybe he had already gone out and I'd missed him. Or left through the underground garage. Maybe I was really stupid to think I could find anything out by trying to follow him.

Clouds danced across the moon, throwing more shadows into the corners. The wind picked up, rustling the trash strewn on the ground. It wasn't freezing, but I wasn't wearing a jacket and I was getting chilly.

I'd wait a few minutes more and if Edmond didn't put in an appearance, I'd head back to Jumbo George's. Maybe work on the shelving in the basement. It'd be nice to have most of that done before I went back to work tomorrow night.

Pulling my hoodie a bit closer around me, I decided I'd waited long enough. As I started to get up, the light went on over the door of the townhouse next to the guard booth.

According to Paydon, that was where Edmond and his dysfunctional family lived.

The door swung open and a person stepped out. Someone else stood in the doorway. I could hear them shouting, but I couldn't make out the words.

The security guard, flashlight in hand, hurried over.

With a decisive bang, the door slammed shut, leaving the person outside.

The pedestrian gate to the public sidewalk opened and Edmond stepped out. The security guard stopped and said something to him, but then turned back into the complex and resumed his rounds.

I got to my feet, careful to stay in the shadow of the big tree. A mosquito buzzed in my ear. Wasn't it early for mosquitoes? And too cold? I swatted at it.

Edmond looked uncertainly up and down the street, then took a few steps away from the gate. He pulled out a cigarette and lit it. Or maybe it was a joint.

A car pulled up to the curb. It was an older model Caddie, black with tinted windows.

Great. If someone was picking him up, I'd never be able to follow.

Edmond walked around the car and leaned down to the driver's window.

Unless I got much closer, I wouldn't be able to see what they were doing, but I didn't want to go out to where I'd be more visible to Edmond or the security guard. I'd have to be content with what little I could make out from here.

They exchanged things. I wasn't close enough to see what.

Possible drug transaction? Sure looked like it. Who was buying and who was selling? I couldn't tell.

Would a kid from a well-to-do family like Edmond take a chance with dealing drugs? Especially out on the public street like that?

I reminded myself that most people don't think about the consequences until they were locked up, facing years of prison. I certainly had not done so myself.

He backed away from the car and it drove off. Then he turned and strode purposefully in the other direction.

I dashed to the edge of the park, vaulted over the low wall and hurried to keep him in sight.

His jeans were designer ones, his hoodie had a brand name splashed over the back, and I'd be willing to bet his boots cost a whole lot more than the fifty nine dollar specials on my feet. He was younger than me by maybe twenty years. Still, with his hair in a pony tail at the nape of his neck, his profile would be indistinguishable from mine.

For a few blocks, we followed the riverfront. Hands shoved in his pockets, head bent down under his hood, Edmond walked along, not paying any attention to his surroundings. Then he turned down a side street.

As we got further away from the waterfront renovation area, the neighborhood changed. More of the streetlights were out, and the curbs were cracked and crumbling. The street led across the railroad tracks and into an area of rundown warehouses and abandoned factory buildings.

The breeze from the river picked up again, rustling the trash strewn around and muffling our footsteps.

I was well aware that my ankle box was broadcasting my location. I didn't think the computer would be manned at this time of the evening, at least by Mr. Ramirez, but what did I know? It would be recording my movements. Not much I could do about that.

Glancing up at the buildings, I decided there wouldn't be too many active security cameras around here. Not much to protect.

Edmond went through an alley and made a few quick turns.

Keeping in the shadows of the buildings, I tried to keep him in sight but walk quietly enough so he wouldn't hear my footsteps. He never turned to look back.

I was losing my sense of where I was.

He stopped outside one of the few occupied buildings. The front window was three quarters boarded up, with only a narrow strip of glass above that. A neon Budweiser sign glowed. When someone opened the door, the loud nasal whines of a country music classic blasted out, along with shouts and laughter. The door shut again.

A bar.

Edmond pulled something out of his pocket and held it to the side of his head. A cellphone?

The door opened. This time a man stepped out. He was old and skinny and walked all bent over. Edmond approached him. They went down an alley next to the bar.

I debated what to do. I still didn't want Edmond to see me, but I did want to know what was going on. I walked by the alley entrance.

The two men were having a heated discussion. I couldn't make out the words, but Edmond towered threateningly over the other guy, his fists clenched.

Shrinking back in the darkness under a fire escape, I tried to watch them. One dismal security light spread a wavering light over the alley by the dumpster.

Edmond raised his voice. "You want me to beat the crap out of you? You'll pay me. Now." He raised his fist.

The old man pulled something from his belt. It gleamed in the uncertain light. From where I stood, it looked like a Saturday night special. A great equalizer.

Edmond backed up quickly toward the entrance to the alley. "Tomorrow night," he said. "I'll be back. You better have the money then. I mean it."

He dashed right by me onto the sidewalk and down the street.

I waited a minute. The old guy didn't move. I followed Edmond. I didn't think he'd noticed me.

He turned along a railroad siding for a few hundred feet. The tracks were old, and the smell of creosote filled the damp night air.

We came back out on a street. I had no idea where we were, so I looked for a street sign. Washington Street.

Hadn't the abandoned car been found in a walled truck yard on Washington Street?

When I looked for Edmond, he was gone.

Where could he have gotten to? I slowed my pace, glancing around. The spot on my ankle where the strap to the monitor rubbed was getting very sore.

A driveway led through a crumbling wall surrounding a warehouse yard. Chunks of broken cinderblock and pieces of plywood were scattered around on the asphalt.

Voices came from the other side of the wall.

I backed into a niche between the end of the wall and the building next to it. A working streetlight lit the area. I pulled a large piece of warped plywood over the opening and crouched behind it.

The wind stirred, blowing a scent of damp rotting wood over the wall. It was mixed with a whiff of weed. Clouds scuttled over the moon.

I held my breath and strained my ears.

"You get it, dude?" a voice said.

"Sure." That sounded like Edmond. "Right here. Anybody else coming?"

"Just Jeremy, and he's got his work cut out for him. Maybe his buddy Staves. Go stash that stuff inside for later."

After a few minutes, they stepped over the rubble and out on the street. "I left my car a block over," the other guy said. "Let's go see if we can't pick up some girls or something."

Shrinking back into the shadows, I listened as their footsteps faded. No point following them now. If they had a car, I would be left behind.

Edmond had stashed something. Since I was already here, I might as well see if I could find out what it was.

I took the tiny flashlight out of my pocket, but I wouldn't turn it on unless I really needed it. I crept down the driveway. A loading dock with its door missing yawned open ahead of me. I hoisted myself up and peered into the gloom, giving my eyes time to adjust.

An odd odor wafted out to meet me. I inhaled. Ammonia? Maybe cats had made the abandoned building their home. I stepped inside and sniffed again. It didn't really smell like cat piss. Acetone?

The floor was covered with trash. I flashed the light quickly to get a better look.

Two liter soda bottles. Over-the-counter cold medicine, the packages ripped open. Lithium batteries.

A meth lab.

My ankle itched.

Not a good place for me to be. I'd better get out of here.

As I turned to go, a huge flashlight flicked on and blinded me.

"And just what the hell are you doing here?" a voice asked from beyond the light.

CHAPTER 19

I froze. All I wanted to do was get out of there. Looked like that was going to be a problem.

The person behind the flashlight didn't move, either. Or say anything else.

He was between me and the exit.

My mind swirled. Was it a cop? He'd have at least one partner somewhere very nearby. Possibly a whole lot of backup.

Or Mr. Ramirez, my parole officer? I knew he was unnervingly conscientious—he often checked out the local bars and such on Saturday nights to see if he ran across anybody on his caseload out where he shouldn't be. He wouldn't be by himself, either. He'd call for backup before entering an apparently deserted warehouse.

Why had I been foolish enough to assume that no one would be monitoring the computer after hours? The GPS box would pinpoint my location. If Mr. Ramirez wanted to know where I was, he'd have no trouble finding me.

Or maybe there was a stakeout on the meth lab, and I'd stumbled into it. If I got charged with manufacture of a controlled dangerous substance, I'd be looking at new charges that could carry twenty years or more. In addition to the backup time on the murder conviction that I'd have to serve. I'd never see the outside of a prison again in this lifetime.

How long could we stand there, not moving or saying anything?

Until dawn, as far as I was concerned.

The blinding flashlight beam looked just like the one that had been shone in my eyes the other night when I was picked up.

If it was a cop, or someone from the parole office, I'd better cooperate. I was in enough trouble without adding any charges of assaulting a law enforcement officer. Or fleeing and eluding. They'd know who I was. I wasn't going to get away for long.

But the guy hadn't announced that he was a cop.

I'd think any self-respecting meth lab operator ought to have a watchdog. Probably a pit bull. Although maybe "self-respecting meth lab operator" was a contradiction in terms. By the time anyone was willing to try the dangerous manufacturing operation, he'd have long lost his self-respect.

He hadn't told me to drop the flashlight or put my hands on my head or lean up against the wall so he could search me.

If he wasn't a cop, maybe I could bluff or shove my way out of here. Especially if he was alone. Unless he had a gun and shot me first.

The chemical scent tickled my nose. Not a good time to sneeze. A breeze came through the broken door back on the truck bay and stirred the trash on the floor.

Why had it seemed so important to me to find out what was in here? It wasn't going to help me much.

Before I did anything, I had to know who I was dealing with. Putting my finger on the button of my small flashlight, I swept it up, shining it at the place where the bright light originated. At the same time, I jumped to the side and crouched down, making a smaller target.

Startled, the guy backed up and knocked into a stack of plastic bottles. In the otherwise silent warehouse, their collapse was surprisingly noisy.

I fervently hoped none of them were already filled with the shake'n'bake components. We could do without an explosion.

But the guy was definitely not a cop. Unless he was in deep undercover. He had unkempt hair flowing over his shoulders and a bushy beard. He wore a sleeveless vest criss-crossed with chains and a black bandana on his head.

And I didn't see a gun in his hand. Or a knife.

"Hey, Jeremy, what's going on out there?" someone shouted from deeper within the warehouse.

I inched along the wall. What was the chance I could get around him and be gone by the time someone else got there?

Not good. Another flashlight rounded a corner. There had to be somebody behind it.

The first guy stepped in front of me and put his arm on the wall, blocking my progress. His flashlight was long and heavy, and he was holding it the way the police were trained to, his hand on the barrel, just behind the head. With a quick flick of the wrist, it made a very effective club.

Scattered overhead lights blinked on and wavered. Another guy, in shorts and a ragged tee shirt that sported a marijuana leaf, stood with his hand on a light switch. He didn't have a gun, either, but he was holding a machete. The blade gleamed in the uncertain light.

I stopped moving. "Now look," I said. "I just want to get out of here. I don't care what you're doing."

"You don't say?" The new arrival glared at me, hefting the machete. "You know what we're doing here?"

"No," I said.

He gave a harsh laugh. "You expect me to believe that?"

"Okay. You're cooking meth. But it's got nothing to do with me."

"How do I know you're not an undercover cop?" he asked, taking a step toward me. "Lots of them poking around these days, trying to find manufacturing operations."

Proving I wasn't a cop shouldn't be hard. I reached down to pull up the leg of my jeans.

The guy raised the machete higher. "You got a ankle holster?" he asked. "Or a blade?"

I paused. "No. I'm just trying to prove I'm not a cop." I hiked the pants leg up.

Jeremy laughed. "A box! You're on monitoring."

"Yeah. So I'm not a cop."

"You're on house arrest. Why aren't you home?"

He was wrong about the house arrest thing, but that wasn't important. I decided not to tell him that this was a GPS device, tracking my movements. "Well." I thought madly. "See, I work in a restaurant that closes late. So my curfew is midnight. Today's my day off. But my PO don't know that."

"Drug charges?" Jeremy asked.

"Yeah." Maybe I'd get a little sympathy.

No such luck. The machete guy nodded toward me. "He knows what we're doing." He took a step forward, the machete poised to strike. He was too far back to hit me if he swung it, but two or three more steps would put me in range. "We can't let him leave."

"What do you want to do?" Jeremy shrugged. "It's a damn shake'n'bake setup. It's portable. We just move to another location."

"But he knows we're working in the area. He could tell the cops."

"I won't." But I didn't sound convincing, even to myself. I cleared my throat and added, "Why would I do that?" It didn't help.

"Trade the info for something," the machete guy said. "Everybody knows how these narcs work. You give them something, they cut your charges. And they like to bust production labs."

"I won't tell anybody," I said again. "For sure I wouldn't snitch to the cops."

Jeremy ignored me and looked at his buddy. "You don't think the cops know there's a number of labs working in the area?"

He had turned, his hand sliding down the wall. With the overhead light, he no longer needed it to see what was going on and he'd let the hand that held the flashlight drop down next to his side.

I calculated the distance to the door. If I pushed by him and made a run for it, I'd have to jump off the loading dock and hit the asphalt running. What was the chance I could do that without falling? And probably breaking my leg. I didn't like my odds.

Only thing to do was get hold of the machete. And hope one of them didn't have a gun or a knife on them.

If they did, though, I was sure they'd have it out by now.

"He's seen our faces," the machete guy was arguing. "He could pick us out. Too much of a risk to take."

"And if we got rid of him, that's not a bigger risk?" Jeremy shifted his weight from one foot to the other.

The other guy grinned. "They'd probably give us a medal if they thought we'd knocked him off. Save them all the grief of keeping an eye on him. And they'd have to find him first. There's a whole river a couple of blocks over. Good place to dump a body. If you got it weighed down good."

Did they really think that it was all that easy to kill somebody? Of course I'd put up a fight.

Time to let them know about the monitor. "This here's a GPS," I said. "They can find it wherever it is. Bottom of the river's not a problem. They got scuba divers."

Jeremy frowned.

"Then I guess we just got to cut the box off," the machete guy said, "and toss it someplace else. Far away from the river."

"Doesn't the computer track where he's been?" Jeremy said. "It'll lead them right here to us. We gotta move anyhow. Just leave all this stuff and start over someplace else."

He had turned to face the machete guy a bit more directly. In doing so, he moved the hand with the flashlight closer to me.

I bent down and snatched it out of his hand.

Startled, he tried to grab it back.

I threw my weight into him, knocking both of us over. At the same time, I flung the flashlight at the machete guy. Hitting him in the head might be most effective, but I used the tried-and-true police tactic of aiming for the biggest body mass and targeted his chest. Less chance of missing.

It hit him in the gut.

"Hey," he gasped, grasping his abdomen with his free hand and hunching his shoulders forward. The machete swooped downward, but didn't hit anything.

I scrambled to my feet.

On the ground beneath me, Jeremy grabbed for my ankle. I stomped on his wrist with my boot and stepped forward to where the machete guy was doubled over.

He still had his hand on the machete, but now it hung limply.

I reached over and grabbed it. At the same time, I tried to knee him in the groin but got his thigh instead.

His grip tightened, but I hammered on his fingers with my fist and pulled the machete away.

As I turned to leave, I stepped on the flashlight. Under my boot, it skidded across the floor. I fell, but rolled away and made it to my feet, still hanging onto the machete.

I ran for the door.

When I reached the loading dock, I paused long enough to sit on the edge and ease myself down to the asphalt, rather than jumping.

I didn't look back until I tripped on something in the rubble-strewn driveway. I shouldn't have turned then. I felt my knee crunch down on a sharp edge.

As I regained my footing, I glanced back at the door.

The feeble light in the warehouse silhouetted both of them as they reached the open door and clambered down.

Holding tight to the machete, which I hoped I wouldn't have to use, I dashed down the street and slipped into the little hidden niche I'd used before. I hunkered down and pulled the piece of plywood in front of me.

I heard footsteps approaching, and crouched, trying to keep out of sight.

The footsteps slowed. "Where the hell did he go?"

"I don't know, but what are we gonna do about it anyhow? Let's get out of here."

They walked away. I listened until I couldn't hear their footsteps anymore, and stayed hidden in the cramped space for a while longer.

I stood up. Stripping off my hoodie and tee shirt, I wiped down the machete as well as I could with the shirt. I didn't want to leave any fingerprints on it if I could help it. Shivering, I put the hoodie back on. I covered the little niche with the plywood.

My knee was damp. I looked down at it. A big gash showed in knee of my pants leg, which was soaked with a dark sticky dampness. Blood.

I tried to examine the injury, but in the poor light and with all the blood, I couldn't really see how much damage had been done. I flexed my leg. It hurt, but it still seemed to work. Probably no permanent damage.

Had I ruined a perfectly good pair of jeans? I hoped not. Even though I got mine used at the thrift shop, they were expensive.

Wrapping my tee shirt around the machete handle, I picked it up. I'd toss it in the next dumpster I saw.

That was more than enough adventure for one night. And I was no closer to figuring out if Edmond had been involved in the carjacking. Or the women's disappearances.

I stuffed the tee shirt in a pocket and headed back home.

CHAPTER 20

When I turned the corner, I saw Kyle's Audi parked out by the curb. No one was in it, but the engine was running and the top was down. Not smart.

Kyle was nowhere in sight. I looked up at his windows. The ragged shades were drawn, but I could see the lights were on behind them.

I stood next to the car for a few seconds, wondering if I should do something. But what? How long was he going to leave it like this? Might as well hang a sign on it saying, "Steal me!"

Maybe that's what he wanted, so he could collect the insurance money for it.

The door to the stairs opened. Kyle stepped out. He was dressed in what seemed to be the neighborhood uniform, jeans and a gray hoodie. They fit snugly, and his hair was newly styled.

He juggled a box, straining to balance it. It seemed to be pretty heavy. He also dangled a small backpack from his fingers. I noticed he was wearing thin gloves.

"You want me to take that?" I asked, reaching for the box. "Where do you want it?"

"No!" He snatched it back.

I dropped my hands to my sides.

He tossed the backpack onto the floor of the car and placed the box carefully on the front passenger seat.

Turning to me, he said, "Hey, when I didn't see you around, I finished up that grant application on my own."

"Oh?"

"Yeah. I just made a lot of the stuff up. Looked up a few prices on the internet, but it's mostly just bullshit. And I took a bunch more pictures to use."

"Okay." If he was going to make stuff up for it, I was just as glad not to be too involved. "So you don't need me to help you with it anymore?"

"Nah. I e-mailed it in today." He smirked. "I'd love to see good old Richmond's face when he discovers that there's stiff competition for his precious grant."

I debated whether to say something about leaving the car running on the street like this. It wasn't really my business, but with his background, I didn't know if Kyle realized just how vulnerable the car was in this neighborhood. If someone made off with it, I'd be sorry I hadn't said something.

"You know, there are lots of people who might take it into their head to take that fancy car of yours for a joyride if you leave it out here. Anybody could just hop in and drive away."

I wasn't sure how it worked with the push button ignition, if someone could really just drive it away or if he'd need the key in his pocket.

"You're right. But they wouldn't get far with it if I reported it stolen. It's pretty conspicuous."

"Somebody could do a lot of damage to it in a short time, though. Or get it to a chop shop."

"I guess. But it's a company car. Sooner or later, they're going to want it back. They may even send a repo man after it."

"So why don't you just return it?"

"No way," he said. "I think I'm gonna park it for now in the underground garage at that condo complex. 'Member I told you about the lady I met?" He winked at me conspiratorially.

"Yeah."

"For the time being, I'm just going to leave it parked in one of her parking spots. Nobody'll find it there."

"Aren't you gonna drive it?" I asked.

"Not much. I'd like to be able to get around a few places without advertising that it's me. I'm going to get a cheapie rental to drive."

"Seems like you're going to a lot of trouble. Just turn it in."

Kyle laughed. "And make it easy for them? No way."

He went around to the driver's side, got in and took off, leaving rubber on the asphalt.

I watched him go and turned toward the head shop.

The front door was locked and the interior dark. I peered in. Jumbo George had gone to bed. Or, to recliner, as the case may be, since that's where he slept.

My key opened both the front door and the back one off the alley. I circled around and let myself in the back, trying to be quiet, and switched on the dim light by the stairs.

The little dog's head popped up. He was snuggled up beside Jumbo George instead of in his bed on the floor.

Hopping down, he came over to meet me, giving his rat-like tail a tentative wag.

"You been out lately, dude?" I asked, keeping my voice low. "Let's take you in the alley."

I clipped the leash on his harness. We went out the back door.

He sniffed around for a few minutes, and took care of his business. I'd forgotten the pooper scooper.

When we got back inside, Snaggletooth went right up to Jumbo George's recliner and tried to scramble up the side, but he wasn't tall enough. He gave a frustrated whine.

"That you, little fella?' Jumbo George stirred and patted the arm of the recliner next to him. "Where'd you get to?"

I knew how hard it was for Jumbo George to get himself settled down for the night. I picked up the dog. The nearly hairless skin was hot and dry on my hands. "Here you go," I said, putting him on Jumbo George's massive torso.

Snaggletooth crept across the stomach, inching his way between Jumbo George's bulk and the arm of the recliner.

A huge hand moved the blanket over and covered the dog completely, then adjusted it so just his head with the strange tuft of hair showed.

"I took him out," I told Jumbo George.

"Thanks."

They both settled in, closing their eyes. A slight smile seemed to play on Jumbo George's lips, but between his scraggly beard and the dim lighting, it was hard to tell.

I opened a cupboard and pulled out a plastic bag to clean up after the dog. Then I made sure I had my keys and flashlight and went back out into the alley.

It was late, but I was still pretty wound up. And come tomorrow night, I would be working the overnight shift again. Might as well stay up now and get something done. Then I could take a nap tomorrow evening and begin to adjust my schedule to the workweek.

After I dumped the bag with the dog poop in the dumpster, I headed for the basement. I'd told Jumbo George that, with Quality Steel closed all week, I'd have no problem getting those shelves put together. I hadn't gotten it done, though. The couple of days in jail hadn't helped.

I tested the door to the basement. It was locked, but it rattled in its frame and I knew a well-placed shove would open it. I opened it with my key and flicked on the light switch.

A cold musty basement smell rose to meet me. I'd have to give some thought to improving the air circulation down there.

The buildings may have been old, but they were solidly constructed. Noise didn't carry. I figured there wasn't much chance I would disturb Jumbo George.

My injured knee was stiffening up. I maneuvered so the light shone on it and examined it.

The jeans were ruined. I sighed. I'd have to get another pair as soon as I could afford it. But at least I could probably wear these ones to the laundromat. Needing to wear one of my pairs of jeans when I went to do laundry was a frustration, since it meant I couldn't wash all of them at once.

My knee was scraped, but the damage was superficial. When I got up to my apartment, I'd wash it well. I was already planning to stop at the drugstore on my way to work to get some gauze and first aid ointment for my ankle. I could use some of it for the knee.

There went my six dollars. I'd better pull ten from my savings stash, in case the six didn't cover it.

I turned to look at the shelving, most of it still in boxes. I put a little bag full of screws and a screwdriver in my pocket, then set to unpacking the shelf parts. I leaned shelf supports against the wall and shelves on top of them. Once I got them propped in place, the parts screwed together easily. I made steady progress and didn't stop until the entire front wall was covered with shelves. A few packages of the shelving were left, so I started along a side wall.

About four in the morning I decided to pack it up. Tomorrow morning, this would be around my lunchtime.

I pulled the basement door shut behind me, and jiggled the doorknob until the bolt settled in the lock. Not secure, but it would have to do for now.

I eased open the back door, using the flashlight rather than switching on any overhead lights. Snaggletooth whined, but he didn't climb down to greet me. I crept up the back stairs to my apartment. Pulling off my jeans, I scrubbed the knee and rinsed out the jeans.

I set the alarm clock for eight and collapsed into the bed.

* * * *

When the alarm sounded, I was dead asleep. I struggled up, totally dazed. Getting back on schedule for work was going to be a chore. It wouldn't do to be so out of it when I had to go to work at midnight. I'd get some stuff done and take a long nap in the evening.

My knee was tight, but it loosened up after a few steps. It was oozing a little, but it didn't look all that bad in the daylight.

Downstairs, Jumbo George had coffee made. He was sitting at the table, reading the Sunday newspaper. Snaggletooth was sitting on a chair next to him, staring forlornly at an empty bowl in front of him.

I poured myself a mug of coffee.

Jumbo George looked up as I sat down. "You go to the girlfriend's house last night after all?"

"Nah. I'll see her tonight at work."

"I seem to remember you coming in at some ungodly hour."

"Wasn't that late. I took the dog out, and he woke you up, trying to climb back up to sleep with you."

Raising his eyebrows, he said, "It *seemed* pretty late. Where'd you go?"

He didn't usually interrogate me like this, but lately he seemed to be more concerned about what I was up to. I wasn't sure how to answer him. Was he worried I'd been doing something that would get me locked up and he'd lose his bail money?

Following Edmond wasn't illegal, but it was weird. And there was the meth lab. That was definitely illegal. If Belkins came snooping around asking questions, how much would Jumbo George tell them?

I didn't want to put him in an awkward position. What he didn't know he couldn't tell anyone.

"Rather not say," I said, blowing on the coffee to cool it. "If it all backfires, the less you know, the better. Then nobody can expect you to answer questions."

Of course, that would just make him more suspicious that I was up to no good. He raised his craggy eyebrows. "But you still got that ankle box, don't you?"

"Yep. I been keeping it charged up good."

He leaned back. "So they'll be able to see where you been."

"They should. I'm not sure how close they can pinpoint the location, but if they want to track my movements, all they got to do is pull up the computer record."

Jumbo George looked at me and stroked his beard. Then he shoved the newspaper in front of me.

The headlines glared up at me.

"Missing Girl Abducted from Riverfront Park."

CHAPTER 21

I grabbed the paper. "When was this?"

"Last night."

"And it made today's paper?"

"Yeah. Sounds like it happened about midnight." Jumbo George reached down and tickled behind Snaggletooth's ear with a thick finger.

By midnight, I was long gone from the park. I hadn't kept close track of the time, but I was pretty sure I'd even left the meth lab by midnight. In fact, I was probably down in the basement working on the shelves.

"Still. How did they find out about it so fast?" I asked. "The other ones weren't discovered until someone reported them missing, were they?"

"Yeah. But this one, the security guard at the condo complex actually saw it. He called 911."

"He didn't try to help her?"

"Said he couldn't leave his post."

I shook my head. "What good is that?"

"Well, it *is* what he's hired for. Keep an eye on the property. If something happened in the condos, he might figure he had to do something. But this was across the street. In the park."

"It wasn't a carjacking?"

"No. The girl was walking. Somebody snatched her and pulled her into a car and took off."

"They get a description of the car?"

"Just a dark sedan."

"No license plate number?" I scanned the article.

"Evidently not."

"And the security guard was sure it wasn't a john picking up a hooker?"

"He said she screamed and fought. Read the whole article."

I set down my coffee mug and read. Carissa had written it, and for once she seemed to be sticking pretty close to reporting, not adding her own creative touches. Straight facts clearly stated, not her usual flowery prose and cleverly phrased half-suggestions.

She must have had to hurry to get it ready for this morning's paper. Not enough time to do much embellishment.

"So were you down there by the park last night?" Jumbo George asked.

I looked up from the newspaper. "Yeah. But it was earlier. I didn't see anything like that at all."

He raised his eyebrows, not saying anything more. Unspoken questions lingered in the air.

I didn't see how I could explain much to him without raising lots of questions I wouldn't want to answer.

Getting to my feet, I said, "I'm gonna go down in the basement and see if I can't get the rest of that shelving put together. I'm almost done."

Jumbo George shifted Snaggletooth in his lap. "And if somebody stops by and asks if I know where you are?"

"You mean, like cops?" I expected them to show up here sooner or later. Probably sooner.

"Well, that's what I had in mind. But I suppose it could be anybody."

I sighed. "Who else is there?"

"Maybe that girlfriend of yours?"

The dull ache in my chest that I'd been trying to ignore throbbed harder. "I doubt she'll stop by."

"Unless she needs a babysitter."

That was a low blow. But not unwarranted. I shrugged. "I'll see her at work tonight."

"So how about if a cop does stop by? Like that detective who's got it in for you?"

"Might as well tell them where I am. No sense making them look for me."

Jumbo George nodded.

"They'd find me anyhow, with the box." I rubbed the raw spot on my ankle. I had to work my regular eight hour shift tonight, sore ankle and stiff knee or not.

I went around back and pulled out my key to open the basement door, but I didn't need it. The door swung open at my touch. The musty basement smell hit me.

The door opened partway and stopped. I eased myself through the opening and looked behind it. A cardboard box sat on the floor, keeping the door from opening fully.

The box hadn't been there last night. I opened the flaps.

Neatly folded clothes were on top. A pair of blue jeans and a bra. Below that was a brightly striped blanket or beach towel or something. It had a few dark stains on it. Maybe blood. Maybe oil. Maybe grape juice.

Someone had discovered how easy it was to get into the basement, and had stored their stuff here. Not good. I hoped no one was sleeping down here.

Uneasy, I closed the box up. This couldn't have anything to do with the women who had gone missing, could it?

All the single doors, front and back, should really be replaced. I wondered if Kyle had included that in the grant application.

For now, though, I could get a padlock and a safety hasp. The kind where the latch covered the screws and secured the whole thing.

The garages didn't lock. Anybody could get into them. I'd have to ask Jumbo George if he wanted me to put padlocks and safety hasps on them, too.

I spent most of the morning assembling the rest of the shelves. When I was done, I picked up the packaging, the plastic bags that had held the hardware, the bits of plastic strapping and carted them upstairs to the dumpster. I left the box where it was, and didn't bother to lock the door behind me.

Back in the shop, Jumbo George was talking to Paydon Norris. Snaggletooth was hunkered on Jumbo George's thigh, his ears laid back. He was staring at Paydon and making a rumbling noise in his throat. With his crooked teeth, it was hard to tell, but it looked to me like the little guy was trying to snarl.

Jumbo George laid a big, soothing hand on him.

"Paydon here says the locks on the two front windows in his apartment don't work." Jumbo George said to me. "Do you think that's something you can fix?"

I poured myself a mug of coffee and sat down. "Prob'ly. I got to go get a hasp for the basement door tomorrow anyhow. Somebody moved some stuff in. Looks like they might be planning to stay there. I can pick up whatever I need then. New window latches or whatever."

"What kind of stuff did he move in?" Jumbo George asked.

"A box." I took a sip of the coffee. It was bitter. "Looks like some clothes and maybe bedding. I didn't go through it, just opened it to take a look. And I think it's a she, not a he. A bra was right on top."

He shifted his weight in the chair. "Okay. Not that I want to see people sleeping out on the street, but I don't want them in my basement, either. And there is the rescue mission."

"And the garages out back—I should put some locks on them."

"Somebody move some stuff in there, too?" Jumbo George asked.

"I haven't looked in them," I said. "But I will."

"Okay." Jumbo George turned to look at Paydon. "Can Jesse take a look at your windows tomorrow?"

Paydon bristled. "I'd like to be there. And tomorrow I have some stuff I got to do."

"How about now, then?" Jumbo George asked, looking from one of us to the other.

"I guess." Paydon shifted from one foot to the other. "But I got to get ready for work soon."

I followed him out to the sidewalk and up the stairs to his apartment.

His two rooms were in the front of the building. The main windows looked out over the street, although a small one in the bathroom and another in the kitchen alcove opened on an airshaft that led to the alley. A fire escape outside the kitchen window led to the ground. It'd be a tight squeeze to get through the window, but at some point, a fire marshal must have passed it. And if the room behind me was on fire, I guess I could have managed to squeeze out.

My apartment was behind this one, but instead of the stairs coming up from the street, they led straight up from Jumbo George's back room. Mine was a bit bigger, with two bedrooms and a central room. Its windows looked out on the alley, except for the ones on the airshaft. It, too, had a window in the kitchen alcove that opened onto the fire escape.

Paydon's view was much more pleasant. And he didn't get garbage smells wafting up from the dumpsters.

But he paid a lot more for it.

He didn't have much in terms of furniture, only a few chairs and a bed. He'd just moved in, so he might be planning to get more. Most of his stuff was in cardboard boxes lined up against a wall.

A girly magazine was open on one of the chairs. This one had a picture of a naked woman tied up on the cover. When he saw me looking toward it, Paydon closed it and turned it over. An ad for sex toys was on the back.

The window latches and locks were in rough shape. They were worn and broken. I couldn't see that it mattered all that much. No way was anyone going to scale the façade of the building and climb in through a window. At least not without a sturdy ladder.

I poked at the rails on the window sashes. They seemed sturdy enough. I could just get new latches and screw them in place.

"I'll take care of that sometime this week," I said.

"Okay. But I don't like people being in my place when I'm not here. So talk to me before you do it, huh?"

"I'm sure we can work it out," I said. "But it might take a few days. I work midnight to eight. Starting tonight. So I get out for the weekend on Friday morning. Although if they offer me an overtime shift on Friday night, I'll take it. How about you?"

"My schedule's not that regular. Usually I work nights, but sometimes I'll work days. Especially weekends. Today I go in for the afternoon. They should have the schedule posted for the whole week."

"Okay. Once you see when you can be here, we'll figure out a time."

I started to leave, then stopped. "Say, remember that kid Edmond you were telling me about?"

"Yeah. What about him?"

"You told me he goes out a lot in the evening. And doesn't come back while you're still on duty."

"So?" Paydon raised his eyebrows quizzically.

"So I just wonder where he goes."

"You got me. None of my business." He turned away.

When I got back into the shop, Jumbo George was still sitting at the table. "Can you fix the windows?"

"Yeah. Just buy a couple of new latches and screw them in."

"Good. Eventually I have to get new windows for all the apartments, but they're pricey. I told Kyle to put them in the grant application."

He laughed. "Fat chance."

"I don't know why Paydon's worried, though," I said. "You'd have to be a monkey to get up to any of those windows."

Jumbo George nodded.

I gave Snaggletooth a pat on the head. One of his little ears perked up and the tuft of hair on his head trembled. He licked my hand.

"After I get the latches, we'll work out a time for me to install them. For now, I'm gonna go take a shower. I need to get back into my work routine."

The front door opened.

Officers Fulton and Jerentolski walked in.

"Looks like you're not getting your shower right now," Jumbo George said to me.

"Jesse Damon?" Officer Fulton asked. She knew who I was.

"Another welfare check?" Jumbo George asked. "I'm still okay."

"Not this time." She turned to me and repeated the question. "Jesse Damon?"

"Yeah," I said.

"We'd like to talk to you for a few minutes. Mind coming outside with us?"

I did mind, but it wouldn't do any good.

She moved back and let me precede them.

When we got out to the sidewalk, she stepped in front of me. I backed up to the wall.

"You got any weapons?" she asked.

At least she didn't tell me to assume the position. "No." I made sure my hands were in plain view.

"Can you tell us where you were last night?"

Of course someone would come questioning me after they checked the computer record of where I'd been last night. I was really expecting Detective Belkins. Probably with Carissa in tow.

If they didn't like my answers to their questions, I was pretty sure they'd take me downtown.

I'd tell them as little as I could, but I had to answer direct questions, or they'd tell Mr. Ramirez I wasn't being cooperative. "I went out for a walk."

"A walk?" Fulton's eyebrows shot up. "At what time?"

"I dunno. About eight or nine, I guess."

"And why would anybody go out for a walk at that time of night?"

"Well, you know, I was locked up for years. So every once in a while, when I'm feeling restless, I go out for a walk." That might sound strange, but it was true. "Just because I can."

"And where did you go?"

They should have that information from the computer record. But maybe they were trying to see if I'd lie. "Along the riverfront for a while. I sat in the park. Then I went along some of the back streets. You know, with all the empty warehouses."

"Strange place to take a walk. Especially at night."

"Yeah, well, sometimes I like to be alone. Usually not too many people around there."

"And were there other people around last night?"

"As a matter of fact, yes. A few. They weren't real friendly types, so I left."

"And went where?" She stared at me.

"Came back here."

"And did what?"

"Got some work done in the basement."

"Who does stuff like that in the middle of the night?"

"Usually I work an overnight shift. So the middle of the night seems like a good time for me to get some stuff done."

"What time was that?"

"I dunno. Maybe around midnight?"

"Okay." She stepped back. "You planning on going anywhere any-time soon?"

"I'm on parole. I can't leave the state. And I don't have a car. So no."

"You make your parole appointments?"

"Haven't missed one yet."

"Somebody might very well be around to talk to you some more."
She gestured to Jerentolski and they left.

I let out a big breath I hadn't realized I'd been holding. They hadn't
arrested me.

* * * *

When my alarm rang that night, I struggled awake and lay there for a
few minutes. I'd set it for ten. Switching back to the overnight work shift
after I'd been off was always a pain.

I didn't want to be late for work, and I was planning to stop at the
drugstore.

I debated taking another shower, and decided against it. For sure I'd
work up a sweat right away anyhow, and need a shower in the morning. I
packed a lunch from my meager supplies and went downstairs.

Jumbo George was lying in his recliner, reading, the dog tucked next
to him. "Early, aren't you?" he asked.

"A little. I want to stop by the drug store before it closes. You need
anything?" It was hard for him to get out to buy anything.

"How about some toothpaste?" he said. "And maybe some foot powder."

"Any special kind?"

"Nah. Whatever's cheapest."

I nodded.

"How about some dog treats of some kind, if they have any." He got
out a twenty and handed it to me. "Whatever you think a dog'll like."

"Okay." I was a bit sorry I'd asked. I'd have to cart everything I
bought to work with me, and stash it somewhere. Stuff it in my lunchbox,
maybe.

"Might be a piece or two of that chicken left you could take for
lunch," Jumbo George said.

"Really? You don't want it?"

"Not that I don't want it," he said. "But I don't need it. And you
ought to have something decent for lunch."

"I made a couple of sandwiches."

"Peanut butter?"

"Cheese."

He snorted. "That's not enough to keep a man going when he's
working all night. Take the chicken."

"Thanks." I put two pieces of chicken in a plastic bag and tucked it
into my lunch box. It would be a welcome treat.

"And grab a can of that root beer."

"I got coffee."

"That nasty instant kind you drink?"

"Well, yeah."

"Take some root beer."

"Thanks." I added a can and snapped the lunchbox closed.

"You *are* going to work, aren't you?" he said.

"Yeah. Where else would I go?"

He shook his head. "Just checking."

I got to the drug store just before it closed. First I picked up a tube of toothpaste on sale. I peered at the foot powder. I should have asked Jumbo George a few questions about what he wanted. The kind that treated athlete's foot was super expensive compared to the other ones. But why would anybody want foot powder if it wasn't to treat athlete's foot? Otherwise why not just use regular bath powder? Or corn starch? Or nothing at all?

Standing here all night thinking about it made no sense. I grabbed the biggest container of the store brand anti-fungus foot powder and headed for the first aid section. I got a roll of gauze, a tube of antibiotic first aid ointment, and some medical tape.

Then I went to the tiny pet section and picked up a bag of bacon-shaped dog treats. It was expensive.

As I approached the checkout counter, an impatient clerk stood by the front door, rattling keys on a big ring in her hand. The big clock said it was exactly 11 p.m. I thought it was a little fast, but not by much.

Someone was already at the cashier, checking out.

Edmond Geer.

He had a roll of duct tape, a box of plastic gloves, and a package of condoms. He asked for two packages of cold medicine, the restricted kind with pseudoephedrine. The kind used to make methamphetamine. The kind the store had to track.

The cashier rolled her eyes and turned to a locked case behind her. She took out two packages and asked Edmond for ID. She checked her watch as he fumbled with his wallet.

I put my purchases on the counter and watched the process idly.

She took the ID, peered at it and scanned it, then scanned the bar code on the medication. A printer sprang to life, spitting out some labels. The clerk pulled a log book out from under the counter. She stuck the labels printed by the scanner onto a blank page and shoved the book toward Edmond. "Please sign."

He took a pen and scribbled a name on a line. I couldn't make out exactly what he wrote, but it definitely wasn't "Edmond Geer."

The clock said five after eleven.

The cashier rang up Edmond's purchases quickly, dumped them in a bag, and grabbed his money.

She did the same to mine, shoving everything haphazardly into a bag.

Edmond was just ahead of me out the door.

The door slammed immediately behind us and the lights dimmed.

A car idled just outside the door. Edmond got in it and it zoomed out of the parking lot, swerving at the last minute to avoid a stop sign at the exit.

CHAPTER 22

I was early for work, and the factory gate was still locked. It couldn't even be eleven thirty.

I thought about walking around to the loading docks to see whether the shipping gate was open for trucks, but John, the foreman, liked to keep an eye on everyone arriving for work. No point doing something that might annoy him.

I sat down on the steps to the office entrance, a few hundred yards away from the gate we used. Only the dim night lights showed through the barred office windows. The office personnel would show up tomorrow morning, just about the time my shift would be leaving.

Unlacing my boot, I pulled down my sock and gingerly felt the raw spot on my ankle. It wasn't too bad now, but if I let it go, by the end of the shift I'd be limping badly. I slathered it with the ointment, then wrapped a few layers of gauze over it before I tucked the sock back up between the strap and my leg. I wrapped more of the gauze around the strap, trying to both pad it and keep it from shifting and rubbing the sore spot. I hoped it would hold until around four, when I'd get my lunch break and could doctor it up again.

Getting to the injury on my knee was trickier. The leg of the jeans was too tight for me to pull it up over my knee. After I looked around to make sure no one was watching, I unzipped my pants and tugged them down a bit so I could reach the knee, bending forward so my hoodie covered what I was doing. I hoped. I rubbed ointment over it, but didn't try to wrap gauze around it. Standing up, I adjusted my pants and rezipped, then sat down again.

I took all the drugstore purchases and jammed them into my lunchbox, rearranging them so they didn't squash the cheese sandwiches or chicken pieces too badly. I leaned back against the wall and closed my eyes. After just a week off work, my body didn't seem to think it should have to be awake at this time of night. I dozed.

The sound of bootsteps and a jangle of keys jerked me awake. For a moment I thought I was back in prison, where bootsteps and keys announced the approach of a CO, and that usually meant I was in some kind of trouble.

But instead of the overheated prison air that smelled of urine, un-washed bodies and disinfectant, I felt the cool night air on my face. The tarry scent of the damp asphalt paving reached my nose.

I wasn't a prison inmate anymore. I fought down the panic in my throat and looked up.

Stebril Jenkins, the watchman, was looming over me. He switched on his flashlight and aimed the beam into my face. "Jesse Damon?" he asked.

I held my hand in front of my eyes to cut the glare and scrambled to my feet. I towered over him. "Yeah?"

"You had my money clip."

How'd he find that out? "Yeah. Could you point that light some place other than my eyes?"

He dropped the flashlight beam onto my chest. "The lady in person-nel gave it back to me," he said.

"Good."

"You had it."

"Who told you it was me?" I deliberately hadn't given my name.

"The personnel lady. She said it was the guy who gets his picture on the front page of the paper all the time. You're the only one I know who gets on the front page of the paper."

Thank you, Carissa, I thought.

He pulled the money clip out of his pocket and waved it at me. "How'd you get it?"

"Found it right out here." I pointed down the street a little ways. "In the dirt by that tree."

He frowned. "Might have fallen out of my pocket when I pulled out my keys. I guess. Or maybe you took it?"

"How could I take it?"

"I dunno. Snuck it out of my pocket or something."

I shook my head. "No way."

"All I know is when I got home and went to put it under my pillow, it was gone. And you turned it in."

"That's a lot of money to be carrying around, Steb."

"I know."

"I hope you're taking better care of it now. Leaving it home or some-thing."

Stebril looked alarmed. "I couldn't leave it home! I live with my sister and her son. If one of them found it…"

"Well, you need something better than a money clip in your pocket. Maybe get a little cloth bag and safety pin it in your pocket. Or one of them cell phone holders to put on your belt. They got them in the dollar store. The clip just loose in your pocket isn't a good idea."

"Yeah. Somebody could just pick my pocket." He glared at me.

"Well, I didn't."

"I know you done time. People learn lots of stuff in prison. What do they call picking pockets? Dipping? You had lots of time to practice."

I sighed. "That's not how it happened, Steb. I found it and stuck it in my pocket. When I got a chance, I turned it in to lost and found."

"Took you a while to turn it in. You could have done it right away."

"No, I couldn't. It was the middle of the night when I found it. I couldn't get back inside. Besides, no one was there to give it to."

"The foreman was still there."

"You're right. He was still there. But he was off somewhere in the shop. He wouldn't have heard it if I'd knocked on the door."

He gestured with the flashlight. "You took *days* to turn it in."

"Yeah. Sorry about that. I got locked up." That wasn't likely to be reassuring to him, but it was true. "I turned it in to personnel as soon as I could."

"Uh huh." He shifted the flashlight so the beam hit my eyes again. "I seen the article in the paper about you carjacking somebody."

I turned away from the glare. "You really think I'd of turned it in if I'd taken it?"

"I thought it out. Bet you was afraid I'd report it stolen. And since you had it on you when you got locked up, the cops would find it. And charge you with stealing it. Besides the other stuff."

"Did you?" I asked.

"Did I what?"

"Report it as stolen?"

He coughed. "Of course not. You think I'm gonna let everybody know I carry that kind of money on me?"

This conversation wasn't making a whole lot of sense. But then, I knew from experience that talking to Steb was often like that.

He'd worked at Quality Steel for years. At some point, he'd been injured on the job. Hit in the head and fell where he breathed in some chemicals that addled his brain, if I recalled correctly. Rather than face a lifetime of paying him worker's comp, they looked for a job he could do.

The fire insurance rates the company had to pay were much lower if they had a fire watchman on duty, making hourly rounds. Nothing in the insurance contract said that the watchman had to be a reasonable person, just a warm body that clocked the rounds. Stebril qualified for that.

I tried to change the subject. "Did you read all the articles in the paper?" I asked.

"Yeah. Said you maybe did something to those women. Didn't sound right to me, though."

That was interesting. "Why didn't it sound right to you?"

He looked thoughtful. "'Cause you're at work in the early morning hours when those other women went missing, weren't you?"

"True, that. But that one girl, that one who got into the accident that night the power went out, she ID'd me as the guy who tried to carjack her and her girlfriend. So they locked me up for that."

"Girl in a gray mini-SUV kind of car?"

I didn't remember reading that in the paper. I tried to think back about the car I'd seen crashed against the utility pole. "That might've been what she was driving. I didn't really get to see it too good. It was pretty well smashed up."

Steb fingered the money in the clip.

"Did you see that car?" I asked him.

"Yep."

"That night? Before it crashed?"

"What, you think she crashed it and then drove back here? Of course before it crashed."

I took a deep breath. Patience. At least he wasn't accusing me of stealing his money any more. "What were they doing?"

"You mean the people in the car?"

"Yes, the people in the car."

"Well, they stopped on the corner—" Steb pointed—"for a little while. Right under the streetlight. I think they were drinking. And smoking something."

"What made you think that?"

"The driver rolled down the window. Smoke poured out. And they threw a bottle out the window. It hit the curb and broke."

"Could you smell the smoke? Was it, like, cigarettes? Or weed?"

Steb wrinkled his nose. "More like cigar smoke, I think. But funny cigar smoke."

Blunts, I thought. Cigars split open to mix marijuana in with the tobacco.

"Was there anybody else around?" I asked.

"I was."

"Anybody else besides you? A man, maybe? Not in the car?"

He stared at me.

I tried to picture Edmond, but I couldn't come up with any distinctive features. "Somebody who looked kind of like me?"

"Somebody who looked like you?"

"Yeah." I felt like grabbing Steb's shoulders and shaking him, but I knew it wouldn't make him answer any faster. In fact, he might shut up completely.

And I might scare him. Then he might report I'd touched him. I really didn't need him saying anything that could be interpreted as me assaulting him.

He scratched his head. "I don't remember."

"Think. This is important, Steb." I tried to keep any hint of annoyance from creeping into my voice.

He was backing away, shaking his head. "I dunno. You was still inside. Maybe there was somebody else there. I'm not sure."

He shoved the money clip into his pocket and turned to walk away.

I'd pushed too hard. "Okay, Steb. Thanks. If you remember anything else, could you let me know?"

"Sure."

"Thanks," I said again.

He stopped and looked back at me. "And then they drove off. The windows were still down, and I could hear them laughing. That's not a good idea, though. You're not supposed to drink and drive."

"You're right about that, Steb."

"All I know's that the car drove away. I was just about to go into the warehouse. I heard a big crash. And the power went out. But the emergency generator started up, so I didn't worry about it. John said he'd take care of it."

He checked his watch. I wasn't sure of all the details of his job, but I knew he had to punch in at checkpoints by a certain time.

"Got to go," he said. "But I don't know how come they arrested you. You couldn't have been out there."

"How do you know?"

"John didn't send you home 'til the power went out. The power didn't go out 'til she hit the pole. If you was in the plant when she hit the pole, how could you try to carjack her after that?"

Jumbo George had said much the same thing. How could it be so clear to them and not to the cops?

"I appreciate that." I wondered if I could get him to repeat that to Detective Belkins. Or another investigator. Doubtful.

He took a few steps and stopped, looking over his shoulder. "And I guess maybe I owe you some thanks for turning the money in. Even if it did take you a few days."

"It must have taken you a while to save that much."

"I been working on it for the last few years now. Might need to get my own place. That's expensive." Checking his watch again, he hurried off around the building.

John swung the door open and looked out. "Jesse. Good to see you. After what's been in the paper, I wasn't sure whether you'd show up, or if I'd need to find another fork lift driver."

"I'm here, at least for now."

"Okay. Punch in right away and go get your lift." He held the door open. "Overtime for the twenty minutes or so when you clock in. We got a lot to do to be ready for day shift."

The overtime was welcome, but it meant I'd be already working when Kelly showed up, and wouldn't have a chance to talk to her before the shift started. Maybe I could manage to get my lunch at the same time she did.

Or see her after work.

John handed me a clipboard with a long list of parts. "Go to the warehouse and get these parts for the platers first. We got to get them up and running by the time day shift clocks in. They take almost eight hours to get completely on line."

I punched my timecard, stowed my lunchbox and donned my hard-hat and gloves. Then I headed back to the charging station to get my assigned lift.

Kelly drove a lift, too, but she wouldn't be here until midnight. Hers was a bigger one than mine. I had to wind my way through all the machinery and equipment on the factory floor, delivering parts and removing pallets of finished products.

She worked mostly in shipping, loading and unloading trucks. That was on the other side of the factory, about as far away from the plating room as it could get.

By the time most of the machine operators on the shift showed up, I had the first round of parts carted out of the warehouse and set up so they could start work. At the midnight whistle, the machinery groaned to life and the air began to fill with sparks and the smells of hot steel and oil. The floor vibrated as the big cutting and forming presses thumped.

I worked steadily through most of the night, not only servicing the stations that were operating on this shift, but setting things up for day shift, which had considerably more machine operators.

John finally sent me to grab my lunch after five. I knew Kelly must have had her break a while ago, but I parked my lift by the rough-hewn picnic bench where the shipping room staff ate, on the off chance that she'd drive by.

She didn't.

I got the last load of parts eased into place just as the whistle blew to end the shift. Since I had to plug my lift in to recharge and do my end-of-shift checklist, I'd be a few minutes late punching out. I wouldn't get paid for that, but I didn't care. What I did care about was maybe missing Kelly completely.

But she was just taking the clipboard off the nail in the wall next to her lift. I pulled into a bay in the charging station.

The four lift drivers on day shift showed up and went to their assigned lifts, beginning their routines. One of them glanced in my direction as he passed and frowned.

Most of the employees at Quality Steel knew the company took advantage of the tax breaks that the state provided for hiring parolees, and my status was no secret.

It might have faded in people's minds, but Carissa's front page articles kept the whole thing fresh. Bucky, the day shift foreman, always picked up a copy of the Rothsburg Register on his way to work and left it on the lunch tables by the timeclock, where everybody got a look at it.

"Hey, Jesse. They let you out of jail again?"

I couldn't tell whether the guy intended the statement as a taunt or a semi-friendly greeting. I knew better than to respond to taunting here at work, if it was indeed taunting.

Narrowing my eyes into a prison yard stare, I faced him, but chose my words to answer as if he were merely inquiring.

"Made bail," I said.

His step faltered. "Did you, really?" he asked.

"Yeah."

"So they did get you on those carjacking charges?"

"Yeah. But it don't mean they're gonna stick," I said. I wished I felt as confident as I sounded.

"Well, congratulations." He grabbed the checklist for his assigned lift and began going over it, ignoring me.

I wasn't sure "congratulations" was an appropriate response, but I let it go. Getting this job was a big break for me. If I lost it, I'd never manage to get anything nearly so good. The last thing I needed was trouble at work.

Kelly waited for me, an amused smirk on her face. We went to punch out together. The noise in the factory made conversation difficult.

John stood next to the timeclock, several envelopes in his hand. Mostly they were the pay stubs for the week before the shutdown, telling people the money had been put in their account. But for me, it was a real paycheck. I didn't have enough money to make a bank account worthwhile. It meant I had to go to the bank that handled Quality Steel's payroll every week to cash my paycheck, but I didn't have to pay the fees charged on small accounts. When I had enough saved up, I'd look into opening a bank account. For now, I lived a cash lifestyle. In some ways, it made things easier. I was never tempted to take on debts I couldn't afford. When I ran out of cash, I had to stop spending. On the rare occasions I couldn't use cash, I went and bought a money order.

Once we got out on the sidewalk, Kelly took my arm and smiled at me.

I felt a foolish grin spread over my face. Maybe she wasn't mad at me anymore. When she thought about it, she must have realized that I hadn't deliberately stayed out of touch. I'd called as soon after I was released as I could. Besides, I'd taken the kids so she could do heaven knows what on Saturday.

I tried not to think about what that might be.

"I got an appointment this morning," she said. "But you want a ride home?"

She didn't say what kind of appointment, and I tried not to care. "Sure," I said. I slipped my arm over her shoulders, pulling her up against me.

I buried my nose in her thick dark hair. A faint whiff of flowery shampoo came through the scent of oil and diesel exhaust that clung to her. And she'd worked up a sweat. The mix of her fragrant hair and the raw woman scent threw my insides into knots. Too bad she had somewhere she had to go. I had trouble keeping my hands from straying down her body.

We crossed the street to the parking lot and got in her car. If I'd had more money, I'd have asked her if she had time for breakfast at the diner. But that would have to wait until after I cashed my check. And even then, since I'd missed a week of work and wouldn't get a check next Friday, I'd have to be really careful with my money.

No diner breakfasts for a while.

"I don't think I said thanks for taking the kids to the street fair on Saturday," she said. "I appreciate it, and they had a really great time."

"Jumbo George had a lot to do with that," I said. "He sprang for lunch and the tickets for the rides."

"Really?"

"Yeah. He likes the kids."

"He doesn't have much family in the area?" she asked.

"Nope. Just his brother, who's in prison right now. And with what he weighs, it's hard for him to get out. So he doesn't get far from the shop much."

Kelly nodded. "I can see that."

"And…" I considered whether I should tell her more.

"And what?"

"And he used to have a family. Wife and kids. Dog, even. But they died in a house fire…"

Kelly glanced over at me. "For real?"

"Yeah. He misses them. For sure he'd rather go home at night and have dinner with his family than sit in the back of the store with me and split a pizza."

We drove on in silence. I wanted to reach over and stroke her leg, but she was driving and she wouldn't appreciate the distraction.

"I wondered if you could come over this evening?" she asked.

My heart jumped. "Sure."

"Maybe just before supper time?" she said. "I could pick you up around five."

"Fine. But I can walk over." It was a hike, but I knew the hours between when the kids got home from school and she had to give them supper was a hectic time. I could get there a little earlier and see if she wanted me to fix dinner, then help the kids with their homework. Maybe read them a few bedtime stories.

Then when they were asleep, we'd have a few hours before the babysitter showed up and we had to leave for work. We were usually pretty good at figuring out how to fill that time.

"Thanks," she said. "I have a meeting that'll run late. The sitter couldn't make it early, and the kids'll be glad to see you. I'll swing by the house and pick you up after the meeting. In plenty of time for work."

The warm feeling that was growing in my chest froze. Babysitting again? With her gone off somewhere?

Was that all she thought I was good for?

But I'd already said I would do it.

She pulled up in front of Jumbo George's place, sitting there with her hands firmly on the steering wheel. "Say hi to Jumbo George for me," she said. "And tell him thanks for treating the kids."

Should I lean over and try to give her a kiss? No. She wasn't even looking at me.

Duped again. I climbed out of the car.

"See you around five?" she said.

"Yeah."

CHAPTER 23

"I'm going over to Kelly's for supper," I told Jumbo George. "You want me to get anything for you before I go?"

"Nah. I'll just order Chinese." He belched. Snaggletooth barked, his naked pink tail whipping wildly from side to side.

"You'll get some, too, little fella," Jumbo George assured him.

"Chinese food? For a dog?" I said doubtfully.

"Just a little. I already gave him some dog food, so he won't be that hungry."

I had a feeling Snaggletooth would not be looking semi-starved and bony for very much longer.

"Kelly gonna cook for you?" he asked.

"We'll see. Sometimes I like to cook in a real kitchen. Chris'll help."

Jumbo George cocked his head to the side. "She gonna be there?"

"Huh?"

"She's got you babysitting again, don't she?" he said.

"Well, she's got a meeting or something. She knows I don't mind keeping an eye on the kids while she goes to AA meetings."

"Or while she goes out with some other guy."

I didn't have an answer for that. I had to admit the thought had occurred to me. As soon as I got there, I'd ask where she was going.

"She gonna come pick you up?" he asked.

"I told her I'd walk."

Jumbo George just shook his head.

Halfway to Kelly's house, I was sorry I hadn't asked her to come pick me up. My ankle was rubbed raw again by the monitor strap. My knee was stiffening up, making it hard to walk.

When I got there, Kelly had already fixed supper for us. Three places were set at the kitchen table. She'd made tuna noodle casserole with mushroom soup and peas.

"Thanks so much for coming over," she said, giving me a hug.

She'd washed her hair. I buried my nose in it, inhaling the lavender scent of her soap and shampoo.

She planted a kiss on my neck. "I'll try not to be too late," she said. "Maybe we'll have a little time before we have to be to work."

I'd heard that before. But I guess I'm really gullible. My heart melted. Much better not to ask her where she was going. I might not like the answer. Or she might lie to me, which would be worse.

She grabbed her keys, gave the kids a quick peck on the cheek, and headed out.

"Where's Mom going?" Brianna asked.

"She didn't say," I answered.

"She's been doing that a lot lately," Chris grumbled.

"Doing what?"

"Going out and not telling us where."

"Who usually stays with you?" I asked.

"Margery, our regular babysitter. She's been coming early a lot of days."

We sat down to supper. Brianna, who often didn't eat much, pushed the food around on her plate. Chris and I did justice to the casserole.

"If you're not gonna eat yours, can I have it?" Chris asked Brianna.

She held her fork motionless for a minute. "No. I'm gonna eat it," she said, and she did.

There was still a lot left in the casserole dish, so I gave him another spoonful.

I finished up the supper dishes while the kids took their baths. Chris was too old to want me to help, and I didn't dare go anywhere near an undressed Brianna. I knew I wasn't going to do anything to hurt her, or any kid, and by now Kelly was sure I could be trusted, or she'd never let me babysit. But I knew the counselor at school saw Brianna, and who knows what she might say if she was asked about me? I didn't want there to be room for misinterpretation.

When the kitchen was cleaned up, I made lunches for tomorrow and put them in the refrigerator. Then I checked the kids' bookbags to make sure they'd gotten all their homework.

Chris had a page of math problems, but he'd already done them.

Brianna's bookbag was a mess. Papers, broken pencils, crumbs, a banana skin, a few envelopes.

I emptied the bookbag and sorted through everything. I threw out the banana skin, followed by outdated notices and scribbled work sheets. If she had homework, I couldn't find it.

The envelopes were from the school. They were addressed to Kelly, but they weren't sealed. It looked like Brianna had ripped them open.

Hesitating, I laid the envelopes and their contents aside while I put Brianna's things back into her bookbag. What should I do about the envelopes? They might be important.

I knew Kelly couldn't read. She'd probably never told that to the people at school. Her unfortunate method of coping with missives from the school was to ignore them. That wasn't the wisest move, especially since family court was going to ask the school to provide records and a report when the next custody hearing came along. And that wasn't far away.

I unfolded the letters.

The first two asked Mrs. Mathias—that was Kelly—to contact a Mrs. Pearson about scheduling a special education meeting for Brianna. They wanted Mrs. Mathias's permission to test Brianna for special education services. A tentative date was included.

The next two were both the same, one marked "4th notice." On the bottom of that one, Mrs. Pearson had added a note that said since they had not heard from Mrs. Mathias about the meeting they wanted to hold, they had finalized the scheduled appointment.

I looked at the date. Tomorrow morning. At nine o'clock. They hoped Mrs. Mathias would be available. She was to contact them if she wanted it rescheduled or if she needed transportation.

I winced. Missing the meeting would look bad for her. Not giving permission to test would look even worse.

At this point, I didn't think there really was much chance that Fred, her ex, would be awarded custody. Just a few months ago, he had been involved in a DUI with the kids in the car.

But he kept requesting these court hearings. Probably just to get back at Kelly. He could afford a lawyer. Kelly had a lawyer, but she struggled to pay the bill. New hearings could cost her hundreds of dollars.

If they decided both parents were unfit, the kids would be placed in foster care.

I was a product of the foster care system. There were some good foster homes—I'd benefited hugely from living with the Colemans for a few stable years—but even under the best of circumstances, it was a precarious, unstable life.

Smoothing those letters out, I put them on the table where Kelly would have to see them when she came in.

Brianna came into the kitchen, carrying her teddy bear and a book. "You gonna read us bedtime stories, Jesse?" she asked.

I grinned. "Of course. Is Chris ready?"

"He's looking for his pajamas."

Mrs. Coleman, the foster mother I had just been thinking about, always said a quick and dirty assessment of the level of a child's care was the condition of his pajamas, if any.

Clean pajamas that fit were a good indicator that the child was well-cared for. Some kids had no pajamas at all, sleeping in whatever they wore during the day or could find. Others had pajamas, but they didn't fit or were torn and stained. And still others had ones that were washed so infrequently, they were grimy and smelled bad.

The pajamas worn by the children in Mrs. Coleman's care weren't often new, but they were always clean, well mended and they fit.

Brianna's were too small and torn. Her spindly arms and legs stuck out, and there was a hole in one shoulder. At least they looked clean.

If someone from Child Protective Services showed up, too small pjs wouldn't be fatal, but it wouldn't look good.

I thought about my little cash fund that I was hoping one day to use for a driver's license and a used pickup truck. Should I raid it to buy the kids pajamas? Did the thrift store have children's pajamas?

Chris came in. He was carrying his book, but he was wearing sweat-pants and a tee shirt.

Definitely time for new pajamas.

We settled onto the couch, one kid on either side of me. Chris got an afghan, and I tucked it over our laps.

The cats, Goddess and her two half-grown kittens, climbed up to join us.

The kids snuggled in close. I inhaled their clean-kid scent. Partly soap, but other things I couldn't put my finger on, too. I could think of nothing that smelled any better. Except maybe Kelly's hair.

Brianna had brought the book "Are You My Mother?" to read. Again. There was probably some unhealthy significance to that as her repeated choice, but I was in no position to judge that.

Feeling warm, comfortable and as content as I'd ever been, I was easily convinced to read an extra two chapters of Harry Potter for Chris. We were working our way through the series. I agreed that when we finished this book, I would see if I could get the video out of the library and we could watch it. Maybe make popcorn and hot chocolate.

Even as I said that, I was mentally kicking myself. I tried not to make definite plans with the kids too much. Suppose I got locked up again? Suppose Kelly had a new boyfriend and I never saw the kids again?

They'd had enough adults in their short lives who'd let them down. I didn't want to be another person in their bitter memories of broken promises.

When I closed the book, we sat there for a little while. The only sounds were the cats purring and wind whipping around the house.

Brianna broke the silence. "When is Mama going to be back?"

"Soon," I said. "But you need to be in bed before that."

"Does she have to work tonight?"

"Yes. I'm sure Margery will be here by then."

"How about you?" she asked.

"Of course I'll stay until Margery gets here."

"No. I mean, do you have to work tonight, too?"

"Yep. Your mom and I work the same schedule."

"So you're not going to be here in the morning when we wake up?"

"No. Doesn't Margery get you off to school in the morning?"

"Yeah." Brianna laid her head against my chest. "I wish you could be here sometimes, though, when I wake up."

So did I. I put my arm around her narrow shoulders and gave her a hug. At the rate Kelly and I were going, that wasn't likely to happen.

Chris turned his face away and stared at the cover of his book. "Jesse?" he said.

"Yes?"

"Did you really kill somebody?"

I couldn't breathe. I'd always known that if I stuck around, he was going to ask me something like that sooner or later. But I hadn't figured out I what I was going to say when he did.

"We've did newspaper stories in school every day last week," he said.

My picture had been on the front page a lot lately.

"There were some articles with your picture."

"True, that," I said.

"It says you've been in prison for killing somebody."

I swallowed hard. "You can't always believe everything you read in the newspaper."

"But I know you've been in prison. Like Grandpa."

"Do you go visit Grandpa sometimes?" I asked.

"We've been," Chris said. "At Christmas. But mostly Mom just goes by herself."

I wondered if Kelly would ever come visit me if I got locked up again. Or bring the kids. I'd love to see the kids. But I wasn't sure that I wanted the kids to remember me as a prison inmate.

"But you *have* been in prison, haven't you?" He wasn't going to drop it. And he did deserve an answer.

"Yes," I said. "When I was younger, I did some stupid things that I never should have done. I got in a lot of trouble for it."

"Did you kill someone?"

"No. Someone was shot and died. But I wasn't the one who shot him."

"Were you there?"

"The man was killed in an apartment. I was outside, so I didn't see what really happened."

"If you didn't kill him, why'd you get sent to prison?" he asked.

That was a question I'd been asking myself for years. "'Member, I told you I was mixed up in some stuff I shouldn't have been," I said. "I was with my brothers, and they were buying drugs. I knew better, but I went anyway."

He was surprised. "You have brothers?"

"Yeah. Two of them. Both older than me."

"Do you ever see them?"

"One's in prison himself. I don't know about the other one."

"You know, you could look him up on the internet and see if you could find him. You can find most people. If you wanted to know how he was doing."

I wasn't sure I wanted to know. "Maybe sometime you can show me how to do that," I said.

Kelly came home shortly after the kids were asleep. She looked tired.

"Good meeting?" I ventured, even though I was pretty sure she hadn't been to an AA meeting.

"Yeah." She shrugged off her jacket and laid it on an arm of the sofa.

"You hungry?" I asked. "There's some of that casserole left over. I put it in the fridge."

"No. I already ate."

Had some guy bought her dinner?

She stepped up to me, put her arms around my waist and laid her head on my shoulder. "Thanks for keeping an eye on the kids. And I'm sorry I've been so distant lately."

She lifted her face up to mine and kissed me gently on the lips. She tasted like coffee and powdered sugar. Maybe she'd been at an AA meeting after all.

I pulled her close to me and laid my head on her softly scented hair, inhaling the mesmerizing clean hair smell.

"We got a few hours before the babysitter gets here and we have to leave for work," Kelly whispered. "Come on upstairs."

She led me up to her warm, soft bed.

My doubts about where she'd been and what she was doing didn't seem important now.

And I forgot all about the notice from the school for the meeting tomorrow morning.

CHAPTER 24

I remembered the letters from school as Kelly was talking to Margery. She was a college student who slept overnight at the house and got the kids off to school in the morning.

The letters were still on the kitchen counter. I grabbed them and followed Kelly out to her car.

"These were in Brianna's bookbag." I held them out to her. "It's about a meeting the school wants to have to see about testing her for special education services."

Kelly shook her head. "She's fine. No need for special education services."

"I dunno. She can't read yet." The way the letters read, I thought she might already be enrolled in special education and getting some services. How could Kelly not realize that?

"She's awfully young for them to be worried about her not reading," Kelly said.

The earlier the problem was addressed, the better, in my opinion. "She's behind the other kids. It bothers her."

"I don't see her being upset about it." Kelly stared straight ahead out the windshield. "I'd know if it bothered her."

I bit my tongue. The school personnel would be able to explain it much better than I ever could. I said, "I think you ought to go to the meeting."

She glanced at me. "They'll just try to tell me she needs extra help or something."

"Good chance they'll say that."

"And I don't want the other kids to see her as different. They'll put a *label* on her. Special education student."

Why couldn't Kelly see that the other kids, at least, already saw Brianna as different? Or, as Brianna put it, "dumb."

"So why should I go?" Kelly asked.

I turned possible arguments over in my mind. Kelly was enough in denial it would do no good to suggest it would be best for Brianna.

"Is the child custody case settled?" I asked, even though I knew it wasn't.

Kelly shifted uncomfortably in her seat. "Not yet. But I don't see how any judge could ever give Fred custody. He's got those DUIs. With the kids in the car, no less. They're gonna say he's unfit."

"But they *are* going to ask the school for a report. And the school is likely to tell the court that you're not involved enough in the kids' education. Suppose the school tells them you haven't come to any meetings to discuss important concerns with the kids?"

"So what if they do?"

"What if they declare you an unfit parent, too?"

"They wouldn't do that." Kelly frowned. "Would they?"

"Well, you know Fred's going to tell them about your drinking. Probably other stuff, too. Might even make up some things. And if the school claims you're not reliable, it's not going to help."

"So what would they do? They won't turn them over to Fred. And there's really nobody else."

"Foster care," I said.

"Foster care?" Kelly's voice rose. "They wouldn't put my kids in foster care. That costs a fortune, and the county don't have enough money to put kids in foster care if they have a place to go."

"They might also decide you need help, and send over somebody to monitor the situation. Maybe even help out."

"Help out? Like how?"

"Housekeeping services or something. Not to do the work, but to teach you and supervise you while you do it."

"I don't need anybody supervising me in my own home."

"You may feel that way. But Child Protective Services don't want to be in trouble for not doing their job. They're supposed to make sure the kids are cared for. If they think you are neglecting the kids, they might think they have to do something."

We rode in silence.

"They also might try to collect child support from you for foster care, if they go in that direction." I said.

"What? How can they do that?"

I shrugged. "They just can."

"Do you really think they might decide to take the kids away from me?" Kelly asked.

"I'd say it was a distinct possibility, the way things look now. But if you go to the meeting, one thing the school can't say is that you haven't responded to their concerns."

"When is this meeting?"

"Tomorrow."

"Tomorrow? What time?" Her voice wavered.

"Nine o'clock."

"I could just get there if I hurried over from work. But I wouldn't have a chance to go take a shower or anything."

"That's not important. Just go."

"I don't know anything about what'll go on in the meeting."

"They will explain it to you."

"I don't know anybody who's ever been to any of those meetings," she said.

"I've been to some," I told her. "When I ended up in Mrs. Coleman's foster home, she insisted I get special education help. I went to all the meetings."

"What kind of help did they give you?"

"Mostly extra help with my school work, to catch me up. But I had a group therapy session every week, too."

"Why?"

"I was identified as emotionally disturbed." I didn't doubt that I probably had been. And I'd have a tough time arguing if someone said that about me now, either.

"Did it do any good?"

"The group therapy, no. The help with my school work, yes."

"Would you come with me to the meeting?" Kelly asked.

"If you'd like."

"That's assuming I decide to go," she said.

* * * *

At the end of the shift, I hurried through my checklist as quickly as I could and still be sure it was accurate.

Kelly seemed to be dragging her feet on hers, but when I went and stood in the aisle behind the charging station, she finished up.

After we punched out, we got in her car. The school was only a few blocks away.

We were early for the IEP meeting. In the parking lot, Kelly sat in the driver's seat, leaning back against the headrest, her eyes closed.

"I really don't want to go to this meeting," she said.

I took a deep breath. "I know you don't *want* to. But you have to. It's to try to come up with a plan for Brianna. She's falling behind in school."

"That's the school's problem. They'll figure something out."

"This is important for Brianna. You can't back out now."

Kelly turned toward me and glared. Then she leaned back against the headrest and closed her eyes again.

"And exactly who are you to tell me what I can and can't do?"

An unexpected wave of white-hot anger welled up in my chest. The silence in the car was as brittle as a thin sheet of ice between us.

I broke it. "Maybe it's not my place," I said. "But I can't sit by and watch you keep doing this."

"Doing what?"

"Doing things that we both know hurt your kids. They need a responsible parent."

"Oh, and you don't think I'm a responsible parent?"

"You're not acting like one now."

She shook her head. "You don't know what you're talking about."

"I know the school wants you to come in to see about helping Brianna. I know she needs help to get by in school. I know she feels like she's dumb. I know that's not good for her."

Kelly stared out the windshield. "She'll be okay. I mean, she's not retarded or anything like that."

"She *won't* be okay. She can't read. And she's not learning."

"*I* can't read. And nobody's worrying about that."

"No? And it's not a problem at work? And everywhere else? You want her to have the same problems?"

A tear trickled down Kelly's cheek. "That's not a fair thing to say."

"It doesn't have to be fair. Things'll *never* be fair. But that don't change the fact that Brianna deserves better than you're doing." So did Chris, but I let that go. Now we were talking about Brianna. Chris seemed to be coping better.

"You have no idea how tough things are for me right now," she said.

"True, that. And I may *never* know how tough things are for you. But I do know that you need to do better for your kids."

She twisted around in the seat, raised her hand, and slapped the side of my face. Hard. "You just don't know."

"Maybe not. But I do know I can't just sit back and watch this anymore." I rubbed my cheek and opened the car door.

"So you're just gonna leave?"

"That's right."

"I thought you cared about the kids," she said.

"I do care about the kids. That's the main reason why I'm leaving."

"That doesn't make any sense."

Halfway out of the car, I paused and looked at Kelly. Her eyes were red.

I held onto the car door. "I can't help them. And this whole thing is tearing me up inside. Only thing I can do is take care of myself. And best thing for me is to not see you hurt your kids anymore."

"I've had a lot on my plate lately."

"Yeah? You think other people don't have a lot on their plate, too?"

"I do the best I can." She rubbed her eyes with the back of her hands.

"Well, then, your best isn't good enough. At least right now."

"What do you want me to do?" she wailed.

"For starters go to this meeting."

"What will that do?"

"Show everyone—especially Brianna—that you care."

"I *do* care."

"Could've fooled me."

By now, tears were streaming down Kelly's face. I glanced at her, then looked away. She was hurting. I knew that. And I was making it worse. I knew that, too.

"I *can't* go in there. They'll make me feel stupid. I'll have a panic attack."

"So you feel stupid. Brianna feels stupid every day. She has to go to school every day, anyhow. And if you have a panic attack—excuse yourself and go in the bathroom 'til you get over it."

"You don't know what it feels like."

I took a deep breath. "I know. You keep saying that. I *don't* know what it feels like to you. But I do know you need to do this."

"You'll come with me?"

"I told you I would."

"Even if they don't want you there?"

"Yeah. I can't be part of the meeting, really—I'm not a parent or anything. But if you want me there, all you got to do is say so. They'll let me stay. They don't have to like it."

Kelly wiped her eyes with the heels of her hands. "I'm a mess."

"So?"

"So I can't go in looking like this."

"Yes, you can." I reached into the back of the car and pulled a tattered blanket up to the front seat. "Wipe your face with this. And as soon as we get in there, tell them you have to go to the bathroom. You can wash your face then."

She took the blanket and rubbed her face. "Is there a comb in the glove compartment?"

I pulled one out and handed it to her. She shook her hair loose and ran the comb through it, then pulled it back into a neater pony tail.

"All set?" I asked.

She shrugged. "As much as I'll ever be."

CHAPTER 25

We got out of the car and crossed the parking lot to the front door of the school, which was locked. I pushed the buzzer.

A disembodied voice answered. "May I help you?"

I leaned close to the speaker. "We're here for Brianna Mathias's IEP meeting."

"Please come straight to the office," the voice said. The latch on the door buzzed.

I opened the door and gave Kelly a little push.

When we got to the office, the secretary shoved over a clipboard. "Please sign in," she said. "And I need your driver's license."

Kelly pulled out her wallet and fished it out.

"I don't got a driver's license," I said.

The woman raised her eyebrows and pulled the clipboard over to her to read my name. I was pretty sure she recognized me from the last time I'd been here, dropping off the kids one day when Kelly was too drunk to bring them in herself.

That hadn't gone well. But as far as I knew, they hadn't gotten a restraining order to keep me away. For sure I would have heard about it if they'd gotten one. Mr. Ramirez would have known and given me a hard time over it.

"Do you have any ID, Mr. Damon?" the secretary asked.

I had two—a work one and my old prison one. I really didn't want to give her the prison one. "Will a work one do?" I asked.

"If it has your picture."

I pulled it out of my wallet and gave her the ID. She took two name tags that had the prominent word, "Visitor" on them, and put our names underneath. Then she handed them over. "Please wear these while you're in the building."

Kelly and I pulled off the backing and stuck them on our shirts.

"Please have a seat in the conference room"—she waved to indicate a room attached to the office—"and someone will be with you shortly."

"Can I use the bathroom?" Kelly asked.

The woman looked at her suspiciously, but got up, picked up a key-ring, and escorted her out to a restroom in the hall. She unlocked the door and Kelly went in.

I sat down at the table in the conference room.

Kelly came back a few minutes later, her face freshly scrubbed and her hair combed again. She sat next to me, rigidly upright.

Three women entered the room, all carrying folders and binders and piles of papers. And pens. I probably should have brought some paper and a pen, so I could take notes. Too late to worry about it now.

"I'm Mrs. Pearson, Brianna's case manager," an older woman said. "This is Mrs. Cryac, her classroom teacher. And Miss Deminsky, the special education teacher in the resource room. Brianna has been visiting the resource room for three hours a week."

Mrs. Pearson waited expectantly.

Kelly shifted in her seat, but didn't say anything. I nudged her. She still didn't say anything.

"This is Kelly Mathias, Brianna's mother," I said.

"And you are…"

I took a deep breath. "I'm Jesse Damon. Friend of the family."

Mrs. Pearson shuffled her paperwork. "We're here to discuss Brianna's educational plan, and whether we should be conducting additional academic testing. Brianna started receiving special education services three years ago, when she was enrolled in the preschool program. She has been diagnosed as learning disabled. I don't believe Mrs. Mathias was present at any of the meetings—the paperwork was all signed by Frederick Mathias. Is that Brianna's father?"

Kelly's nod was barely perceptible.

The three women took turns droning on. Below grade level. Lack of motivation. Poor peer interaction. I could tell Kelly wasn't following what they were saying, but I paid close attention.

"So," Mrs. Pearson said, "we propose continuing resource room support for Brianna, and are evaluating a few other supports. We'd like to conduct academic testing to see where Brianna falls compared to other students her age, and speech testing. Brianna doesn't talk much, and we feel it's important to assess whether there's an underlying problem with her mastery of language."

I frowned and looked at Kelly. Her eyes were glazed over.

"Exactly what kind of testing will you do?" I asked. "What would it tell us?"

Mrs. Pearson looked at me like I was some kind of alien intruder. Which I guess I was.

"We would give a standardized academic assessment, perhaps the Woodcock-Johnson," she said. "We know Brianna is operating below grade level in both reading and math. That's what the resource room support is intended to address, but we want to be sure we are targeting the appropriate areas."

"How about the speech testing?" I asked.

"We have a speech pathologist, and we'd like to have her evaluate Brianna's language skills. If there is an underlying problem there, especially in receptive or expressive language, it could impact her ability to understand and respond to her schoolwork. And in social situations."

I looked at Kelly, who wouldn't meet my eyes. "Could she be mentally retarded?" I didn't think she was, but Kelly had brought that up. Brianna was so quiet and shy, she might come across that way.

Mrs. Pearson bit her lip. "We don't use that term. We say cognitively challenged."

"Could Brianna be cognitively challenged?" I asked.

She shuffled her paperwork. "We have seen no evidence of that."

"Does that mean she's never been tested?"

"She has not had a formal IQ test, no."

"Might it be a good idea if she did?" I asked.

"I'm not sure what we could expect that to tell us."

"Whether she was capable of the work?"

Miss Deminsky said, "She will seldom attempt the tasks I give her. But when she does, she is capable of doing them."

I remembered helping Brianna with her homework. She needed lots of help, or she'd stop working. "By herself?" I asked. "Or with somebody working with her?"

"She does better when someone assists her on a one-to-one basis," Miss Deminsky conceded.

"So maybe she needs an assistant available to help her?" I said.

Mrs. Pearson sniffed and frowned. "Brianna's disabling conditions are not severe enough to justify a one-to-one assistant, Mr..." she looked down at her notes. "Damon."

I said, "And since an IQ test is given by a school psychologist—" at least they had been years ago when I'd been tested—"maybe an evaluation for emotional disturbance? She's been going through an awful lot with her parents getting divorced and all."

Mrs. Pearson looked at the other women.

I nudged Kelly. "Do you think maybe some more testing would be helpful?" I asked her.

"Huh?" she looked around.

"We're discussing additional testing. We know Brianna's below grade level in reading and math. We expect some tests will tell us exactly where she is. And speech. But maybe it would be a good idea to get an IQ test and a psychological assessment."

"I guess that would be a good idea," Kelly said.

Mrs. Pearson sighed. "Are you requesting this further testing, Mrs. Mathias?"

"Yes."

"We'll need to get the psychologist in," Mrs. Pearson said, standing up and going to the door. "Would you please see if Dr. Eugene is available to come in for a few minutes?" she asked the secretary.

She sat down again. "While we're waiting, let's go over the rest of this paperwork," she said.

Once again she droned on, talking about standardized testing, modifications to the curriculum and accommodations.

A middle aged man, bearded and dressed in a business suit, appeared in the doorway.

"I'm Dr. Eugene, the school psychologist," he said, leaning over the table and offering his hand to Kelly.

When she just sat there, I shook it. "Jesse Damon. And this is Kelly Mathias, Brianna's mother."

Kelly took the cue and limply took his hand.

"Mrs. Mathias, here, is requesting IQ testing for Brianna," Mrs. Pearson said. "And a psychological evaluation."

"Oh? I don't know that I'm familiar with Brianna's record," Dr. Eugene said. "What are the concerns?"

Everyone looked expectantly at Kelly. She got that deer-in-the-headlight look in her eyes.

"Brianna isn't doing well in school," I said. "She goes to the resource room, but I think she's falling further and further behind. She says it's because she's dumb, and that the other kids tease her. I don't think she's dumb—just shy—but I think it would be important to know if she's able to do the work, or if we're expecting too much of her."

"I see." Dr. Eugene made some notes.

"She's had a rough time of it, too," I said, turning away from Kelly, who was going to be furious with me. "Her parents are divorced, and there's an ongoing custody battle. It's a lot for a kid to deal with. Child Protective Services has been involved."

Dr. Eugene continued to make notes. "So I take it you're not the father?"

"No."

"What's your relationship to Brianna?"

Not an easy question to answer. I gave the same answer I had before. "Friend of the family."

Dr. Eugene was a bit more astute than the women had been. Or more willing to ask the troubling question. "Mother's boyfriend?"

I nodded.

"Do you live in the household?"

"No."

He scribbled a few more notes. "Okay. We can run a battery of tests, give us an idea of where Brianna's functioning. And some academic testing, too, to see where she is academically. Speech to see if some therapy is called for."

The other people from the school seemed to have let him take over the meeting. He said, "Do we need anything else?"

I couldn't imagine what else there could be.

"No problem with motor skills? Or other areas?"

"No."

He looked across the table and said, "Mrs. Pearson, can you fill out the permission to test forms for Mrs. Mathias to sign?"

Mrs. Pearson's face was tight. She'd probably expected a quick meeting with no family present. Now not only was the meeting going on for much longer. there would be a lot more testing than she'd planned on. It would be time consuming and expensive for the school to get it done. "Yes."

"Good," Dr. Eugene said. "We can reconvene in about three months with the results and see where we go from there. The IEP will be extended as written until that time. Is that satisfactory to everyone?"

The three women from the school nodded.

I looked at Kelly. She stared at the paperwork in front of her. "Brianna's way behind in reading," I said. "And three months is a long time. Is there some way to get her extra reading help right away?"

Dr. Eugene nodded. "I'd think we could get her assigned to a reading specialist on a temporary basis."

Mrs. Pearson looked pained, but she wrote a note on the paper in front of her. "Is that what you'd like, Mrs. Mathias?"

I nudged Kelly. "Is that okay?"

"Yeah."

They passed around papers for everyone to sign.

"You don't have to sign, Mr. Damon." Mrs. Pearson glared at me. "You have no official standing in this meeting."

That was fine with me. As long as they were going to look into Brianna's problems.

When we got back out to the car, Kelly sat for a few minutes, keys dangling from her fingers.

"That wasn't so bad, was it?" I asked.

She snorted. "What if they discover she *is* retarded?"

"Then at least you'll know what you and the school are dealing with. And can figure out the best way to help her."

"And did you have to bring up the custody fight and Child Protective Services?"

"Yes. They'll find out about it, if they don't already know. And it might be a big part of why Brianna's not doing well in school. Or anywhere else, for that matter."

"What do you mean, anywhere else?" She looked out the windshield.

"She doesn't want to do much but watch TV. That's not normal for a kid." I didn't go into the no friends and everybody teasing her.

Kelly slammed her palms on the steering wheel. "She's *fine*. Except for the reading. And that's not such a big deal."

I didn't say anything.

"I'm her mother. You think you and some school people who hardly know Brianna can tell me what's best for her?"

"I'm saying that before Brianna gets so far behind she can't ever catch up, *somebody* better do *something*."

"You?"

"Maybe not me." It was hard to talk with the lump forming in my throat. "If these carjacking charges go through, I'll be locked up again. And I don't know what's going to happen between you and me. So maybe it's best if I don't become a big part of her life. Or Chris's."

She started the engine, put the car in reverse and stomped on the gas pedal. The car shot out of the parking space. "Are you saying you don't want to see me anymore?"

I swallowed. "That's not what I meant, but maybe that's a good idea, the way things are right now. Unless we can make some changes."

"Like what?"

"Like we don't spend hardly any time together. Me and the kids, a little. But not you and me."

"You don't call what we did last night 'spending time together?'" she asked.

"Last night was great. But it was the first time in a while. And let's face it, we didn't do much talking."

"I been busy," she said. "And I thought you *liked* the kids."

"I do. And I don't want to see them hurt. That's why I think I shouldn't get too close to them. Not good for them. And not good for me."

Kelly was crying now. "What about me? I thought you maybe cared about me. At least a little."

"Yeah, I got to tell you. I *do* care. There's no place I'd rather be than be with you."

"You like the sex," she said. "And that's all. You don't love me."

"The sex is great. I won't deny that. But I don't think I know what love really is." I didn't add that the lump in my throat was dissolving into a bottomless pit, or that I knew I'd never forget about her. No matter what happened.

"What do you want me to do?" she asked.

"Do what you need to do. Take care of your kids."

"And for you…"

"I don't need anything." That wasn't true. "But I'd love to get together with you again, if that's what you want. Give it some thought. You got to be willing to put something into a relationship, though."

She tossed her head. "You know, I've had a lot on my mind lately."

I felt a knife twist in my heart, and I resisted the urge to take her hand. "Hey, things are tough all over. I'm probably going back to prison."

"If that was gonna happen, I think you'd be locked up by now. You'll beat those charges."

"I hope you're right."

"Look, I know I've left the kids with you when you thought we were gonna do stuff together. I'm sorry."

"Not just with me. With the babysitter, too. Don't tell *me* you're sorry. Tell the kids."

"I've been going to AA meetings."

"A couple of evenings a week? And all day Saturday?"

"Well, not exactly." She wiped her eyes.

"But you have been going to AA?"

"Yeah. At least twice a week. And I'm sober now for almost a month."

"That's good to hear." I tried to remember the last time I'd smelled alcohol on her breath. Was it a whole month ago? "You been trying to help some of the other members?"

"Kind of," she said.

"It's important to think about other people sometimes. Not just concentrate on what *you* want."

She glared at me. "But there's something else…"

"Yeah, I know. Sucker that I am, I've been babysitting while you go out with somebody else."

"No! Let me tell you what I've been doing…"

"I don't think I want to hear." I'd just torture myself if I knew the specifics.

"Too bad. I'm gonna tell you. Will you listen?"

I sighed. "All right."

"You remember me telling you what happened to my mother?"

"I think so. She died when you were a kid. So did mine."

"And how my dad kept me?" She stared at the road ahead. "Mostly for the social security check?"

My father had done much the same thing, when he got out of prison. I was sixteen at the time, and he took me out of the Coleman's stable foster home. Where I'd been doing well. I wondered how different my life would have been had he left me there, and I'd gone on to the community college. Instead of the state prison.

Kelly sighed. "He was the treasurer of the Predators Bike Club at the time, and we lived in the biker clubhouse. He didn't pay much attention to me, but I was kind of a pet for everybody. So I got by," she said.

"Did you ever know what happened to your mother?" I asked.

"Not really. Dad just said she was dead. I was afraid to ask what happened. Mostly I was afraid I'd find out he'd killed her."

"Do you still think that?"

"No. I got a letter from her."

"What?"

"A letter. She's been in a nursing home all these years. Paralyzed. And brain damage—her mind isn't clear. I went to see her. She doesn't remember what happened to her."

"So what did you do?" My mind was reeling. I could just imagine how she must have felt.

"I went to see my dad in prison. He said she'd been in a bike accident. Riding with one of his buddies. No helmet."

"And he told you she was dead?"

"He said it was like she was dead to him, especially when he discovered she'd been cheating on him with his buddy. He's sorry he told me that when I was a kid, but once he did, he didn't know how to go back and say she was still alive. He even went to see her once, but at that point she was in a coma."

"I take it she's not in a coma anymore?"

"No, and I guess she hasn't been for years. But she's pretty confused. She thinks I'm about twelve years old."

"Why all of a sudden did she send a letter?"

"She got moved to a new place. They have a lot of volunteers. One of them tracked us down—me and Dad. He said he'd gotten a letter, too. So he wasn't surprised to see me coming around, asking questions."

She pulled up in front of the head shop. "I've been going to see her. Here all these years I didn't know I had a mother. I needed a mother!" She was crying in earnest now.

It was all I could do to keep from gathering her against me and telling her it would be all right.

But deep down, I knew it wouldn't be all right.

"Ain't a whole lot you can do now about that. But your kids need a mother, too. And there's plenty you can do there."

CHAPTER 26

I wanted to calm down before I saw Jumbo George, so I walked down to the coffee shop. It was a little late to pick up breakfast for us, but he was always ready to eat.

Standing in front of the glass cases, I studied what Stanley offered besides donuts.

A few different kinds of pastries. Cupcakes. Some muffins. Slices of something that had to be quiche. Individual containers of fresh fruit.

We should be eating healthier than we did. The quiche and the fresh fruit had to be better than the donuts and cupcakes and pastries.

I looked at the little price tags. The quiche and fruit were by far the most expensive things there. No wonder so many poor people are both poorly nourished and fat.

Stanley finished making a latte for another customer, who took it and left. He came over to where I stood. "Some cop's been asking about you, Jesse."

"That so?"

"Yeah. Come in twice now. Wants to know how much I know about you."

"What'd you tell him?"

He wiped his hands on his apron. "Not much. Just that I saw you around. But you know, he made a point of making sure I knew you were on parole."

"You knew that, didn't you?" I never saw any point in trying to keep anyone from finding out. Even if I'd tried, Carissa did a pretty good job of pointing it out to everybody.

"Yeah. He made sure I knew it was a murder conviction."

"No secret there."

Stanley leaned on the counter. "*I* didn't know that."

Didn't he read the newspapers he got for his customers? "Does it make a difference?" I asked.

"I guess not."

"You think Jumbo George'd eat some of that quiche?" I asked. "And maybe some of that fruit?"

"Jumbo George'll eat anything. Didn't he tell you to get donuts, though?"

"I'm just getting in from work. He hasn't had a chance to tell me what to get."

He laughed. "Yeah. Get some quiche and fruit. But get a couple of muffins or something, too. You wouldn't want his whole system to go into shock over the healthy stuff."

I grinned and put a ten on the counter. "What can I get for that?"

Stanley pulled a quiche with two pieces missing and put it in a box. "I made that yesterday," he said. "It's still good, but I got another one in the oven now. I can't keep this one much past lunch time anyhow." He added four fruit salads—which, by my reckoning, should have cost over ten dollars all by themselves—and half a dozen bran muffins.

He closed the box and pushed it toward me. "Here you go."

"Thanks."

Two cars were parked in front of the head shop. Kyle's red Audi was one of them.

Well, I had enough food that he could eat, too, if he wanted.

As I walked by the other car, the door opened and the driver got out. A familiar voice said, "Jesse."

I stopped short. Mr. Ramirez, my parole officer.

He had a file folder in his hand.

What was he doing here? I knew he often made field visits to check up on people on his case load. Once he'd shown up at Quality Steel at 2 in the morning to see if I was really working. But he'd never stopped by where I lived before.

He walked over. "Just thought it was about time I checked up on your residence." His gaze swept over the storefronts. "I've been meaning to get over here ever since I found out you were living over a head shop. This it?"

"Yes, sir. I live upstairs, in the back."

"Here?" He nodded toward the 214 ½ door.

"No, sir. That's the front apartment. You got to go through the store to get to my place. The stairs go up from the back room of the shop."

"Really?" Mr. Ramirez grinned. "That's interesting." He checked his watch. "You got out of work over three hours ago. I thought maybe you weren't coming home this morning."

He didn't directly ask where I'd been, so I didn't offer any explanations.

"Let's go in and take a look around," he said.

When I opened the door, the patchouli scent billowed out. Mr. Ramirez inhaled. "Sure *smells* like a head shop."

No way could I give Jumbo George much warning about this. I shoved the door all the way open and called out, "I got some breakfast for us!"

Jumbo George and Kyle were sitting at the table, papers spread out in front of them.

"It really looks good." Kyle gestured at the papers. "But they might postpone the decision. They were supposed to make an announcement tomorrow. Somebody asked for an extension."

"Your Mr. Richmond?" Jumbo George asked.

Kyle leaned back. "Probably. But you got it covered." His eyes glittered brightly and his movements were jerky.

I glanced at Mr. Ramirez to see if he noticed.

If he did, he didn't give any indication.

I put the box down on the table. "Mr. Ramirez, this is George Stenski, my landlord. And Kyle Staten, a neighbor."

Gesturing back toward Mr. Ramirez, I said, "This is Mr. Ramirez, my parole officer." I figured Jumbo George would be cool, but Kyle might say any stupid thing that came into his head. Especially if he was drunk or high. He seemed like he might be.

Snaggletooth sniffed around our feet and started yipping.

I slipped my hand under his belly and deposited him onto Jumbo George's lap, where he burrowed his face under the beard, leaving his naked butt and tail sticking out.

Mr. Ramirez looked at Jumbo George and the little dog. He didn't often run into people who were wider around than he was, but Jumbo George definitely qualified. Mr. Ramirez blinked twice, and grinned again. "Is that a dog?" he asked.

"Yeah. What can I do for you, Mr. Ramirez?" Jumbo George asked.

"Just want to look around," Mr. Ramirez said. "Routine check. Do I have your permission to search?"

"Sure," Jumbo George said. "I got nothing I shouldn't. All the pipes and rolling papers and stuff are legal. I got a good supply of tobacco."

"Any spice or K-2 or anything?"

"Nothing like that. But go ahead and look."

"Thank you. And I'd like to take a look at your apartment, too, Jesse."

He was being very polite. For the apartment, at least, all he had to do was announce a parole search, and he could look all he wanted. Maybe that was why Jumbo George wasn't giving him a hard time, like he'd done with Officers Fulton and Jerentolski.

"Would you like a cup of coffee, Mr. Ramirez?" Jumbo George asked.

"No, thank you." Mr. Ramirez looked around. "Any places locked?"

"Some of the cabinets and drawers," Jumbo George said. "And the basement door. Jesse, give him the keys."

I stepped over to the cabinet in the kitchen, took the keys off the hook, and handed them over to Mr. Ramirez, who went into the shop and stepped behind the counter.

"Might as well have a real breakfast, Jesse," Jumbo George said, opening the box. "My lord, you're going to poison us all! Where's the donuts?"

I shrugged. "I thought maybe we could have something different today."

"Well, get yourself some coffee. I'm not sure this stuff is really edible. I want to see you eat some first."

I wasn't hungry now—my gut was all tied up in knots—but I picked up a slice of the quiche and took a bite. I'd never had quiche before. This had cheese and bacon and something green in it. Maybe spinach. Despite my churning stomach, it was surprisingly tasty.

"You want some?" Jumbo George asked Kyle.

He was gathering up all the paperwork, his hands moving spastically. "No, thanks. I'm not hungry. You know what? I'll be back later." He stuffed everything in his briefcase and headed out the front door, past where Mr. Ramirez was opening drawers and glancing at the contents.

I finished the piece of quiche. "What did Kyle want?"

Jumbo George coaxed Snaggletooth out with a bit of quiche. "He says I should have the grant, but that they delay it for a few days. He's pleased as punch. Not that I probably got it, but that his father-in-law maybe didn't. There's gonna be a press conference tomorrow. Either announce the grant, or to say there's been an extension granted for applications and the entire process has been postponed."

"Well, at least you're still in the running," I said.

"Yeah. Kyle says I ought to go to the press conference."

I laughed. "Then it might be your picture in the paper for a change, not mine."

"I guess maybe I got to go buy some new clothes. Maybe I can get away with jeans, but I can't go in a stained tee shirt. I could go down to the thrift shop this afternoon. If you didn't mind watching the store."

"Sure." Would they have clothes big enough for Jumbo George? I didn't know.

"And if we get the grant, I won't be able to have you paint the trim scarlet. Or purple."

"But it'll be well worth it, if you get it," I pointed out. "You could get all the work done right away and start renting out the rest of the storefronts and the apartments."

He shoveled an entire slice of quiche in his mouth, chewed and swallowed. "That's not really that bad," he said.

After he'd given the shop a quick once-over, Mr. Ramirez came back to the table. "How do I get upstairs?" he asked.

"That door right there," Jumbo George said, nodding to it.

Mr. Ramirez opened the door and stared at the narrow, steep flight of stairs. "Can I even fit?" he asked.

Jumbo George shrugged. "I stopped trying a while ago. But maybe you can make it. The railing's strong."

After giving us a disgusted look, Mr. Ramirez hoisted himself up the first couple of steps. "I almost hope I find something up here to make this worthwhile, Jesse," he said.

I was pretty sure he wouldn't.

We sat at the table, listening to him clomping around upstairs. The apartment was sparsely furnished, and I didn't own much stuff.

The search didn't take long. Mr. Ramirez started down the stairs, holding tight to the railing and putting both feet gingerly on each step before he descended to the next one. When he got downstairs, he was sweating profusely and sat down at the table.

He wasn't carrying the file folder any more.

I wasn't sure I should say anything, but I decided it was better to point it out than have him forget it. "You don't have your folder."

"Oh, shit." Mr. Ramirez rubbed the back of his neck.

"Want me to run up and get it?" I started to get up.

He peered up at me. "No. I'll go back and get it."

I sat down again.

"You need a cup of coffee," Jumbo George said.

Mr. Ramirez pulled out a handkerchief and mopped his forehead. He looked a little gray. "I shouldn't..."

"Jesse, get him a glass of water. And a cup of coffee."

I did so and placed them on the table in front of Mr. Ramirez, who took a generous gulp of water. "Thank you."

Snaggletooth put his front paws on the table and sniffed at Mr. Ramirez.

"Now," Mr. Ramirez said, taking a smaller sip of the water, "I've got a few questions I want to ask you. Is there an office or something?"

"Here's okay. I got no secrets from Jumbo George." That wasn't entirely true, since I hadn't told him much about what I was doing last Saturday night when I followed Edmond.

"Okay." Mr. Ramirez picked up the coffee mug and cradled it in his hands. "If I'm going to violate best practices, I might as well really do it."

He took a drink. "Jesse, want to tell me where you were Saturday night, and what you were doing?"

I wasn't about to be the one who brought up Edmond or the meth lab. I tried to remember exactly what I'd been doing when. Of course he had the computer record. Probably a printout right in that folder.

"I went out to sit in the park for a little bit," I started.

Mr. Ramirez took a deep breath. "Out to sit in the park."

"Yeah. You know, down by the river. It's kind of neat to have that so close. Watching the water calms me down."

"You needed calming down?"

"Uh huh."

"Why is that?"

"Well, not calming down, exactly. I mean, it gets kind of close in here. Jumbo George isn't used to having someone around all the time. And when you been locked up for as many years as I was, just being able to go out and look at the water and the sky is a big deal. So that's what I did."

"And then?"

"Then I walked around for a while."

"Go anywhere special?"

"Not really. I hung around a few warehouses for a little while."

"Why?"

Why indeed? I couldn't tell him about the meth lab, although he might know about it already. "Couple of raccoons there," I said, making it up as I went. "They were kind of cute. Somebody'd left a couple of bags from a hamburger place. Must have been some food in there. They were tearing open the bags and eating stuff. Picking it up in their little hands."

"You go into the warehouse?"

How much could he tell? "A few feet, maybe. Not all the way in."

"You hung around there for quite a while."

"Didn't seem to me like it was that long."

"Loitering?"

I shrugged.

"Then what?"

"I came back here."

"And did what?"

"I went down the basement to put some shelving together. Jumbo George wants to use it for storage."

Mr. Ramirez put down his coffee mug. "Late at night, well after midnight, you come home. And instead of going to bed, you decide to put up shelving in a storeroom."

That part was true, although it did seem a little far-fetched. "Well, you know I usually work that midnight shift. It means I'm not doing things the same time as most people. Yeah, I was working on the shelves for a few hours."

"You see anybody else when you were in the park?"

"Not really. A few people walking around, maybe. But nobody to talk to."

"How about at the condo complex across the street?"

"I saw the security guard. At the condos. And a few people coming and going."

"You see any women? Especially a woman walking by herself?"

"Not that I remember."

"You know what happened down there that night?"

I could feel my face flush. "Another woman disappeared."

"Did you have anything to do with that?"

"No. I think I was long gone by the time it happened."

He leaned back in his chair. "It happened just about the time the computer lost track of your signal."

CHAPTER 27

I shifted uncomfortably. "I dunno how that could happen. I been following the instructions to keep it charged and all."

Mr. Ramirez wrapped his hands around the coffee mug. "I've been off for a few days," he said. "And when I checked the records, your signal had gone blank a few times. Usually not a huge problem, but when it happens at the same time as a woman disappears…"

I tried to say, "I had nothing to do with that," but he ignored me.

"And in the same neighborhood…" He pushed his chair back from the table. He was breathing hard. "I got to get that file."

We watched him open the door. He paused at the bottom of the stairs, wiping his forehead. He turned around to look at us. His face was pale. He began to lumber up the stairs.

"Prob'ly some notes on you in that file, that you're not s'posed to see," Jumbo George said. "Or he'd of let you go get it for him."

We heard someone pounding out front. The whole building shook.

"What the…?" Jumbo George said, struggling to his feet and hurrying to the front of the store. Or at least moving at a pace that qualified as hurrying for him.

Snaggletooth barked frantically.

I picked him up and followed.

Several people, some in uniform, stood on the sidewalk around the door to Paydon's apartment.

"Police! Open up!"

Jumbo George stepped out onto the sidewalk. "Lord. They're gonna break that door down." He glanced back at me. "Go get the keys, Jesse. If they're gonna go in, maybe they'll use the keys."

Scurrying back inside, I yanked the huge ring of spare keys to all the buildings and apartments in the block off its hook and brought them to Jumbo George.

"You wait inside, Jesse," he said.

I turned off the bright overhead lights in the store and stood just inside, where I could see and hear most of what was happening. Snaggletooth cowered in my arms.

I didn't blame him.

"Don't break the door down!" Jumbo George said to the cop who seemed to be in charge. "I got the keys."

Too late. I heard the sound of cracking wood.

"You damn well better have a warrant for this," Jumbo George said.

"Who are you?" the cop asked.

"I'm the landlord. You gonna show me that warrant?"

The cop handed him a piece of paper.

Jumbo George nodded. "Search warrant for 214 ½ Second Street, all right. The upstairs apartment. Why the hell would you be searching it?"

The cop shook his head. "Information received."

"And you couldn't wait for me to open it with a key?"

"That'd take too long. Can't give the subject time to destroy evidence."

Jumbo George waved the warrant. "The tenant's not here. I think he left early for work. He was in his uniform."

"I was told he works nights."

"Sometimes he does. But it's different every week."

The cop shrugged. "I was told he worked a steady midnight to eight during the week."

"You was told wrong. His shift varies. And he works a lot of weekends. He'll probably be home shortly after midnight."

The cop shrugged again.

"What're you looking for?" Jumbo George scanned the paper in his hand.

"It's right there in the warrant."

"That's so general, you could take anything you wanted to and say it was covered."

"We have a warrant and it's our job to execute it, sir. If you have a complaint, you're certainly free to file it."

Jumbo George ran his fingers through his straggly hair. "I ran a background check on this guy just last month before I rented to him." That was an exaggeration of what he'd done, but how would the cop know that? "Nothing much showed up. No credit report or criminal background or anything."

The cop smirked. "You'd better find someone else to use for background checks. That one sure missed a lot."

"Yeah?"

"Suppose I told you that your tenant is on parole for murder? We probably didn't need to get a search warrant. Could have just done a parole search. But the detective in charge of the investigation wanted to be sure anything we find won't be thrown out of court on a technicality."

Jumbo George rocked back on his heels. "I hate to tell you this, dude, but I think you've got the wrong apartment. The convicted murderer lives in the back apartment, not the front one here. 214, not 214 ½."

"You sure about that?" The cop chuckled.

"Damn straight I'm sure. Jesse Damon is the ex-con. Paydon Norris lives in the apartment you're searching."

"Well, well. Won't Detective Belkins be surprised." He looked around. "He was supposed to be here by now. But I got to follow through on this search anyhow."

"Could you at least take the keys and unlock the door upstairs? It's gonna be expensive to fix those doors."

The cop stepped over toward the stairwell, took a look up and came back. "Too late, I'm afraid."

"You gonna give me an inventory of everything you take?"

"We'll leave one in the apartment."

Jumbo George came back in and slumped down on a chair. "Gonna need new doors."

"Too bad," I said. "But you were probably gonna need new ones anyhow. At least the outside one."

"I sure as hell hope Paydon don't have some weed or meth or something tucked away up there."

"Yeah." I had no idea whether Paydon was likely to have something like that or not.

"They thought it was your place. But they didn't tell me why they were searching it."

Since Mr. Ramirez had already searched my place, I couldn't see that it mattered much.

Another couple of cars pulled up.

Detective Belkins climbed out of one and came into the shop, unlit cigar clenched firmly in his teeth. He stopped when he saw me standing there. Turning to the door, he hollered, "Get a uniform in here. Now."

Officer Jerentolski walked in. The overwhelming scent of patchouli set him to coughing.

"Why the hell isn't he in cuffs?" Belkins demanded, nodding his head toward me.

Jerentolski started to say something but stopped and shrugged. He stepped up to me. "I'm gonna search you. And put you in cuffs. For everyone's safety. You're not under arrest."

"Yet," Belkins added.

I didn't really think anybody was much concerned about my safety. But protesting wouldn't do any good.

"Let me give this dog to somebody," I said, holding Snaggletooth up.

"That's a dog?"

"Yeah. Can I take him over to Jumbo George?"

"Okay," Jerentolski said. He put his hand on his holster and followed closely as I went back to put Snaggletooth on the table in front of Jumbo George, who reached out with his massive hand and pulled the dog into his lap.

I spread my feet and put my hands on my head.

"You got any weapons?" Jerentolski asked me.

"Box cutter. Right front pocket."

He reached in and took it out, tossing it on the table. "What do you have that for?"

I was tempted to say, "Cutting boxes," but they would think I was being sarcastic. They'd be right.

So I said, "For work."

"Mind if we have a look around the shop here," Belkins said. It wasn't a question.

"You got a warrant?" Jumbo George asked.

Belkins zeroed in on him, took in his size, and blinked a few times. "And just who are you?"

"George Stenski. I own this place."

"This is a public accommodation. We don't need a warrant to search public areas."

"Then stick to the public areas."

"Damon is on parole. We can do a parole search, whether we have a warrant or not," Belkins said.

"Then be sure you limit your search to his place. And the premises covered by that warrant." He didn't mention that they had a warrant for the wrong address.

Or that Mr. Ramirez was upstairs in my apartment this very moment, getting the folder he'd left behind. He hadn't come down yet. Had he found something?

I was surprised that Jumbo George was giving Belkins a hard time. He'd told Mr. Ramirez to go ahead and search, no problem.

Probably came down to attitude. Mr. Ramirez had asked nicely. Belkins was being a jerk.

"Damon here," Belkins jerked a thumb toward me, "seems to have access to the rest of the place, doesn't he?"

"So get a warrant," Jumbo George said. "Meanwhile, I'll call my lawyer."

Belkins chomped on the cigar. Then he shrugged. He turned back to where I stood, my hands now cuffed behind my back, Jerentolski gripping my upper arm firmly.

Carissa slipped in. Just what I needed.

Belkins stared at her, then cast a final glance around. "Bring Damon outside," he said to Jerentolski.

Carissa, her eyes watering from the patchouli, slid up to Jumbo George and simpered at him. "Your shop is fascinating. Maybe I could do a feature article on it."

Not surprisingly, there was no foot traffic on the sidewalk. One person came out of the coffee shop, took a look at the patrol cars with their light bars flashing, and went back inside.

"So." Belkins stepped in front of me. "You gonna tell me what's going on?"

"What'd ya mean?" I asked.

"You have something to do with these women who've been disappearing. I just don't know what. Or how. Yet."

"I haven't had anything to do with any of that."

"No? How about the attempted carjacking? We have a positive ID there."

If I tried to tell him that I hadn't gotten out of work until after the car crashed, he wouldn't listen anyhow, but he might take anything I did say and twist it around. Since Mr. Ramirez was right here—he had to be coming downstairs any time now—it wouldn't matter if Belkins told him I was being uncooperative. Mr. Ramirez could ask me questions himself.

"I'll talk to you later," he said to me. To Jerentolski, he said, "Put him in a car."

Jerentolski led me over to a patrol car and opened the back door. He held his hand to keep me from bumping my head. When I was seated, he reached in and fastened the seat belt. Then he closed the door.

Two cops crossed the sidewalk from the 214 ½ entrance to a car. They carried some stuff, but it was all in bags so I couldn't see what it was.

They carted out an old computer tower.

A computer? Lots of people had computers. I remembered the magazines Paydon had in his apartment. I hoped he didn't have any child pornography or anything like that on the computer.

Belkins stepped over and knocked on the barred car window next to me.

I tried to ignore him.

He took the cigar out of his mouth and grinned. He raised his voice so I could hear him through the glass. "We're finding lots of stuff. You're gonna have some explaining to do."

I didn't bother to tell him it wasn't my stuff. That would come out as soon as Mr. Ramirez talked to him.

Where was Mr. Ramirez? He'd been short of breath and kind of grayish-looking before he'd started back up the stairs. Was he okay?

Jerentolski, who was keeping an eye on me, came over. "I'm gonna put this window down," he said. "The sun's out. It might get hot in there."

"Hey," I said, not sure how to say I was worried about Mr. Ramirez.

He leaned into the front seat and pressed the button that lowered the window. "What?"

"My PO—Mr. Ramirez—he went upstairs to my apartment a little while ago. He hasn't come down."

"What was he doing in your apartment?"

"Parole search."

"He part of this search?"

"I don't know. He showed up maybe fifteen minutes ago. A little while before you guys."

"Well, if he's up there, he's probably helping them look around."

"No. That's not my place they're searching. Mine is in the back. You have to go up the stairs in the back room of the store. I don't think anybody else is up there with him."

"Yeah? So?"

"So I'm kind of worried about him."

"*You're* worried about *him*?" Jerentolski grinned. "Usually it's the other way around."

"He didn't look so good. And those stairs are steep. Could you go check up on him?"

Jerentolski shook his head. "Check up on him? Why?"

"I'm afraid he might need some help or something."

"What's it to you?"

I didn't have a good answer to that.

He went over to talk to someone else, who went into the store.

Belkins gestured to the cop who was directing the search. He came over.

"How much are you finding?" Belkins asked.

"A lot." The cop glanced over to where I was sitting in the car, a few feet away. "Maybe we should move."

Belkins spit on the sidewalk. "Nah. The window's up. He won't hear."

With an effort, I wiped all expression from my face and stared out the windshield. I could hear perfectly well.

"What do you have?"

"A box of women's clothes. Matches the description of the missing items. Duct tape. Latex gloves. Rope."

Belkins grinned. "Sounds like we got him good."

"Well, certainly probable cause to find and arrest the resident."

Belkins nodded in my direction. "We got him right there."

"No," the cop said. "That's the resident of the back apartment. 214, not 214 ½."

A screaming siren split the air. An advanced life support ambulance screeched to a halt, double parking beyond the patrol cars. The medics jumped out, grabbed their equipment and a gurney, and dashed into the store.

"What the hell?" Belkins said.

"Some guy upstairs in the back apartment. They think he's having a heart attack."

"Who is he?"

"ID says Carlos Ramirez. Parole officer."

"What's he doing here?"

"From what that big guy says, conducting a parole search of Damon's residence."

"How did he get involved?"

"Well, he *is* Damon's PO."

Yet another car pulled up, paused momentarily, then continued down the block and parked in a legal space. The driver got out and fed the meter.

Mr. Billings. Jumbo George's lawyer. He was dressed in another impressive suit and carrying his briefcase.

"Gentlemen." He nodded at Belkins and the cop as he headed toward the door of the shop.

"I'm afraid you can't go in there," Belkins said. "Search underway."

Mr. Billings stopped and raised his eyebrows. "Oh? May I see the warrant?"

"Warrant's for the apartment," Belkins said. "But we're interested in the entire premises. We have a couple of suspects in there. No one is allowed to enter or leave."

"Really? Is my client, George Stenski, a suspect?"

"We'd like to ask him a few questions."

"Then isn't it fortunate that I'm here? I'm his attorney."

Belkins threw his cigar on the sidewalk but didn't say anything.

Mr. Billings peered through the big display window, into the shop. "It appears to me that a reporter for the Rothsburg Register is in there, too. Is she a suspect?"

"No comment."

"Then I see no reason why I shouldn't be permitted to enter. Not only is my client there, waiting to be questioned, but you have allowed a media representative in." He took a step toward the door.

When Belkins made no effort to stop him, he continued to the door, but stepped back and held it open.

The medics pulled the gurney out and over to their ambulance. I couldn't see well, but a large someone, presumably Mr. Ramirez, lay on it and was attached to an array of blinking equipment and monitors.

They loaded the patient in the back of the ambulance. One medic climbed in the back with him. The other shut the doors and got into the driver's seat, slamming that door behind himself. The siren wailed again as they peeled away from the bevy of patrol cars.

Belkins watched it go and then followed Mr. Billings into the shop.

I sat in the car. As the sun crept overhead, Jerentolski stepped into the entry of a vacant store, where there was some shade. I was grateful for the open car window.

Two of the patrol cars left.

Belkins emerged from the shop, Carissa right behind him. He nodded to me. "Take the cuffs off," he said to Jerentolski.

"You mean let him go?" Jerentolski headed for the car.

"Yeah. We'll be able to find him again if we need to." Belkins stomped over to his car and drove away.

Carissa, perched on stiletto heels beneath her bird legs, watched as Jerentolski got me out of the car and removed the cuffs. Her layered blond hair ruffling in the breeze.

"Here you are," he said, putting the cuffs back on his belt. "You're free to go."

"Thanks," I said, resisting the urge to rub my wrists. He hadn't tightened the cuffs to the point where they'd cut off circulation.

He got into his car and followed the others.

Carissa grabbed my arm. I tensed, but didn't shake her off.

"This is gonna be such a great front page on tomorrow's paper," she said. "And all mine!"

I didn't say anything.

"I've got to check some stuff out, but I'm sure I'll have the lead story," she said. "And I'll also have a great feature! The whole front page'll be mine. You'll just love the feature!"

"Oh?" I said. After everything she'd been putting in those stories, I doubted I would love it.

She leaned in confidentially. "I came up with some great info! It's terrific. But it's an exclusive. You'll have to wait with everybody else until it's in the paper tomorrow. I want it to be a surprise! So I didn't even tell Roger."

Roger was Belkins. I wondered what kind of information she was withholding from him and me. And everybody else.

She gave me a quick kiss on the cheek. "Thanks, Jesse. You're a great subject to write about! I'm going to try to get my feature series on the Riverfront Rapist nominated for a journalism award. If it is, I'll invite you to the presentation dinner in New York! You can sit with me and Roger."

Like I'd really want to go someplace like that. Especially with her. Or Belkins. "I can't leave the state," I reminded her.

"Oh, I'm sure you could get permission for something like this." She disengaged her arm from mine. "See you around soon, I'm sure."

She left.

The curb in front of the shop was empty. No patrol cars, no ambulance, no puke-green hybrid.

Inside the shop, Jumbo George and Mr. Billings sat at the table. Snaggletooth came over and sniffed me as I walked in.

Mr. Billings shook his head. "So they did turn you loose."

"Yeah. They didn't tell me why, but I'm not gonna argue about it."

He grinned. "I pushed them about why they were planning to arrest you. So I think they thought better of it."

"Thanks," I said.

"I have to say things haven't been dull since I've been representing George. He gets himself into some serious spots. And he hangs around with some interesting people."

Jumbo George leaned back in his chair. "I knew I could count on you."

"But." Mr. Billings eyed me. "I'm not a criminal lawyer. I still think you're going to need a good one."

One that I couldn't afford. I'd be stuck with a public defender. But Mr. Billings had already saved my bacon at least twice.

"I heard it was you told them to check on Ramirez upstairs," Jumbo George said.

"Yeah. He didn't look all that good to me when he had to go back upstairs. And when he didn't come down..." My voice trailed off. "I wonder if that folder's still up there?"

"What folder?" Mr. Billings asked.

"He had a manila folder with him, that he forgot the first time he came down. He wouldn't let me go get it, so I figured it had to have some kind of confidential information in it. Or notes about me."

"You're probably right." Mr. Billings got to his feet and started toward the stairs. "As an officer of the court, I can bring it down to the courthouse. Don't worry; I won't read it myself."

"They think Paydon is the Riverfront Rapist?" I asked.

"Looks like it. So much of their evidence pointed to this neighborhood and even this building. Cell phone calls, computer searches, plus just the proximity to the comings and goings of the culprit."

"But they thought it was you," Jumbo George said. "And they'd be able to track you here. Then sometimes your monitor signal died. I wonder what's up with that."

"It happens. A poor signal, probably," Mr. Billings said. "Did you go down in the basement much?"

"Yeah. I was putting up shelving there."

"Underground. That's when they'd lose their signal. Your PO probably figured that one out. But Belkins didn't want to hear it. He's looking for some way you could have disabled it so you could got out and do things."

I shivered. "Like kidnap women?"

"Exactly."

CHAPTER 28

Work didn't go well. I was tired and distracted.

Even if Paydon was the Riverside Rapist, he'd been at work when the alleged attempted carjacking took place. So while I might be exonerated in most of the cases, the one in which I was actually charged was still open to question.

Working around heavy machinery was no place to be distracted. After I almost ran off the side of a ramp, carrying a full load on my forks, I turned my attention firmly to my tasks at hand, quashing any stray thoughts about kidnappings or carjackings.

I was exhausted when I got home, and collapsed onto my bed in my grimy work clothes.

By late afternoon, I was wide awake. I took a shower, carefully washing and drying the sore knee and the inflamed skin on my ankle, and went downstairs.

Jumbo George was out in the shop. He actually had a customer. A well-dressed one. They were discussing the Civil War cannons in the window.

The newspaper, still rolled up in its rubber band, sat on the counter. I could read the headlines.

I carried it over to the table. The lead story was about Paydon. I wondered if they'd managed to find him to arrest. And how airtight the case against him was.

If his DNA matched, there wouldn't be much doubt that he was involved. I had trouble picturing him as the Riverfront Rapist. He'd seemed like an okay guy, if a bit hot-tempered. But then, so did a lot of serial sex offenders.

I wasn't at all sure I really wanted to know what Carissa's wonderful surprise story was, so I left the newspaper rolled up. I figured I should read it before I went to work tonight, since half the people there would have seen it. At least I'd have some idea what people were thinking about me.

Snaggletooth was hiding in the back room, but he looked at me and went over to the back door. I snapped his leash on his harness, grabbed the pooper scooper and a plastic bag, and took him out the back door.

After he was done, I turned to go back in. A car pulled up to the loading dock.

Kelly.

I watched as she and the kids got out. She opened the back and took out a grocery bag, which she handed to Chris, and picked up a covered aluminum tray.

"Hi," she said, leaning over to give me a kiss. "Is it okay to leave the car by the loading dock for now?"

"I think so," I said, returning the smooch. "Too late for any deliveries today."

She looked down at Snaggletooth. "What in the world is *that*?"

"A dog."

"It doesn't look much like a dog," she said doubtfully.

"Well, that's what it is. And it's a *he*. Somebody didn't want him, and I think Jumbo George is going to keep him."

Brianna clutched a book in both hands. She switched it to one and bent down to pat the dog's head. "What's his name?"

"Snaggletooth."

"That's a funny name." She ran her hand down his naked back. Snaggletooth wiggled delightedly under her gentle touch. "What happened to his hair?"

"I don't think he ever had much," I said. "He's part something called Chinese Crested. They don't have much hair."

"He's ugly," Kelly said.

"No, he isn't," Brianna said. "You'll hurt his feelings. He's cute."

"Can we come in?" Kelly juggled the tray in her hands. "This is hot."

I went to take it from her, but she said, "Just open the door."

Inside, she put it on the table. "Lasagna." She took the bag from Chris and put it down next to the lasagna. "I thought about what you said. That I never do things for other people. Even when they've done nice things for me."

Jumbo George's customer was gone, and he waddled into the back room, sniffing. The scent of tomato sauce with garlic filled the air, even overpowering the patchouli scent. He peeled up a corner of the aluminum foil covering the tray. "Lasagna? Did you make it?"

"Yeah. Kind of a thank you for doing so much for the kids at the street fair," Kelly said. "And I brought some Italian bread and stuff for salad, too." She nodded toward the grocery bag.

Jumbo George peered into it. "Is everything ready to eat?"

"Should be. Or you can put it in the refrigerator for later."

"Why would we save it for later?"

Kelly laughed.

"Can't we eat it now?"

"Sure."

"You're gonna have some, too, aren't you?" Jumbo George asked. "You and the kids?"

"We'd love to," Kelly said.

Jumbo George glanced over at me. "We got enough plates for every-body, don't we? And some milk and root beer?"

"Yeah."

"So okay. Let's have dinner."

"I'll make the salad," Kelly said. "Jesse, you set the table."

The kids stood quietly, looking at us.

"Hey, Chris," Jumbo George said. "Come over and look at this here catalog. This guy, just moved into the area, he was asking about Civil War soldiers. Maybe we should get some. Put them on the other side of the window. Get some more knights on horseback, too, for outside the castle. And," he cast a glance in my direction, "a trebuchet or two. We can move the cannons over by the Civil War soldiers."

Brianna stood next to me as I unhooked Snaggletooth's leash from his harness. She held her hand down for him to sniff. "Hello, dog," she said. "Do you want to come sit with me?"

I picked up the dog and followed Brianna into the shop. She pulled a cushion from the shelf under the counter and plopped herself down on it.

"Now, he's kind of shy," I said. "And I don't know if he's used to children. So he may not want to stay with you." I put him down beside her.

"Come cuddle, Snags," she said, patting her lap.

The dog climbed onto her and snuggled down.

"I'm going to read you this book, Snags," she said.

I smiled. "Has it got good pictures, Brianna?"

"It's got some pictures," she said. "But it's mostly words. The lady at school who's my new reading teacher gave it to me. She said pretty soon I'll be able to read all the words myself."

"Really?"

"Yes. Now I'm in recovery."

"Recovery?" The only recovery that came to my mind was drug re-hab. Couldn't be what she was talking about.

"Every day, I'm supposed to go with the recovery teacher. She gives me books and she's helping me learn to read them."

"And are you learning?"

"Yes. After she helps. She gave me a book of my own." Brianna held up the book she was carrying. "See? And I can already read most of the words in it. When I can do all of it, she'll give me another book. But I can keep this one."

"That's great, Brianna."

"It's better than the resource room. I'm the only kid in my recovery class. So I don't cry so much."

I felt a pang. "Do you cry a lot at school?"

"Only in the resource room. Sometimes. If I cry in the regular class, everybody makes fun of me."

She opened the book. "Now, Snags," she said. "You listen while I read this to you. And then maybe next time, you can read it to me."

I grinned. "I don't know that he'll ever be able to read, honey. No matter how good you teach him."

"That's okay. He can listen." She leaned down and planted a kiss on the scraggly tuft of hair on his head. "He's a good dog. Even if he never learns how to read."

Jumbo George and Chris stood behind the counter in the store. Chris stared at the miniature figures in the catalog. "You really gonna get these, Mr. Jumbo?"

"I imagine." Jumbo George settled his bulk on a stool. "This guy was saying he'd like to buy some. You can come over when they come in, if you want. And set them up in the window."

Kelly took two loaves of bread, a cutting board and a sharp knife. She sliced the bread. Then she looked up at me.

"After we eat, I thought maybe you'd want to come back to the house with me," she said. "We could get the kids to bed. And have a couple of hours before Margery gets there and we had to leave for work…"

Jumbo George came into the back room and smiled. He grabbed a slice of bread and stuffed it into his mouth and shoved the rest of it to the middle of the table. "You and Jesse?" he said. "Sounds like a plan to me."

Kelly laughed. "I wasn't exactly asking for your approval But I'm glad you think it's a good idea."

"Sounds like a plan to me, too," I said.

She cast a wicked grin in my direction.

Jumbo George sat down and reached for the newspaper. He unrolled it and stared at the top of the page. "I guess they got Paydon good."

I felt a little sorry for Paydon. Although if he'd been abducting women, he didn't deserve it. Still, it's no fun going through the criminal justice system. And then onto prison, especially as a despised sex offender.

"Hey, Jesse." Jumbo George looked up at me. "Did you see the newspaper today?"

"Not really. Just took a quick glance."

"Carissa wrote something you'd be interested in," he said.

"She said she was gonna."

"Well, you should read it." He shoved the paper in my direction.

Reluctantly, I took it and looked down to the bottom of the front page where her feature articles usually were.

There was a picture of the two girls who'd claimed I'd tried to carjack them.

The headline screamed, "They Lied!"

I looked closer. "Two girls who claimed they were victims of an attempted carjacking confess they 'didn't want to get in trouble' after they crashed the car into a utility pole. So they made up a story about an attempted carjacking."

I skimmed the article quickly, then went back and read it carefully. The two girls, both 19, were out without their parents' permission or knowledge. They were adults, but underage for drinking. And, if Steb was to be believed, smoking marijuana.

When they crashed the car, they were afraid they'd be in big trouble. So they tried to deflect attention away from themselves and claimed that someone had tried to carjack them.

I tried to make sense of that. There had been no attempted carjacking? Then there would be no valid charges against me.

Brianna came over, carrying the dog, who had tucked his head in her armpit.

"Is it time to eat? Snags is hungry."

"Oh, he is, is he?" Jumbo George said.

"Yeah. And I am, too." She sat down at the table, and stroked the dog's hairless back. "You can come out, Snags. It's gonna be okay. But you can't hide all the time. You got to do your part, too."